This work is as fictional as anything else can be when we cannot even agree on what is "is."

Names, characters, places and incidents are the product of the author's experiences real or imaginary. I mean, damn! The author is just a character too, after all.

Cover design by Monica The Flower

ISBN: 978-1543272918

cc me

BITCOIN BELLE

Dester Lyaya

Dude - you can't be

Shoting the Belle. Juchig -

Shoot Blash.

Best.

Bitcoin Belle

Aist, do no ham.

"Things are not as they seem; the first appearance deceives many; the intelligence of a few perceives what has been carefully hidden."

Phaedrus

Prologue

She entered through the arched doorway with the glow of the late afternoon sun creating a silhouette of curves draped in a sheath. The vision was all I had hoped for. Sunlight danced off her hair, long and smooth; I could hardly wait to mess it up. We had agreed to meet in the café early enough to work up an appetite but by the appearance of erect nipples poking through her silk blouse and the way she was biting her lip, I could see she was already hungry for me. I liked that. I liked her.

I had intentionally seated myself so I would have the best line of sight when she arrived. Sure it was exciting to me that I would be paying her to satisfy me, but I also wanted to unnerve her. And I succeeded. Once her eyes found me and she realized I'd been staring at her while she scanned the room, a mild look of distress drew her eyebrows together; the confident and powerful woman in front of me blushed. It turned me on. Oh God this was going to be fun.

It was important that she come to me. My chest puffed as I watched the eyes of every man and woman follow her then look at me with envy. She was stunning. Bending my neck to rest my lips upon her hair, I inhaled her scent into me. Clean hair mixed with the subtle hint of the perfume I'd told her to wear along with her faint, natural musk caused me to stiffen slightly. She was intoxicating.

"Thank you for wearing the perfume I sent you as well as dressing in that slinky silk." She smiled demurely and cast her eyes down.

"It's really my pleasure," she said and smiled. Ahh, what a delight—such unabashed obedience in a woman like this. "I enjoyed watching you look at me as I came to you. I could tell you were admiring the way the fabric moved across my body."

"Yes, it is a lovely skirt you are wearing. It looks as though it could just slip right off of you with a single tug of that tie." I felt ravenous as I looked at her. The movement of her chest caused by her quickening breath tugged at me. "Change of plans." I motioned for the waiter and instructed him to send Champagne to the room.

"Oh I just love Champagne!" she purred. How could this woman be so fucking enchanting while at the same time captivating onlookers, turning spectator into a predator in the mind? "Maybe you should order two," she said with a bat of her lashes. "You might want to pour some on my pussy."

"Affirmative." Reaching into my suit jacket, I pulled out a stack of lira and handed it to her. "As per our agreement—half now and half when I've finished." With the instructions adjusted, and to the sound of a collective sigh from the room, I escorted my property from the bar to the private sanctuary of the fancy rent-a-bed I'd purchased. It seemed a shame that we'd only be enjoying it for a short while but we had lives to return to. Until then, however, I was going to relish the taste of this goddess.

"You may fill me with your desires and I will drink your nectar Mr. What-was-your-name-again, one swallow at a time." She said this while passing in front of me as we ascended the stairs close enough so that her hip brushed against my growing cock.

I gave her a swat on her bottom and moaned. "You are such a sexy bitch!" She just laughed and walked on ahead leaving me in the wake of her scent. Ha! A funny girl with a smoldering body. I could just make out her tiny waist as the curve of her hips swaying below it lured me in, mesmerizing me with their hypnotic rhythm. I let her walk on ahead past the room so I could enjoy the view. "Uh hem. You've gone too far. Come back here." The same swaying of the hips below the tiny waist, plus the erect nipples and hungry look on that pretty face were keeping me hard.

As I opened the door, the feel of my prize's breasts rubbed tauntingly against my arm. I gave her a sideways glance before the sound of a click turned both of our attention to what was on the other side of the threshold. Stepping inside to where I had prepared the room, she mocked me. "This looks more like a love nest than it does a pleasure palace" she said and walked across to where the doors opened out to a balcony. Below us were gondoliers guiding couples through the tight waterways.

A knock on the door signaled the Champagne had arrived, which saved me from having to find the appropriate retort to this wanton little hussy. Besides, it was rather amusing to watch her strut so confidently, certain she had control of the situation. Her misconception would soon be remedied. Handing her a glass of bubbly and kissing the inside of her wrist as she accepted it, I could not help but let out a moan at the feel of her skin and smell of her scent. I said, "You may call it whatever you want, my pet. But call me 'Sir'."

I brushed across her nipples with the back of my hand and watched her lips part as her breath caught. She suddenly appeared nervous as she downed the glass. I rewarded her by toying with the tie of her skirt. I marveled, "Look at you, all wrapped up like a present. Show me what's inside, honey." I watched admiringly as her eyes locked mine. I could see the wheels turning in that pretty little head of hers as she composed herself. Her irises actually changed color from a soft amber to a deep auburn, the exact color of her hair. Astounding.

"I would be happy to . . . Sir." She twirled away from me toward the open doorway. The breeze caught the material of her clothes and forced the silk to cling to her. The outline of her body pressed against the fabric. Her soft breasts hung gently above her little waist begging for me to take them into my mouth. She caught me staring and slowly traced the outline of her lips. That sweet, strawberry-flavored tongue. Plump and moist. I wanted to suck on it.

She stared straight into my eyes as she undid the tie and unwound herself from the wrap. As she did, a layer peeled away, and the backlit, filmy fabric revealed her secret. She wasn't wearing any panties. She let the skirt slip to the floor and as it did, my attention followed. Down over the curve of her hip, her thigh, slipping down her calf; the fabric puddled at her feet. I wanted to trace the line it had traveled with my tongue.

"Do you like what you see?" The words dripped from her lips as her blouse dripped to the floor. Staring at her titian mound, I caught the tip of the triangle glistening with her moistness. All I could think was how much I wanted to taste her. Freckles danced along her fair skin, the shade and smoothness reminding me of the inside of a seashell. What a little siren she was. This woman could be the death of me.

I surprised her as I scooped her up and tossed her onto the bed. She started to open her mouth in protest but was silenced as I placed my hand across her lips. "Don't. Do not say a word." Her eyes narrowed. This was a woman used to getting what she wanted. I let her watch me undress myself, not willing to give her the gratification in playing the seductress. I felt a great deal of satisfaction as she tried to maintain eye contact. She could see I was mocking her and her pretty little chin jutted out defiantly while I just smiled. But she was going to toy with me if she could. I knew underneath the veneer of sweetness and coquettish deference, she was a smoldering inferno ready to erupt.

"Come here and open your mouth, please." She just looked at me, mouth closed. "I won't ask twice." She pulled her legs behind her, making sure to let me catch a glimpse of her pink pussy before she slowly crawled over to the edge of the bed and opened her mouth slightly while I waited. Leaning back on her heels as she knelt in front of me, she opened her mouth wider, then as wide as she could. "Good girl!" I cupped her chin with my hand and squeezed her cheeks until her lips pursed, distorting them so she had a laughable fish face. And though it must have been slightly uncomfortable, her eyes twinkled. "You are a beautiful fish," I told her and bent down to finally let our lips meet. Wet and juicy, her luscious tongue tasted like ripe fruit.

"I bet you taste that good everywhere."

"I bet you'd like to find out."

"Yes. Yes I would. But first, let's see that pretty little mouth of yours swallow up my cock. Let's see if the back of your throat is ticklish, shall we?" Wrapping her fingers around me, with her tongue flattened out, she licked from under my balls, up the length of my shaft and over the head like it was an ice cream she didn't want to miss a drop of. Her moist, warm tongue made little beating movements, giving pressure in a beckoning way. It reminded me of a vagina opening and closing. Just then, her mouth closed down around me and she engulfed my thick, throbbing penis in one devouring swallow. Fuck me if this was not the hottest woman imaginable!

With a handful of hair, I gently pulled her head back. "Darling you are magnificent!" She smiled with a mouthful of cock the best she could and pulled up and back with a trail of spit dripping from her mouth.

"I'm so glad you're pleased," she said. "Now why don't you come fill me up and get the taste of my juice all over you and I'll happily lick it off."

"You read my mind," I said. We both inched up onto the bed, her like a teasing minx backing away, and me as a predator desperate to ravish her.

She opened her legs with knees bent and I could see her plump lips, wet and swollen, totally bare but for a cute little, downy-like patch at the top — her "fig leaf" was more of a temptation than it was shield. Parting the lips, I felt her moan as I put first one and then two fingers inside while her hips made the slightest movement toward my hand. With my other hand exposing her clit, I leaned in and nibbled on her hard, enlarged bean. Sucking on it, I continued to finger her until I felt her body tighten and warm liquid flood over my hand, animal-like sounds escaping from her mouth.

As she caught her breath and with her face awash with exposed vulnerability, I climbed on top of her, letting my cock find its way to the tip of her opening.

With my two hands on either side of her head, fingers entangled in her mane, I stared straight into her eyes as I slowly entered her, her mouth parting as her vagina also did. "I'm going to fill you with cum." She just nodded before she reached up and pulled my mouth onto hers.

With one hand cradling her head and the other one holding firmly to her hip, I pushed and pulled at her body as she grasped me with her legs wrapped around my back. I could smell her lust as it filled my nose. With each thrust, I felt her expertly tighten around my cock, making it difficult to pull out before once again filling her until my balls pressed against her opening. I was not going to be able to continue like this much longer without letting my load escape, and this was my last thought before my body was wracked with a violent convulsion that erupted inside her just before I collapsed with our lips still touching.

Both of us were silent for a moment, and I pulled away to retrieve the Champagne. Round one deserved a toast. Pouring each of us a glass, I asked confidently, "So what did you think?" taking a mouthful, before turning around to find her in a shoulder stand with legs up above her head: the queen of all poses. As hot as it was to see wetness all over the bottom of her ass, the overall look caused me to spew my drink, laughing so hard I snorted.

"Hey! I read it's best to do this to increase chances of fertilization," she said matter-of-factly, keeping her eyes focused straight ahead. "We know you are a good swimmer but I'm not sure that is hereditary," she added with a giggle. "I need to stay like this for about ten minutes."

"And then we can do that again?" I asked eagerly, knowing I never had to ask, as my wife was always willing.

"We sure can" she said with a smile. "You were such a good boy to get this all worked out with such short notice darling.

"And you were so sweet to play my naughty hooker, though we really didn't get very far with that little act, did we?" I dabbed Champagne onto her lips before positioning myself so I could hold her legs up for her.

"I wonder if those people downstairs thought I was really a hooker!" she gushed excitedly.

Laughing at my little hippy chick, I was more in love with her than ever — nearly twenty years later and never a dull moment. As exciting and free-spirited as the day I met her when I was a shy, awkward, college student and she, a precocious and sassy, wisp of a girl, soon-to-be artist extraordinaire. "I doubt anyone would mistake you for a hooker." I smiled when I saw her face cloud over. "Honey, we're in Italy. It's not so strange for a man to have a lover. Especially if he is as handsome as I am."

She feigned offense. "And you need to give me more money. There is no way the stack of lire is going to cover groceries and the laundry, even for a non-hooker girl like me!" How many women would be disappointed at not being a convincing prostitute?

"How about I give you a baby?" I offered. "But only if you are sure you are ready."

She squealed, let her legs come down, and pulled me close. "Yes, John. I am ready." She nestled sweetly against me and whispered the very thing that I was thinking. "I hope we make a girl."

Chapter 1

How often do we take a path we've travelled all our lives, knowing it is the very last time we will ever walk that way again?

I stared at the foot-worn passage that connected me like an umbilical cord to the home where my mother had given birth to me, and wound to my parents' workshop, where they had created their masterpieces. Day and night, they worked, while I grew up at their heels, following in their footsteps. I was my mother's greatest creation, she said.

I turned from the attic window to take in one last look at the magical wonderland that had been my mother's private sanctuary. The room was filled with evidence of a wild and adventurous spirit. There were photos of exotic places with tapestries and costumes she had collected along the way. I closed my eyes and pressed my face to them. With each inhalation, I was transported to the faraway land that had inspired my mother to carry home each object as a token, encapsulating an experience worth breathing in again and again.

Renderings of sculptures she'd completed were encased in crafted frames my dad had forged, and they were displayed on the walls of the little alcove that had been my nursery. My heart sank as I looked at the empty space where the drawing of the twenty-first sculpture from her *Crypto Chaos* series would have hung—the final piece to a project she had worked on for ten years.

Dad built the Womb Room, as he called it, to be her sacred space where she could welcome their love child. I was the result of one day in Venice, when he claims they "wished me into existence." Mom told a completely different story. Something that involved headstands, timing, and pretending to be a call girl. I tried not to think about it.

The story was way too much for me to hear the summer I turned fifteen, but I am forever grateful to know it now, because it was so her, so him, so them. And then there was me. Even after we moved one story down to our respective rooms, the attic remained Mom's. I melted to think it continued to be a nursery, since these projects were her "babies."

I visited it as a young child would a fort. It felt like a cocoon to me. Since Mom died, Dad visited it on nights when he drank a bottle of Scotch and hoped answers would come to him. The answers definitely weren't in the bottle and by the look of him the next day, he had not found them in the attic room either. He never was able to wrap his head around her death.

It wasn't a place of solace for him, but a puzzle box where I think he felt somehow lay the answer to a question he'd never shared. I would see his eyes cloud as they did when he was trying to figure out a problem. The fog would roll across his face, followed by a wave of recognition that was gone before it was fully realized.

Once a month, he would climb the stairs as part of his bottom-to-top maintenance inspection. I knew he was finished when I would see . . . or hear him . . . screaming through the air. In my home, even something as simple as exiting a room transformed into an event.

In addition to the door that led to the landing of the third-floor staircase, the room had a second exit—a Tyrolean traverse zip line. Tucked into the window seat bench were climbing harnesses and carabineers. A single click and one could swoop across the backyard like Tinkerbell.

"You never want to have a single point of failure, Phalaen," said Mom. She handed out oracles like most moms told kids to tuck their shirts in or brush their teeth.

I once asked Dad why he'd built the second exit, thinking Mom's answer was unoriginal. His response was equally as boring: "A happy wife is a happy life." He was known for dorky sayings, dolling out sage advice like you'd find in a fortune cookie.

Though their answers made me yawn at the time, the reality was that my dad and mom were wildly and passionately in love and he'd have done anything to make her laugh. He was a practical man with a wonderful sense of humor who saw an opportunity for play in everything. He had been her ideal man.

They had met Thanksgiving weekend in 1976, introduced by Peter, of course. He and Peter were roommates at Stanford, both on the rowing team, and both taking a class on metallurgy, which had become an obsession of Mom's.

The story goes that the two tall, muscular, college boys walked into the kitchen where Mom's aunt was whipping up a dinner to end all Thanksgiving dinners.

3

The first thing Peter said was not, "Hey, we're here! Happy Thanksgiving!" but instead, "What? No chocolate pie?"

From under the kitchen table came an annoyed voice, "Would you like some whine to go with that cheese?"

Peter and John bent down and lifted the blue and white checkered cloth and the two of them peered under it at a boy who was being entertained by a feathered and painted squaw. She looked at them both, raised her hand and said, "Hau!"

"With great precision and immaculate attention to detail," was my father's response. He won Mom over immediately. She proceeded to crawl out from under the makeshift tent, and as he would tell it, gaze longingly at him. She never denied it.

Peter said beaming, "Six, meet my roommate and second best friend, crew partner, and ideal man. John, meet my best friend, favorite girl, and the smartest person I know, Vivienne Lane."

John leaned over and whispered into Peter's ear something that caused Peter to throw back his head, burst with laughter and say, "Yeah, she's closer to a seven."

"Oh shut up, Peter! I told you that was a stupid nickname!" giving him a little kick to the shins. Patiently explaining to John, who was standing there flummoxed, she said, "Nobody except my dad ever called me Vivienne. Instead they called me Vi, which I never liked. Clever Peter here started calling me 'Six' because of the Roman numerals. Get it?"

"Can I still call you 'Seven'?" Dad asked in a low voice, with what Mom said was the most dashing smile and twinkling eyes.

"No wonder you like him so much, Peter; his eyes look like they're made of chocolate." She winked and told John he could call her anything he wanted, just so long as he called her.

Mom was forward like that. She always knew what she wanted and according to her, she had decided right there and then that she wanted John Lundgren. She said she could tell there was no bad thing in him. And she liked his hands.

It took Dad a little longer. Although he instantly found her enchanting, he was and is the type of man who has to work out everything in his head before moving forward. The two of them were nothing alike and absolutely perfect for each other. Thirty-four years after their first kiss, he was still charmed.

I took one last look around the Womb Room. Everything was exactly as she had left it. I had even kept my music box on her drawing table. I never knew why she had placed it there in the first place, but I didn't want to change anything. I liked imagining her walking into my childhood bedroom to pick it up from my nightstand and carry it upstairs. The image was fresh and original. And just mine.

As I descended the eighteen steps to the entry, I paused at my teenage bedroom, where there was a sign on the door from when puberty hit me hard that read, "Welcome Fly, I'm Spider" — a testimony to the unapologetic boundary by which I had defined my personal space.

My parents valued privacy above nearly all else. That didn't stop them though from flying in, costumed as flies, buzzing about my room, while I was laid up with fresh holes where wisdom teeth had been. The three of us lay snuggled on my bed that afternoon watching Jeff Goldblum mutate while my winged mom fed me ice cream. Dad tickled my face with antennae.

My bedroom resembled two brain hemispheres. To the right were mirrors with a ballet bar attached to one, with a springy wood floor that edged up on three sides. Whereas some people record a growing child's height on a kitchen door post, we hung my ballet slippers — the smallest practically fit my thumb.

My mom's record player rested on a fifties-style TV tray in the corner. Just below was a row of vinyl records I'd inherited from her. After her dad returned from Vietnam, he used to eat his dinner on the tray while listening to his favorite album. I kept it as a showpiece in front of all the others: Astrud and Joao Gilberto, with legendary sax player, Stan Getz, performing "Girl from Ipanema." The song had been written the year his darling Vivienne was born.

In the center of the room was my bed. Above it was a skylight through which I stared into space every night. The sky enveloped me but if I got cold, there was always the standard-issue army blanket my mother had kept of her father's from his two tours, or one of the many Moroccan blankets Mom had collected as one might collect shells from a seashore vacation. Mom and her blankets!

On the opposite side of the room was an L-shaped desk that had formerly held graphing paper and an assortment of pens and pencils. I had kept the Skittlescolored abacus that I'd had as long as I could remember, but I'd replaced the hardback dictionaries and thesauruses with monitors, towers, and crypto mining rigs.

Mom had maintained a strict "no digital devices in the house" policy. I thought it was silly. Especially considering that when I wasn't dancing or riding my bike, I was writing code or playing online games. Dad never objected, so I took it as tacit agreement that it was fine, and I brought all the equipment in from the workshop dungeon.

I liked that the space still felt and looked like a cave. I think my mom would have appreciated the velvet painting of *Dogs Playing Poker* I recently added. I had become the eighth seat at the card table, once my dad made it through the initial shock of losing more than just his wife. The art piece was a gift from the group who gathered weekly to drink and play cards at our house.

There was also an oversized poster of Einstein sticking his tongue out. I had grown a patch of chia on it. I wondered if my dad noticed it was there. He never said anything if he did.

From this room, I had grown a network of friends in the online gaming world. Living in a town with a population of 200 wasn't so bad for a girl like me when I had best buddies with names like Dookie and Gizmo. The fact that they lived in the interweb was just fine with me. I lived there, too. Or, well, "Ms. P." did.

I was pretty certain Dookie and Gizmo were boys and that they were related, because of how they bantered with each other. They were funny. I felt a special bond with the two of them that I couldn't explain other than we just seemed to recognize each other.

They were the ones who had told me about mining for cryptocurrency. They also seemed to know I was a girl, although I am not sure why I thought that exactly, or how they would know, since my avatar was a pretzel.

Of everyone I knew in the gaming world, they were the only people I had told I accepted an offer from MIT. I was supposed to go last year, but six months was too soon after Mom's accident to think of leaving my dad.

My work on peer-to-peer networks and decentralized systems had made me a popular nerd — if there could be such a thing. So despite not having a high school diploma, I was accepted into college. Finishing high school had never been a goal of mine.

Like Mom said, "Learn the rules. Then learn how, when, and why to break them." Going to MIT without a diploma hardly seemed like an act of rebellion, but it did crack me up. In 2008, Mom heard President Obama say everyone should go to college. I remember my mom talking to the TV, ranting that the systemized institutionalization of Americans was the downfall of Western society.

Shortly thereafter, Dad had heard enough and he worried Mom might have an aneurysm, so he put the brain-sucking machine into the fire. She rescued it and turned it into a sculpture that we now have where the TV once stood. She begrudged people's unwillingness to think critically or creatively.

As I descended the final steps toward the kitchen, I thought now about how saying goodbye to Dad loomed in front of me.

He loved making knives and was, in fact, a famous knife maker. With me gone, he'd be able to travel and lecture as he had done before I was born. And truth be told, I hoped he would start dating again.

I could hear Dad rattling around in the kitchen. I smelled the piney scent of cleanser before I saw the splattered mess that had erupted from the mixer.

"Whoa! What happened here?" I asked with genuine concern. It was not like my dad to make a mess in the kitchen. He kept it pristine when he wasn't creating a masterpiece, and even when he was, it was a tidy mess at worst.

He glanced up from where he was mopping up the spill and paused. I could see the look of hurt in his eyes as he took in my traveling attire, with backpack and suitcase in hand.

"Going somewhere?" he asked quietly.

"Just give me a minute to clean this up. I've got lunch for us out in the workshop. You do have time for lunch?" He glanced at me, looked down, and muttered, "I was going to make a cake for your going-away party tonight.

"Yeah Dad, about that," I started to say before he looked up at me sharply. "I was actually thinking I'd head out today . . ." I began and then sat down on the arm of his leather chair where I'd rubbed it worn sitting on it when I was too big to be curled up in his lap.

I thought of how much I was going to miss this space. Where other people had sofas and coffee tables in their living rooms, we had arcade games: Asteroids for Dad, Ms. Pac-Man for me, and a vintage 1973 pinball machine for Mom—High Hand. Mom loved to play cards, so of course she would favor a poker theme. They had not been played since Mom died.

I started to feel guilty about leaving Dad out of my plans, so I stared at my bags and pretended I was taking inventory. Stuffed inside my backpack was everything I could possibly need for three days of travel. Clothes, my laptops, and three bedside books: *Ethics of Liberty,* by Murray Rothbard, *Alice in Wonderland,* and *Purgatorio,* the second book in the trilogy by Dante, and of course my bike gear. Thoughts of riding my Pink Lady on the train filled my head. I wondered if it could get me thrown off.

I was allowed one more suitcase without paying extra for the trip. "K.I.S.S.," a motto of Dad's, echoed in my head. Rolled up and stuffed inside my backpack were tights and leotards, workout clothes, underwear, two skirts, three of Mom's cashmere cardigans, and two pairs of jeans. In addition, there were five T-shirts that displayed my favorite bands, including one of Fleetwood Mac from the cover of their *Rumors* album and a pink vintage tee of Heart.

The last two had been retro gifts from Mom. She had scrolled a note left within them that she had saved for my eighteenth birthday, along with a marijuana cigarette, which I still had, and a homemade video that had long ago been transferred to a floppy disc, then a CD, then a thumb drive, and now to a tiny chip I kept in my music box, where a lopsided ballerina pirouetted to *Fur Elise.*

Although I had opened the gift, I had still not watched the video. I wanted to hold onto the last fresh encounter as long as I could. How funny to think this experience, too, was in front of me, and yet I was

10

avoiding it as long as possible, rather than getting it over with. Of course, Dad was still here and Mom was not.

The whimsy of Stevie Nicks, combined with the passionate intensity of the sister rock band had seemed to encapsulate my Mom's, teenage experience. The tees came from her concert calling of 1977, which she laughingly referred to as the "summer of her Miss Spent Youth." She, Peter, and my dad had toured the West Coast in a VW bus, following their favorite bands. When I told her I thought it should be "misspent," she smiled and said, "No baby, I wasted nothing, but spent it all!"

That was her: drink deep from the well of life until your thirst is quenched. And then add salt. "Gotta stay thirsty, Phalaen," she would tell me, if I ever showed signs of placid contentment.

Across from me, hanging on the wall, was a cross-stitch I'd made for my mom, which read, "No Bitchin in My Kitchin." It was a joke—Mom didn't cook. Dad used to say she was the only person who could burn water. Of course, one can't burn water.

She did manage to destroy more than one pot in an effort to reheat leftovers. Her defense was that her idea of cooking involved melting and shaping metal. "I was made to do a few things well, so I do," she said with a hair flip when teased.

Back when they were on their summer concert tour, Dad made a comment about the two guys doing all of the food preparation. The story goes Peter looked at John and just shook his head laughing. Fifteen-year-old sassy-pants stood up and walked away from the campfire, undressing as she did. She flung her panties at John and asked, "Can you smell what I'm cookin' now?"

I overheard that story one time when my parents were having their weekly dinner for eight. I had snuck down to the kitchen long after they thought me asleep. Hearing my dad say, "That was the meal that sealed the deal," sent me scurrying back upstairs.

I nearly barfed, saying aloud, "Nobody wants to imagine their parents having sex." They must have heard me because a round of hysterical laughter followed.

Sex was not on my bucket list per se, but it was certainly on my to-do list. However, I wasn't like my mom—a free spirit, confident in her feminine strength and sexuality. I had about as much sex appeal as a rock.

Mom told me I was made for one man, just as she had been, and that I would recognize him when I saw him. I told her how absurd that seemed to me, considering I would have to know someone first in order to recognize them. It made her laugh that certain laugh she used to have, which made me so irritated. It wasn't condescending exactly, but it annoyed me.

I'd give anything to tell her about my friends Gizmo and Dookie, and how I feel I recognize them even though we've never met. And I wanted to tell her she was right. Again.

Dad finished mopping the slop and asked me if I'd please join him for lunch one last time in the workshop before he reluctantly drove me to the airport. I just stood still, feeling a little bit ashamed for not cluing him in on my change of plans.

He removed my backpack from my shoulder and easily picked up my fifty-pound suitcase as we walked out the door. "Don't tell me you don't want me to drive you to the airport, honey," he said, more as a non-negotiable, matter-of-fact statement than a question.

"It's not that, Daddy. It's just, well, it's just . . . It's just that I am not flying to Boston," I blurted, hoping my perkiness would smooth over any concern or worry he might have. "I am going to take the train!"

Following the pathway and taking in all of the familiar sights, my dad and I walked in sync and in silence. I felt a twinge of nervousness. Had I made the wrong decision to leave early? Should I have gone to Stanford like he had, or at least somewhere closer?

I could hear my mom saying, "Stop it, Phalaen! Don't second-guess yourself. You are a brave, smart, and capable young woman and you can do anything you set your mind to." I breathed a sigh of relief.

"Mom talking to you?" Dad asked, his eyes shining. "I love it when she does that," he said.

I looked up at his warm smile and handsome face. I was going to miss him so much. I nodded my head, since words could not get past the tightness in my throat.

"Look, PAL," as he called me. "You know how much I love you and that I knew this day was coming." His eyes shone like glistening moons of freshly made chocolate.

"Oh Dad, come on! I am going to be fine. Besides, think about how happy Mom would be that I am avoiding the public raping by the TSA." I could feel him smiling.

"In that case," he began as he reached into his back pocket, "here is an upgrade to a sleeper car." He winked at me as he handed me a first-class ticket that would give me dining car privileges and my own room. And my own bathroom!

"What? But how did you know I was taking a train and not flying?" I wasn't mad at all and in no way felt as though he'd violated my privacy, but I was flabbergasted that he had pulled one over on me. He was so bad at keeping secrets that Mom had to hide our presents, for fear he'd open them early and show me.

"Dad, you are the best! And I am so tickled you surprised me," I told him with genuine delight. Mom had always been the one who could fool anyone. "This is a nice treat. Thanks!" I stopped, twirled, and did a happy dance.

We approached the workshop door, his face aglow with an "I got you" look of satisfaction. He opened the door and I stepped over the threshold to a crowd of people who shouted, "Surprise!" I looked up at his grinning face with my mouth agape. He had gotten me twice.

The lounge-like area of the workshop—where my family would often eat meals cooked with blow torches or in a cast-iron pot set over a fire, alongside whatever project my parents were working on—was filled with a crowd of standing-room-only townies.

Among them were the usual suspects. There was the mail mistress and gamer, Jan, Dad's hunting partner, and her lover, Misty, who was his web designer and chief brownie-maker. They were both teary eyed.

My mouth dropped when I saw Jan standing tall as a statue and nearly as perfect. In all the years I had known her, I had only seen her in mail-carrier blues or cargo pants, camo, or khaki. And there she and Misty stood, both wearing dresses, with their hair done and makeup flawlessly applied.

Misty stepped forward and wrapped her arms around me. "Vivienne told Jan she could wear whatever she wanted to her weekly dinner parties, as long as she wore a dress for your graduation and your wedding." I burst out crying. Only my mother could illicit this sort of devotion from people.

Laughing through tears that were now streaming down my face, I stuttered in awe at how beautiful they both looked. I was used to seeing Misty dressed up. But Jan's transformation caught me completely off guard. It was somehow unsettling. Like maybe I didn't know her as well as I thought.

Jan gathered me up in her arms and hoisted me above her head to cheers from the whole room. When she set me down, she whispered into my ear, "Things are rarely what they seem."

Later I opened a card from the two of them. It was filled with cash. They had inscribed the following oracle: "Remember, if you can determine the energy of a system, you can learn everything there is to know about it." That had to have been something they'd heard from my mom.

The Vet stood sheepishly with his hands in his pockets. After all these years, I still didn't know his real name. He was like an animal whisperer. He had helped me train my puppy, Baby Harry.

Next to the Vet stood his wife, Aunt DeeDee, who used to grow Mom's "medicine." His wife was as sweet and kind a person as there ever was, and a natural healer. Her heart was so beautiful that once people got to know her, they stopped noticing the burn scar that covered half of her face and neck.

My dance teacher stood front and center with his wife, looking ridiculous; both had cheesy grins on their faces. His son, Steven, had been my dance partner until he was paralyzed in a diving accident. Now he was my master of disaster and trouble-making twin. I was going to miss him terribly.

Two years younger than I, Steven would pretty much go along with whatever cockamamie idea I had, and I had a lot of them. He had been my surrogate brother since I was seven years old, when his family had moved to town. His father replaced my previous dance teacher, who had fallen in love with a circus performer. What a romantic story! Dancer runs off with circus strongman to make circus babies.

Steven's stepmother, Ng, had been our academic advisor of sorts. Raised by a foster mother after she was orphaned, Ng understood the loss of a parent, and she stepped up to fill the gap when Mom died. She was a computer programmer and my mentor, teaching me nearly everything I knew about coding.

Looking at my extended family, I was impressed they'd all kept quiet about this soiree. I had always figured they were terrible secret keepers because they seemed to always know what I was up to. Nosy Nellies, I called them.

In addition to this motley crew stood the rest of the townspeople. Literally the entire population stood inside our family workshop, shoulder to shoulder. The space was really the size of a small warehouse, but with all of the forging, melting, and sculpting equipment, it felt packed. Everyone from gardeners to grocers and lawyers to Laundromat owners was present.

The only time this group would all get together at our house was for Dad's annual cherry blossom party. His mother was Japanese, and the party was the one thing he did without fail to celebrate her life. Dad roasted lambs on a spit—a nod to mom's Welsh ancestry—and everyone brought a side dish or dessert and two bottles of wine. Misty, of course, brought brownies.

The next morning, bodies could be found camped out or passed out and strewn throughout the yard, atop and under the trampoline. It was appropriately held around Mother's Day and was a gala not to be missed.

The story of Dad's mother and father was a sorrowful one that he never discussed, but Mom had shared it with me. Dad's parents met in Hawaii while Papa was stationed there. A delicate and diminutive girl of eighteen, my grandmother Nana captivated the much older, second-generation Swede who towered over her, making her appear as a little girl in all of their photos. They both had lost everyone they loved in the war.

Mom made a sculpture of me sitting on Papa's shoulders, with Nana standing next to him. She was laughing and looking up at me. It was the only piece Mom had kept. Nana died of cancer when I was quite young and shortly after, her husband followed, destitute without the joy of his life. Mom said he'd died of heartache.

Looking around, I could see everyone was there. Everyone except the people I wished more than anything could be—my mom and my best friend, Q, along with Q's family. All in all, it was truly a great send-off and I was ready to go.

I was ready to leave home and do my part to change the world. I was sure decentralized systems were the key to greater self-ownership and a more peaceful existence. I wanted to be involved and in the center of the technology that would change everything. As it turned out, I was at the center more than I could have ever imagined.

Chapter 2

"What would you like for your birthday, Scary Ari? I know! How about if I turn you into a human catapult and hurl you through the air?"

"Would I land on a cloud of cotton candy, Johnny?" I asked. "One I could eat as much of as I wanted and not get cavities?"

Picking me up by my wrists, the naughty twin, Johnny, began to spin me around. I tried grasping at his hands or arms, certain if he let go, I would sail off into the air and float away. I tried to focus on one still object like my dance teacher had told me to, do so I wouldn't get dizzy. But I failed to do both. Suddenly, the shapes melded into a rainbow that I was flying through and they became a kaleidoscope of terror.

"Stop, Johnny! I am going to be sick" I tried to say. What came out instead was gibberish, perhaps because my laughter had turned to crying and my smiles to tears. And then he let go of me. I was falling and falling and falling.

Jacob caught me in his arms, cradling me like a baby, whispering, "Ssshhh, I've got you, sweet girl. I've got you."

I sobbed, "I tried to hang onto Johnny's hands, but I couldn't do it, Jacob."

I wanted so much to be a big girl and play with the boys, but they were always faster and stronger. And they just kept getting taller. I felt like I would never catch up.

"Johnny tried to make me throw up!" I said. Of course, I knew it wasn't true, but I said it anyway.

"He did? Well, what should I do about it, Princess Phalaen?" Jacob always fixed everything. He was the biggest of the family.

"Turn him into a dookie-ball mud pie and then feed him to the trolls!" I said.

"A dookie ball? What is that? It sounds dreadful!"

Johnny stood behind Jacob and taunted me. "No, not THAT, Scary Ari!" I knew he was playing with me, but I still wanted to see if Jacob would do whatever I asked.

"Make him stop calling me that!" I said to Jacob. I stuck my tongue out at Johnny, and he stuck his right back out at me.

"Do you want me to turn him into a dookie-ball mud pie and feed him to the trolls, or do you want me to make him stop?" asked Jacob.

He sounded serious and I was afraid he might actually do it. Johnny looked scared.

"Never mind.' I said. "It is more powerful if I forgive him, so I will just do that."

Johnny expressed his undying gratitude and fell to his knees, bowing down to the ground. "Thank you, Princess Phalaen. I am forever in your debt."

"I think that's the best course of action in this case. It is very mature of you, sweet girl. Do you think that way because you are seven now?" asked Jacob.

"No. I think it is what Daddy would tell me to do. And he is the smartest man in the whole universe!"

Johnny asked, "The smartest? Even smarter than your hero Jacob?" He had that look in his eye like he was going to start teasing me again.

"Jacob is the second smartest and that is why I am going to marry him someday. And then I won't be a princess anymore. I'll be a queen!"

Wrapping my arms around Jacob's neck, I whispered in his ear, "Momma says you are the king of hearts."

"You are the queen of my heart, little princess. Now, off you go for a nap, or you will stay this size forever. You have a big party this afternoon and you don't want to be a cranky girl." I gave him one more hug around the neck, and I wriggled out of his arms.

"Okay, but first I have to find Q. We don't want her to stay this size forever." I tried to wink at him like his little sister — my best friend — had taught me, but only my lips and cheeks moved. Jacob laughed. He had the best laugh.

"Well, she is right over there, Scary Ari," said Johnny.

I stuck my tongue out at the recalcitrant twin. "And Momma says you have the attention span of a squirrel, Johnny Harrison!" Both he and Jacob laughed even harder.

Under the giant apple tree, leaning up against a large, wooden crate stood the youngest of the Harrison clan. She was nothing like the boisterous boys who were more than five years her senior. Even though she was the youngest, her brothers all did as she asked of them. Of course, she didn't talk very much and asked for very little. But when she talked, they listened; and when she asked, they did as she bid.

We girls were given our particular names in honor of a bet my mom and Q's dad made when they were young enough to make silly bets without thinking they might lose. My name was Phalaenopsis Ariel Lundgren and hers was Quaking Aspen Harrison. But nobody actually called us Phalaenopsis or Quaking.

Mom called me Phalaen, Dad called me PAL, and nearly everyone else, including the beasty boys, called me Ari, mostly so they could attach Scary in front of it, even though I was hardly scary. Everyone called Q, well "Q."

Johnny once suggested she go by "Q and A," or just "A." He thought he was so funny. Q didn't seem to notice he was teasing her. And being the perfectly logical person she was, she reasoned that if she went by "A," she'd always be at the front of the line, and she didn't like being in front.

The two of us were practically inseparable when our families got together each summer and over the Christmas holidays. Mom said we were of the same tribe. It was a ridiculous thing to say: neither of us were Indians.

"What is in the box?" I asked. I knew it must be a present because it had a big bow wrapped around it. Pink, my favorite color!

Before Q could answer me, a whizzing sound above us startled us both. The perilous adventurer, Patrick—the other twin—zoomed down the zip line.

Upside down, naturally. He never did anything like other people.

He righted himself, as he slowed to a stop, and unclipped his harness, in midair. Waving his arms with a flourish, he bowed. "I am so sorry to be late, ladies. I hope I haven't missed you opening your present."

"No, Padi. You arrived just in time!" I assured him. And he had. As per usual. Never early, never late. Always at the right time. Everyone called it "P-time."

By now, everyone had gathered around. Standing behind Q were our parents and her brothers. They all looked at me and seemed just as excited as I was to see what was inside the box.

"You get three guesses, honey." Mom beamed.

I always got three guesses. If I was wrong, I got to open the present. And if I was right, I got to open the present. It was a game we played, just for fun. Mommy always said it was like the Game of Life, because no matter what happened, I could always win. I just had to be willing to accept the gift.

I went to shake the box and heard a round of nos from the crowd around me, the force of which was startling. Q came around to the other side and pressed her nose against mine. "Phalaen doesn't like nos, do you, sweetie?" She was right; I didn't like the word no at all.

"I wasn't really going to shake it. I was just testing you. Now I know it can break!" I said. The adults all looked at me with approval, as if I was so clever. Q gave me a kiss on my nose and told me to make my guesses.

"So it is not a hat?" I asked. I couldn't help but laugh. Everyone knew I hated hats. They couldn't even get me to wear one for the spring recital, so we all wore a feather in our hair instead.

"Is it an Everlasting Gobstopper?" Our families had just watched *Willy Wonka and the Chocolate Factory* together. Afterwards, we had taken turns being Veruca Salt. At the mention of candy, we all started singing "Give it to me, give to me . . . I want it now!" and laughed at the funny song and at the thought of Veruca, the silly girl.

Johnny said, "This is your last and final guess, Scary Ari." The words were barely out of his mouth when a glare from his mom made him sink a bit.

"Oh, don't worry about him, Aunt Jenny," I said. He's just jealous because I am going to marry Jacob." I looked at Q, and we giggled.

"For my last and final guess . . . drum roll, please, Padi. Is it a puppy?"

Mommy couldn't believe I had guessed correctly. I looked up at my dad who was trying very hard not to laugh.

"See, Daddy, I told you I could keep it secret."

"John! You didn't!" Mom wasn't really mad at him but she was good at pretending.

"Thanks a lot, PAL," he said, laughing. "I just couldn't help myself, honey. Besides, our little Sherlock here saw the puppy food and asked me. You know I can't lie to her."

"You are incorrigible!" said Mom. It was true. Daddy couldn't keep secrets. He always said keeping secrets is like telling lies—hard to know what the truth is when you can't remember what you've said or were supposed to say.

"That's okay, Daddy. I think you have lots of courage," I said, trying to console him.

"Oh, Phalaen! You silly goose. I adore you. Now open that box and show us your new puppy." Mom was all smiles. She never got mad at little things.

I handed one end of the ribbon to Q and I took the other. Together we pulled, and when we did, the sides of the box all came down. And inside was not a puppy. Inside the crate was a stuffed animal. It looked like a puppy but it was definitely not a puppy.

Nobody made a sound. I could feel my throat start to hurt. This wasn't what I thought I was getting. I looked up at my dad and he looked as confused as I felt. We all turned to Mom, who was laughing hysterically.

"Gotcha!" She pointed toward the back of the house. Walking around the corner were the Vet and Aunt DeeDee, carrying a ball of fluff. I took off running across the yard, as I heard Daddy call Mommy "rotten."

"She's not rotten," I yelled back over my shoulder. "She's just a joker, Daddy."

The puppy must have known I was his mommy, because as soon as he was put down, he ran straight for me. He was so excited, prancing about. His front paws had white socks on them; he did the cutest little dance.

"He looks just like you when you dance, Daddy!" It was true. My father's free-styling resembled someone having a seizure. He would gawkily step about with his 6'3" frame, hands out flailing, while wearing the biggest grin ever.

"Is that an invitation to dance with my birthday girl?" he asked.

"Oh, Daddy, don't be silly. I have a baby to take care of now." Just then, the puppy let out a wide yawn and his pink tongue stretched out like the unfurling of a fruit roll-up. "I think he needs a nap."

24

"Come on, Q," I said. Let's take the baby up to the nest." As I gathered my new obsession into my arms, I coddled him a little bit until he had found a comfortable place entangled in my long hair.

With my free hand, I took hold of Q and we trudged together up to Mom's craft room, leaving behind our families, including my "future husband."

"Looks like you've been replaced by a four-legged face-licker as the favorite in Scary Ari's heart, dear brother," teased Johnny.

I just looked back over my shoulder and stuck my nose in the air before flipping my tresses and walking off. I left them all behind, with the whole group shaking their heads and mumbling something about an apple not falling far from the tree.

"Of course an apple can't fall far from the tree," I hollered. We trudged upstairs, happily leaving behind everyone else.

"What are you going to name your new puppy, Phalaen?" Q asked.

She arranged the Moroccan wedding blanket I'd pulled from my parents' bed to make a spot for us to rest. The fabric was soft with talismanic cymbals sewn into little tufts of material to ward off the evil eye. Daddy called it a baby-making blanket, which made it perfect for my purposes.

We snuggled up together, as the coins made jingly sounds like the tinkling of wind chimes. Mommy said if you listened close enough you could hear the call to prayer like you can hear the sound of the sea in a conch shell. All I could hear were the cute noises of my new puppy calling me to comfort him.

"I am going to call him Baby Harry, because he is the baby and he was a gift from the Harrison Family."

Q liked my pragmatism. "That sounds perfectly logical," she said. I watched her face in silence as she gazed up at the ceiling. She was doing numbers in her head. She was only eight but she already did math from the college.

"You do know Johnny will probably always call you Scary Ari because he knows how much it drives you crazy," she said. We rolled our eyes in unison. "Boys are weird, except for Jacob. He's perfect. You can marry him some day and then we will be sisters."

"Oooh, that reminds me. Jacob said I had to take a nap or I would stay this small forever. Do you think grown-ups actually believe the silly things they say? Things like, 'If you cross your eyes like that, they will stay that way,'?"

Q crossed her eyes and they went right back.

Light flooded in through stained glass windows, filling our attic hideaway with a soft pink glow. I was too excited to sleep, with a puppy breathing heavily against my chest, and the anticipation of my birthday party. Baby Harry let out a big yawn and nestled deeper in between the two of us. I still felt restless. "Hey Q, are you tired?" I asked.

"No, actually, I'm not tired at all," she admitted candidly. One thing about Q, she never lied. Not directly.

"I'll be right back." I tiptoed downstairs and caught sight of my dad, Uncle Peter, and Q's brothers outside the library window. They were trying to rotate their hips with hula hoops around them.

They were not succeeding and kept dropping the rings to the ground. Mom snapped photographs of everyone, including Aunt Jenny, who was doubled over holding her belly, begging them to stop.

I found the yearbook I wanted among the photo albums, and I glanced quickly out the window before making my getaway. Nobody caught me.

Imitating the boys' failed attempts at hooping, Q and I shared a moment of gloating. We were expert hoopers, especially Q, who could spin more than one hoop at a time! It felt good to be better than the boys at something for once.

My spot was still warm next to my little fur ball who was tucked in against my friend. I licked my finger and began to turn through the slick photo paper. The faint scent of earth rose up like a vapor from the slightly warped pages. I wrinkled my nose. The smell reminded me of the abandoned house we had snuck into last summer. That was the day Q had seen a ghost.

Our fathers stood side by side in one photo, wearing what looked like old-fashioned, one-piece women's bathing suits. Daddy leaned toward Uncle Peter, his teammate, and whispered something, while Uncle Peter had his eyes closed; his head was tilted back with a huge smile on his face.

"Do you know that's the boat race where your dad met your mom? Daddy said she was a dachshund," I said.

"Oh, Phalaen. "You say the funniest things! Mama was a 'coxswain'! She told the rowers how to steer. A dachshund is a type of dog."

My eyes grew big. Aunt Jenny was definitely not a dog. Q looked thoughtful for a moment and brought her hand to her chin, like she did sometimes when she was thinking hard, and said her dad did sometimes call her mom a tiger.

"Yeah, but not a dog!" I said. We both laughed. It was okay to be a big roaring cat.

The long, skinny boat in which they had won their race hung in the workshop collecting dust. "Mommy keeps teasing Daddy that she is going to turn the shell into an art piece if he doesn't start to row again. He says his butt is too big."

"That's funny," I said. "Mama tells Papa that since he retired from the army, his belly is as soft as her behind. He says that after twenty years of being a 'lean, mean, fighting machine,' it's time for him to 'enjoy the good life' AND her behind."

Both Q's and my hands flew to our mouths. We knew he was talking about S-E-X. We had found a picture book in their bedroom once that had naked people.

"Maybe there will be another war so Uncle Peter can go back into the army and be a lean, mean, fighting machine again."

"I hope not, Phalaen. Papa says war is about killing people, leaving behind the living ones to pay for it. I like having my papa home. Besides, he is teaching me a lot of stuff on computers."

"Maybe Uncle Peter will teach me 'puters too," I mumbled before drifting off to sleep.

Chapter 3

At first glance, there was nothing remarkable-looking about the teenage girl. She wore a faded blue baseball shirt with a number six on the back. She had long legs that filled out a pair of vintage, button-up 501s, the frayed bottom edges rested upon a pair of well-worn leather boots. Her magenta-colored hair was the only distinguishing quality about her appearance. A bright orange bandana was wrapped twice around her right wrist, covering most of her forearm. On her left was an assortment of beaded macramé friendship bracelets. She looked average.

But unlike most kids her age, she had perfect posture, her chin perfectly parallel to the floor. She moved gracefully, almost gliding as she walked alongside a man who, based upon their strong resemblance, I figured to be her father.

The notes in the file said she was a dancer. But there was more to her almost regal posture than just good genetics and well-developed musculature. She carried herself with a dignity that was the function of a self-awareness and confidence that far surpassed her years. She appeared nothing like what one would expect a geek girl to appear, but then again, I hardly resembled the stereotypical drug dealer.

I felt a twinge of warmth as I witnessed the charming sight of the man's masculinity drip away into a puddle of tears at the simple touch of his daughter's goodbye peck upon his whiskered face. I could not claim to know the tenderness that a daughter's touch could invoke in a father's heart. But it was enough for me that the woman I loved had stolen my heart with a gentle press of her fingers upon my arm as she slid my biology books across a library desk, so that I knew the power of the feminine. I could still feel it now, fifteen years later.

But there was no room for sentimentality. All I had to do for the next four days was observe her and answer the calls to the burner phone I'd been given. Four days of watching and reporting, then I would be off the hook, free to return to my wife. I hated lying to Angie, but I was sure she'd forgive me. After all, I was doing this for our son. I had done it all for our son.

Yearning for my wife made me feel antsy, as did the rumbling in my stomach. Phalaenopsis Ariel Lundgren was obviously boarding the train, so the dining car was my next target. I had to admit I was grateful the girl had upgraded from coach to business class.

I don't care who you are and how humble you may be—coach sucks. Having the private dining car was a real plus in addition to the roomy seats. I had spent weeks of my life sleeping on the floor in a lab or on the hard ground, so I was accustomed to finding rest in uncomfortable situations. But there was no replacing good food.

With one more peak, I caught sight of the girl lifting her pink tresses, as her dad fastened a clasp at the nape of her neck. Her hand reached for the pendant, and something about her seemed familiar. I told myself to focus.

The dining car was empty except for a French couple who were heatedly discussing the Fort Hood massacre; a seemingly annoyed businessman—probably a right winger—and a spry-looking, white-haired woman who had a patch over one eye. A patch! I had never seen anyone who actually wore a patch.

The businessman sat in the far corner and had the best seat to people watch, but he was without a window. The French couple was on the wrong side of the train. So that left Patch.

She would have been my first choice regardless. The notes said the hacker girl ate dinner every night with her family, so I was pretty certain she would make her way here eventually. And old people tended to eat slowly, so I'd be able to linger under the pretense of good manners. As I approached the table, the woman's one good eye locked on mine, and with sincere pleasure, I asked to join her.

"Yes, you may. Please, sit down," she said, and then went back to looking at whatever had her attention captured outside.

I did as I was bid. The rapscallion in me wanted to sit beside her to watch her head swivel like an owl. My wife both hated and loved my demented humor. I refrained and set myself across from the bird with the patch. The only disadvantage from where I sat was its less-than-optimal vantage point if Miss Lundgren should happen to choose a table behind me. It was sixes.

With a broad smile, the steward introduced himself to me as Karl, took my drink order, handed me the dinner menu, and then gave an attentive glance toward Patch. She made no indication that she was aware of his presence.

As soon as Karl withdrew from the table, Patch zeroed in on me with deliberate precision, as if her head were a honing device that had just tracked her target. I was rather caught off guard by how much her movement resembled an owl. Was I projecting my ornithologist training onto her?

"Normally I would never eat fish upon a train or an airplane," said Patch, "but in this case, I can recommend it highly. It is Coho season so you are guaranteed a fresh catch. There is nothing quite as delicious as the unique flavor of salmon. Assuming, that is, it is not overcooked." Her nostrils flared slightly at the thought.

"Well, I appreciate the suggestion," I said. Not passing up the opportunity to watch her wince, I added, "I am, however, a vegetarian." I was rewarded with a slight constriction of her pupil. This was a woman with definite opinions and absolute certainty they were correct.

Karl returned with my Tanqueray and tonic and a notepad. Deferring to my dining companion, I listened, amused, as she ordered her meal. And I do mean "ordered."

In all my life, I had never seen nor heard anyone ask to see their animal protein prior to it being cooked, in order to instruct the waiter on what to say to the chef regarding how long and at what temperature to cook it.

Karl was certainly going to earn his money tonight. He listened politely, appearing to be unmoved by her demand. "Of course, Madame. And may I suggest a wine to pair with your meal?"

She turned back to face me, while telling him curtly that she didn't indulge. I indeed felt judged and had to clear my throat to hold back from laughing.

I requested the vegetarian pasta with a side of broccoli. "However the chef prepares it is just fine. Just keep these coming," I pleaded, pointing to my nearly emptied rocks glass.

Karl smiled. "The vegetables will be snappy, I assure you."

The woman and I studied each other in silence for a few minutes. I was quite accustomed to staring contests with old birds; I could do this all day. But did I really want to? "So what were you studying out there?" I asked. She continued to look at me the same way my aunt did when I spilled milk on her tatted table cloth.

Just when I thought she might never answer, she said she had been looking at the sculpture set in the middle of the depot courtyard. "The thing is ugly. It has no purpose. According to the article in *Trains*, it was commissioned to honor the four sister cities of Eugene, Oregon: Irkutsk, Osaka, Kathmandu, and Jinju. How is such a blob an honor to anything?"

Her tone was flat and I could detect nothing from her face. Maybe she was teasing or testing me. Did I dare tell her that I found it to be quite an amusing piece and that the bench that was at the base encircling the inverted cone seemed quite purposeful? My stomach rumbled, giving me a reason to focus on buttering a piece of roll Karl had snuck onto my bread plate.

"I am not sure how a volcano with fruit and animals on it is supposed to represent anything of value," she said.

Chewing and swallowing gave me a moment to ponder my words carefully. To look at her, you would just think her a sweet, old lady . . . with a patch. But something about her made my neck hairs stand up. "Did the article say what that cone is supposed to be? Because it looks like a witch's hat to me."

"A witch's hat?" she hissed. "That is absolutely absurd!"

One would think I was saying the hat belonged on her head. I had no idea of how to neutralize this situation. I felt bad having disrupted her peace, though my intention was to leave room for others to use the open tables. No good deed goes unpunished. Fortunately, Karl walked toward us with two steaming bowls of consommé. Fancy! Maybe she liked to eat in silence. As it was, we were stuck together for the time being.

The dining car filled with passengers. There were two families with young children who were behaving delightfully. Behind them, an elderly couple had reached the point in their lives when a half century of living together had caused them to look alike. Then there were some nerd types who were bent over handheld computer devices, clicking away as they traveled from Seattle to Silicon Valley. They each sat with ear buds in place, at different tables, enabling them to be solitary. Angie called that "voluntary solitary confinement."

The kids obviously knew each other quite well and were able to communicate with a series of gestures and facial expressions that would make Jim Carey envious. Their giggles were contagious and they had to stifle them behind the palms of their hands to keep from erupting into hysterics. However, when Karl approached, they sat up straight, made direct eye contact, let their meal requests known, prefacing them with "may"; not even the youngest demanded with a "give me."

I may have been raised on a shoestring budget, but my mother was a stickler for good manners and etiquette. My father, who had been killed in action in Vietnam, left behind wealthy parents with a lot of preferences they called rules. Mom was determined that we know the rules for when we visited them.

Her pedigreed in-laws had looked down upon her as a mutt ever since she had licked the drip from the lip of her coffee cup. Funny that she should remarry a man whose nickname means "mutt."

Mom's innate confidence, combined with her sensitivities to the insecure needs of others for artificial meanings, made for an interesting upbringing. We kids were encouraged to see the world from others' perspectives, as a basic tenet to critical thinking. An unexpected consequence to this education was that we learned how to easily spot people's strengths and vulnerabilities.

I had become a watcher. I watched and studied. And then I made a career out of it. As I was doing here, I reported my findings to someone else. What they did with that information was of no consequence to me.

I discovered the truth at a young age that we often cannot know someone's intentions and we have very little power over their decisions once their mind is set.

My life approach and best defense was to do my job, keep my head down, and take care of my family.

And that was exactly what I was here to do. Sato would have told me to check my premises. But he wasn't the one whose family was in peril.

Watching the joyful interactions of the children made me miss my family. I would kill for my sister, Tracy's, homemade linguini and tomato ice cream sauce. Despite the fact that the train's chef cooked my broccoli trees to perfection, my meal lacked the flavor and baked-in affection of home.

"Are you not going to eat that?" Patch inquired as if annoyed. Clearly she was taking personal offense to the slow pace at which I was eating, though it seemed like Karl had only just set down my plate.

My appetite seemed to have vanished. The rumbling in my stomach was replaced by an ache in my heart. Everything about this situation suddenly felt wrong.

"To tell you the truth, this is the first time I've been away from my family and I am missing them very much," I said. Placing my knife and fork across my plate to indicate that I was finished, I waited for the next wave of judgment. I was almost disappointed when instead her eye darted over my shoulder.

"Excuse me, would you mind if I join you?" said someone behind me. I must have looked ridiculous as I spurted out the first good swig from my second drink. That voice! I would have recognized it anywhere, even in a crowd. I craned my neck and looked up into the eyes of my childhood crush. Only it wasn't her; it was Phalaenopsis Ariel Lundgren—the hacker girl I was being blackmailed to watch. She looked and sounded just like my Phi-Phi.

Chapter 4

My head reeled. The hacker girl politely asked if
she could slide in and sit at the window. "It's my first
train ride. You don't mind, do you?" Her voice was
smooth like velvet, almost sultry, just like Phi-Phi's. I
stood and automatically let her in.

"Hello, I am Phalaen Lundgren," she said,
introducing herself first to the old woman and then to
me. Her posture was as perfect when sitting as when
standing, I thought, as I watched her delicately place the
napkin I had not been using upon her lap. It then
occurred to me that neither Patch nor I had exchanged
names, much less the usual pleasantries that civilized
people do when first introduced.

"What an interesting name, Phalaen," Patch
responded. "You may call me Ms. Foster." Although her
mouth said "Interesting," I heard, "stupid."

Phalaen inched her finger toward a tired tot of one
of the families, who hid flirtatiously behind his sister,
and explained that her name was short for Phalaenopsis
and that she was given the name as a result of her
mother losing a bet.

Turning to see what was delighting the young
lady so, Ms. Foster remarked with barely concealed

disdain, "Oh, yes, they are born charmers," adding casually that it must have been a stupid bet that her mother regretted.

"She could have called you Rose, Lily, or even Iris. Those are all acceptable."

Phalaen smiled and simply said, "Yes, she could have."

"Well, Phalaen, it's my pleasure," I said. "I am Richard Fleming and I love your name. Orchids have always been my favorite flowers."

I imagined Ms. Foster's blood began to curdle as her fingers gripped her tea cup so tightly the blue in her veins darkened. Patch didn't find me any more affable than I found her, apparently. Or maybe she just didn't like orchids.

The old woman said, "Maybe you can help us solve our debate. We were just discussing the sculpture that was at the train station one stop back." Mockery filmed over Patch's one eye like a wedding veil hiding the face of a harlot. "Was the sculpture a witch's hat, or not?"

Our good steward placed a third cocktail in front of me. "Good evening and welcome aboard the Coast Starlight," Karl oozed with southern graciousness.

He added, "We are no longer offering the salmon, I'm afraid." He leaned in to whisper to all three of us in the strictest of confidence that it had made a passenger ill. I had noticed the businessman leave abruptly only moments ago.

"He must have a weak constitution," said Ms. Foster. "I ate it and as you can see I am perfectly fine." Challenging Phalaen to test her strength against her own, Patch tried to insist that Phalaen too order the salmon.

"Well, thank you for the suggestion, but I will not be ordering the fish," said Phalaen. A wave of relief flooded Karl's face. "No offense to the chef, but the only fish I eat is that which I, or someone I know, catches." Phalaen smiled impishly as she realized she inadvertently offended the older woman and tried to make up for it by explaining that she was a "compassionate carnivore" who only consumes meat that has died an honorable death.

I burst out laughing.

Patch stared while her lips pursed with bitterness. "When I was your age," she said, "I was happy to have any sort of meat, whether caught humanely, as you kids like to call it, or not. Humans are at the top of the food chain and the industrial farming practices of this century have nearly solved starvation."

There was a brief moment of quiet during which time I hoped that Ms. Foster would choke on her own string of insults and criticisms.

"Anyway," Phalaen said, quickly moving on, "it's nice to meet you, Karl. I was just about to solve a mystery for my fellow travelers." She turned to me squarely and said, "You were about to ask me to solve a debate about my mother's sculpture."

"Did you just say that your mother created that?" There had been no mention of her mom in the file so I just assumed her parents were divorced and she lived with her father. "Who is your mother?"

"She signed her art VSix7, but her actual name was Vivienne Lane Lundgren." The young girl was radiant with pride.

Did she just say "her mother"? So that meant that my Phi-Phi forged that beauty. But of course she did. And of course something she created would irritate the woman sitting across from me—they were total opposites.

In fact, they would have hated each other. I chuckled to myself, almost feeling sorry for the old lady. I once heard my mom say the fun and playful Phi-Phi I loved was the fiercest person she'd ever known.

"Oh, I am sorry but I didn't notice a sculpture," Karl apologized with total sincerity. "I am always so busy running around here. Can I get you a drink to get you started, hon?"

It seemed incredibly odd that Karl could have missed seeing the sculpture, since it had been there since the remodel several years back. It would be pretty hard to miss a blackish, thirty-foot-high witch's hat in the middle of a train depot. And now that I knew who created it, I was sure it was a witch's hat because Phi-Phi loved Stevie Nicks.

Phalaen told Karl she would appreciate it if he would get her a hobo and some dope, which sent him into gales of laughter, while Ms. Foster offered another one of her looks of disapproval.

"Wouldn't we all like that, honey?" He sashayed off telling her he'd give her a second to look at the menu and then would return with some water.

The young woman sat back, folded her hands in her lap and said to Ms. Foster, "Indeed it is true that by every quantifiable metric, poverty has decreased by over one third in the last century. However, I do not think your point addresses the relevancy of inhumane farming practices, nor is it a valid argument that could possibly dissuade me from consuming only animals that I, or another honorable person, kill."

Wow! This young woman was my hero! She was able to sweetly, politely, and logically put Patch in her place, without a hint of malice or snarky insolence. Was that fear I saw cross Patch's face like a dark shadow? How did this mere girl incite an emotional response in just seconds and without seeming to even try? She was definitely her mother's daughter.

Phalaen continued her scolding. "It is strange to me when I hear older people talk about younger people as if the monsters raised themselves." She smiled at Karl as she accepted a glass of water and added, "My mom always said war brought about a shortage of good mothers and that if there was anything to blame for society's ills, it was that—a lack of good mothers."

The four of us were quiet as the words hung in the air like a noose waiting for someone to stick their neck out.

Karl once again saved us all as a good host will do, jumped in, and said, "So you say your mother was the artist of that incredibly fun sculpture at the Eugene train station? I just looked it up in one of the brochures. It's faaaabulous!"

"Yes! It is Merlin's hat," Phalaen said. She pulled out a pamphlet from her back pocket and unfolded it to the page that described the piece. "See, if you look here, you can see the Dungeness crabs that are meant to be reminiscent of spiders crawling all over it, with bunches of blueberries hanging off as well. Those are meant to pay homage to Jinju, South Korea, with whom there was a significant trade agreement." She looked up as though she was fully expecting all of us share in her enthusiasm.

"How droll," Patch remarked, unimpressed. "And the other three sister cities? How is it that they are reflected in the piece? And more importantly, what actual purpose does it serve? The directional column that was there previously was at least informative." Her resentment of the erection seemed personal.

Phalaen grinned like the Cheshire Cat. "I'm so glad you asked. You are going to love it! My mom was so playful. She believed purpose, when wrapped in childlike wonder, provided the sense of awe necessary to keep the delusion of self-importance at bay, while making learning fun." We all stared at her for different reasons.

Turning the brochure so we could get a better look, Phalaen pointed out how the bench, purposeful indeed, was carved from a single myrtle tree, just as the Kasthamandap, the Hindu temple in Kathmandu had been. "Also, it is still a directional column," she said proudly. "The tiger or beaver that is the mascot for Irkutsk sits on top, pointing north." She giggled like a teenager.

"Oh, that is clever!" Karl clapped. "Thank you for sharing. I feel like we have a celebrity among us."

Still not won over, Patch pointed out that Osaka, Japan, was not represented and even so, the entire spectacle was riddled in silliness. She conceded that a bench was useful, but hardly required an entirely new piece to be built. The money spent on that alone could have been used by the city to pay for something else like a new school.

"Actually," said Phalaen, "if you look closely, there is a cryptographical message covering the hat." She covered her mouth so she wouldn't spoil the punchline. "It's the rice and the grapes . . . they are zeroes and ones!" She seemed tickled with a childlike delight. "And as for the cost, well the city didn't pay for it and my mom didn't believe in public good, so..."

All of this seemed perfectly reasonable when I recalled Phi-Phi, my adopted sister, who made everything magical—everything except the cryptography. That was not her, but I knew who it could be and it made me smile. "However did she come up with the idea for the cryptographical messages?"

"Cryptography is an integral part of each of her pieces. It was her way of including her best childhood friend in her art. They had their own language that they developed to talk to one another. He ended up studying computer science in school and is a well-known cryptographer."

Until Phalaen had mentioned Phi-Phi's friend, I had had no recollection of him. But then I remembered the long-haired guy who used to sit at the kitchen table with Mom, Dad, and Phi-Phi late at night, always engrossed in philosophical debate. This was all coming together, even as it was blowing up.

"And what about your mother? Is she a programmer, too?" Ms. Foster asked.

"No, she was not a programmer, Ms. Foster. She was an artist."

Just then, we were distracted by the two families who stood up to leave. Phalaen exchanged signals with several of the children as, one by one, the little cherubs filed past us, with our steward patting the youngest on the head like he was a little puppy.

The parents nodded and smiled with great pride, as if to say, "Yes, they are adorable, aren't they? We are blessed." As the last of the family exited, Karl sighed almost enviously and turned back to us.

Patch took the opportunity to excuse herself to "stretch her legs." She said she would be back for coffee and dessert. The area warmed considerably the further she got from the table.

"Whew! It's a bit airish in here," Phalaen said, mimicking Karl's accent.

"Airish?" I asked, as Karl stood, smiling and seeming to not hear the mimicry. With a shrug of his shoulders, he indicated that he too did not understand the word.

"Huh. Well it really is a fantastic word. It means 'chilly'." And then with a style altogether different from my other female dining companion, she handed the menu back to Karl and melodically requested her dinner. In French! "Pour commencer, une salade César. Et ensuite, je voudrais avoir un steak frites avec des tomates grillées et d'asperges à la sauce béarnaise, s'il vous plaît."

"Oui, Madamoiselle, bien sur!" Karl did an about-face, nearly clicking his heels together.

Moving into the spot that had been occupied by frosty Ms. Foster, I took note of the fact that the cushion was cold. It was another clue that the woman was reptilian.

"I thought you were a 'compassionate carnivore,' only consuming meat that died an honorable death," I said.

"Is that a question, Mr. Fleming?" Phalaen asked.

"Please call me Richard. And yes, I suppose it is."

"Wellll . . . Ms. Foster was rude and I am a teenager unable to resist the opportunity to put a muggle in her place." She grinned and asked if I knew what a muggle was.

"Yes, Phalaen, I do. I have a six-year-old son who is convinced the librarian is really a teacher at Hogwarts and he breathlessly anticipates her taking him along when he's ready."

"That is super cute! And yes, it is true that I make it a rule to eat only meat that has been raised roaming and happy, contrary to some of those assembly-line practices 'her generation' designed. But the Australian beef served here has a 'Happy Cow' stamp-of-approval rating, so I'm good."

Ahh, clever girl! "And how did you know that Karl could speak French?" I asked. "You speak it very well yourself, by the way."

"Thanks. Computer languages are my favorite, but I do speak French and Japanese fluently. As for Karl, I noticed he spoke with a French accent, so I assumed."

Of course a girl so young had not traveled much, so any accent—other than the lack of one, a unique characteristic that Oregonians could claim—must have sounded exotic to her. I said, "I think you are detecting his Blue Ridge Mountain hillbilly accent. His name tag says he is from Asheville, North Carolina." I tried hard not to sound condescending as I told her this fact with the presumption that I knew better than she because I was older. It was a mistake I would make again, but only once.

"No, he speaks Blue Ridge Mountain hillbilly, though not very well, with a French accent. His first language is definitely French and he is most likely Moroccan, not Appalachian." There was a resolute confidence in her tone that was familiar.

I started to ask her whether she was sure, but quickly shut my mouth, confident in her confidence. Instead, I said, "Wow, I had no idea." Typically, I would have been slightly embarrassed at my ignorance, but it was easy to accept her correction.

Karl arrived just then and placed a Caesar salad in front of her. She discretely felt the edge of the plate and smiled. "I just knew you would appreciate that," said Karl and he stood a little taller. "I must say, it is a real treat to have someone who notices subtle distinctions like a chilled salad plate. Thank you, dear."

"Thank you, Karl! Now if you would just be so kind as to get me some dope."

"Well now, I really cannot do that while I am working." He whispered and mouthed the words with great exaggeration. "But if you come by at the end of my shift, I can probably have a little something for you then."

He put his finger to the side of his nose. The young girl just sat nodding her head. He winked and was off again. He would make a terrible spy.

"You handle yourself quite well for someone so young, Phalaen," I said. She smiled at me and laughed at herself, as a drop of dressing landed with a plop in her lap. Her eyes traced its descent, her mouth full with romaine, as it fell from her fork tines to somewhere below the table.

"Good that you took my napkin," I told her. She blushed a little and smiled, green leaves and all. "You were telling me about Karl and his French accent."

She took another bite, picked up an anchovy filet with her fingers, dragged it through a puddle of sauce, dropped it into her mouth, dabbed her lips, and swallowed. She didn't just consume food, she devoured it. I should have waited to eat with her. Maybe if she'd ordered it for me in French, I would have enjoyed it more.

"Yes, well Karl, if that is even his name, is an imposter. It is unclear to me why he would be pretending to be the man who is the regular steward, but he is not him." She continued chomping salad, expertly picking out the heart pieces that were firm enough to hold the creamy mixture so as to avoid loose-leaf limpage and subsequent lap splatting.

How could she possibly know who the regular steward was? I wondered. I thought she said this was her first train ride. A buzz against my left thigh interrupted my thoughts.

It was the cell I was given for Operation Get My Life Back, but I could not very well answer it in front of her. I begged off to take the call. I had to tell her something, and wishing my son goodnight seemed a reasonable excuse to jump up from the table mid-conversation.

The device buzzed me again with the annoyance of a mosquito. This time, I grabbed it from my pocket. It read, "Restricted." I said, "Hello?"

"You were instructed to watch her," bellowed a voice that was mechanized like Darth Vader's.

"I am watching her. She asked to sit at my table in a dining car that was filled," I responded defensively. Shit! Am I being watched? I shook my head as the reality sunk in. This was not a casual observance; this was a stakeout. There was no point in asking how the caller knew what I was doing, since it was clear he knew exactly where and with whom I was sitting.

"Your trip will be ending in Colorado," the voice on the other end of the phone said.

"Colorado? But, we had a deal." I felt a surge of panic.

"Change of plans."

I did not know what to do. I had no plan B.

Chapter 5

Peaking at 10,000 feet, Mt. Shasta was the perfect backdrop to my feelings of elation. They contradicted the supposed insignificance of a single human being. But one person can make a difference in the life of others, and the change ripples. Like a spark that sets off a stream of lava that creates a mountain.

I considered what effects my actions would cause, as I admired the patches of ice fields. They had outlasted the summer heat and glowed white with the light of the full moon amplifying the brightness of the glaciers on the mountain's north side. The fortitude of the staying power of the glaciers deprived the night from shrouding us all in darkness.

We rolled along the seventeen-mile base, with cars whirring against the track, synched with the racing of my heart. It had been some time since I'd felt this adrenaline surge, and holding my dinner down seemed unlikely.

I yearned in that moment for Mom's caress. I could almost feel the touch of her fingers tracing across my forehead, relaxing me in unison with the train's bellowing tone. I wrapped my own finger around the pendant holding the magical stone that had been Dad's parting gift to me. It was a crucial piece to a puzzle.

The events of the evening were far too involved for a string of texts, and the cell service had been nearly nonexistent for the last hour. And though I promised Dad I would take a break from my keyboard for the train ride, and it seemed perfectly reasonable at the time, it now left me shaking my head.

Parents, even with the best of intentions, put us kids in the position of having to lie to them. If I broke out the keyboard and typed an explanation for all that had happened, I would be violating my promise. It was a silly promise in the first place, but I was willing to make it because Amtrak blocked VPNs. Though the odds of me being hacked were slim, I just couldn't support free Wi-Fi that lacked the ability to log in securely.

I looked at the pen and paper on the table in front of me and thought once again of Mom saying, "Learn the rules. Then learn why and how to break them, darling." Funny how even in this moment, she was the one I thought of to determine my course of action. As crazy as the evening had been, it wasn't sufficient cause to break my promise. It would just be convenient.

Mom's insistence that I learn how to write cursive had caused more than one morning of frustration at the kitchen table where I practiced writing while she heated water to pour over oatmeal. It was the one day a week she made me breakfast, while Dad went hunting or target shooting.

Maybe if she hadn't made me oatmeal, which I hated, it would have been less brutal but she really could only boil water. At this moment, I felt grateful she insisted, and I wished I hadn't given her such a hard time about it. I did have lovely penmanship. I gave one more glance toward the breathtaking view from my private room and set about writing to explain to Dad all that had occurred in the first few hours of my trip, while I myself reflected and tried to digest it, along with my dinner.

My salad had tasted delicious, with little pieces of anchovy in the dressing making the sauce extra salty. Richard had excused himself from the table. It worked out well, since I was able to get the skinny on Karl, whose real name was Karim.

He was definitely not the steward whom I'd heard stories of from his flame dames, Jan and Misty. Nope, Karim was Karl's lover! He just happened to be wearing Karl's name tag, which caused confusion.

I was surprised that he'd still not caught the idiosyncratic words I had cleverly incorporated into our dialogue. But according to Karim, his dearest had worked fastidiously to rid his speech of the country. When I told him that "dope" was what Blue Ridge Mountain Folk called "soda," he had laughed at having offered me some pot.

"Today happens to be my last day, so it's not like I am going to get fired for weed peddling," he said with a smirk and sat down to join me.

He placed before me a NY strip with fries and a ramekin of the rich sauce that served as a measurement of a good cook to my dad, and therefore to me also. Chervil, shallot, tarragon, and peppercorn all crushed together for flavoring were expertly strained out of the vinegar and egg yolk mixture until the creamy sauce remained; clear of specks of spices.

I removed a knife from my purse and glanced up to see a look of surprise on Karim's face. With our eyes locked, I said casually, "I made this myself," as I sliced through the pink-centered steak and dabbled a bit more sauce on it before I placed it in my mouth. I closed my eyes; or maybe they just rolled back into my head.

"I'm quite impressed! That is quite a piece of cutlery you have there," said Karim. He paused and let me finish chewing. "Should I be scared?" he asked. I smiled and raised my brows, drawing a hearty laugh from him.

"So what do you mean that today is your last day?" I didn't feel like I was being nosy, considering he had invited himself to sit down. And most of the diners had left. There remained just the old couple ogling each other with a look of young love; and the Silicon Valley commuters, who were all still locked in their own worlds, hidden behind screens, and shut off from the rest of us via earplugs.

"I would have told you earlier," Karim said, "if you'd introduced yourself as 'Ariel, Queen of the Flower Fairies." He gave me a wink as my jaw dropped. "Yes, yes, yes, of course I know Jan and Misty," he said to my surprise.

He continued, "They happened to have been the ones who introduced Karl and me years ago. I am actually a bit surprised they didn't think to inform you I may be on the route." He wasn't offended in a way that his feelings were hurt for being forgotten. It was more like he couldn't imagine the reason "why."

"Well, that's easy! They didn't know that I was taking the train," I said. His puzzled look told me that he found that hard to believe. Apparently, he did know Jan. She was such a talker and had she known, she would have made a big to-do over it.

Jan was the town informant: mail carrier by day and gossip by night. She was keen on drinking bullshots at the tavern just outside of town, while using her never-ending billiard skills to earn money off people passing through. In between racking and cracking balls, she filled everyone in on what everyone else was doing.

"Oh don't look so surprised," Karim said, smacking my hand gently. "When you said your mother was the one who had sculpted the piece at the train depot, I knew exactly who you were."

His face fell and for the first time, I felt like I was seeing him, not the person I had expected him to be. I also felt like I was about to be introduced to aspects of my mother I had never known. It left me feeling both curious and slightly defensive.

"We were all so devastated when she left you and your dad," he said. His eyes teared up and he drew his hand around his throat as if he could physically push back the lump. "We were real sorry to miss her memorial service, but Karl was just so very ill. We did, however, donate to the mission she started in Morocco."

"She started a mission? In Morocco?" I asked. "My mother, Vivienne Lane Lundgren?"

"Well yes, yes, she did. She created a safe place for teens to go for the day, the night, or longer, if they wanted."

"I have never heard about this, Karim. You would think my mother would have told me. But to be honest, the only connection I knew my mother to have in Morocco was a love of their wedding blankets."

His face lit up like a Christmas tree. "Yes! The kids make those. She and some local women taught the kids years ago how to weave and decorate blankets as a fun

54

craft. By the next time she visited, they had made enough to start a business."

He obviously knew my mom, but borrowing his lover's identity and his job seemed a little weird, even for people she would find interesting. And what was with the accent? It was almost as if he is trying to cover up his French accent with a hillbilly one. For a person as colorful as he, that did seem to be a step in the wrong direction.

"I myself lived on the streets of Morocco as a teen," he said. "It was where I met your mother years ago. . . . Let's see. . . . Oh, gawd, it's been decades now." He lifted a knife, looked at his reflection in the blade, and gave a slight shudder.

"I was caught with my pants down with my best friend," he continued. "There was no kafala for me, so I had to learn to adapt and overcome. Fortunately, your mother spoke French and interceded when she happened upon a deal that had gone bad. I was able to escape to the US with her help."

"I'm sorry to interrupt, but what is 'kafala'?" I asked.

"Oh, no apologies, habibi! Kafala is the adoption process in Morocco. I was thrown out of my home and orphaned at age ten because of my homosexual act. But adoption is not possible for anyone who is not Muslim. And Islam does not allow homosexuality."

"So Allah and Jehovah are down with stoning people, and having multiple wives, just not same-sex partnerships. That seems perfectly reasonable," I said. I offered an exaggerated eye roll so he'd be sure to know I was being sarcastic. He smiled tenderly.

I continued talking while chewing and absentmindedly pointing my knife at him. "The ways that groups pick and choose the parts of sacred texts they maintain as inviolate, while forgetting the very ones that cover all the rest, annoys me."

"You are your mother's daughter!" he said and smirked, nodding toward the knife.

"Actually, that part is my dad. He is pretty big on grace and forgiveness. And knife throwing." We both laughed at how opportunity had given me a joke.

"You know something? I have never met John."

"That's odd. He and my mom were nearly inseparable."

"After you were born, that is true. Your mother traveled a lot while your father was studying abroad, but she never missed one of his speaking engagements. She always said it was his voice that had first drawn her. So romantic," he sighed.

"Okay, I am confused, but we'll get back to all that. What is with the accent? You are hardly from Appalachia, but your speech has some of the nuance without the vocabulary. And why are you wearing Karl's nametag and using his identity?"

"Karl and I have been together for ten years and have sort of merged, as they say. I don't intentionally hide an accent but I did unintentionally pick up a bit of his."

"And where is Karl now and why are you doing his route?"

The kind look in Karim's eyes was unmistakable—it was similar to how my dad looked at me when I'd said or done something that crossed a line of etiquette I didn't really understand. Dad told me it was a result of me being American.

"Well, honey, he's had HIV for over twenty years. And though he's been perfectly healthy, thanks to caring for his immune system and utilizing some non-FDA-approved remedies, he contracted cancer two years ago. His health has been declining rapidly since."

Karim looked so vulnerable. He fiddled with his tie and flattened it out against his chest, petting his heart to offer himself solace, though none could be had. He had that look of inevitability that crushes some and gives resolve to others.

"I knew everyone that worked Karl's routes," he said, "and I made a deal, so he could keep his insurance and get his retirement benefits. I am him! We keep it on the down low though, so sshhh . . . don't tell anyone I'm not really a dining car steward." He winked at me as if it was necessary to actually keep the secret.

He breathed in deeply, lifted his chin and said, "You know what Debbie Reynolds says . . . 'Chin up, tits out!'" and he smiled like a clown. There is nothing quite as sad as a clown.

I was very much enjoying our chat, as well as my perfectly cooked piece of meat, when Richard returned looking terribly haggard. Karim jumped up to make room for him and ran off saying he'd be right back with another Tanqueray and tonic. Richard mumbled an expression of gratitude. I didn't feel it appropriate to ask if there was a problem at home, so I chewed while lost in my own thoughts, trying to digest my meal along with the new information about my mother.

With elbows on the table, Richard pressed his pointer and middle fingers against his temples, making circling movements, while I concentrated on forming the perfect bite of tomato and asparagus. Karim returned, setting a rocks glass of elixir before Richard, and then slid onto the bench seat next to him, resting a hand upon his shoulder in a very maternal way. We three seemed an odd mix, but somehow we fit.

Richard looked up at me with bloodshot eyes. "Everything is really messed up, and . . . and . . . and I have made such a terrible mistake," he choked out before he began to sob. Karim patted his shoulder while I sat immobile. First my dad, and now this man in front of me, blubbering like babies. It was nearly more than I could take and I was glad my new acquaintance was here to console him.

Karim fished a clean handkerchief from his pocket, which Richard graciously accepted, before wiping his eyes and blowing his nose with it. Karim and I made eye contact and he gave a little shrug as I looked down onto my plate at the béarnaise sauce that had suddenly lost its appeal. At least I'd been able to finish most of my dinner. Karim removed my plate and de-crumbed my place setting.

The spectacle was kind of weird. What was weirder, though, was that nobody in the dining car even noticed. I felt thankful to my dad for suggesting that I stay AFK during the trip out to Boston. Seeing the way the techies were missing out on some real-life drama brought home to me the point that my parents made when I was certain I would be into computers: face-to-face interaction is where we experience compassion and empathy.

The techies were immersed in their virtual worlds and were oblivious to Richard's pain and present meltdown. The old couple, on the other hand, came from that time when people were prone to mind their own business and offer privacy as a courtesy. Or maybe they were hard of hearing.

"Is everything okay with your son?" I finally asked, feeling that to not say something would somehow be rude. I was really not good at this sort of thing. Dad and Mom used to say that I was like a Vulcan, ruled by logic, and not real gooey with emotions. I presumed Richard's child had to be the root of the distress, since he'd left to wish him goodnight, and even I understood that the parental bond causes intense passions.

Richard nodded his head. He reached out, took my hand, and with his other one covered his eyes as he wept. And though I hadn't really thought about Q in this way for a very long time, I wished she were here. She'd know exactly what to say. She was definitely the more empathic of the two of us when we were young, and she could offer the exact thing to sooth a sorrow.

Karim returned with a tray carrying a teapot and three cups and saucers, a small bowl filled with Turkish delight, and another one with tangerines. He placed a little bit of sugar in each cup while telling us how his grandma had made this drink for him when he was a little boy and it had comforted him.

The aroma of mint filled the air as he poured the hot concoction into our cups, while steam rose to fill our noses. The effect was immediate and reminded me of my mom's own version that she had invented to sooth the heartache of a young boy she had babysat when she was a teenager. She said he had buck teeth.

"Thanks, Karl," Richard said as he once again wiped the tears from his face with the gifted hanky.

"His name is 'Karim'" I told him and then winced slightly at the disapproving look I got. It was as though Karim was trying to telepathically communicate something and I wasn't quite catching on. Richard didn't notice.

"This smells terrific and reminds me of something my Phi-Phi made for me." Richard said this while his left hand tilted the cup and his right thumb and forefinger raised the delicate drink to his lips. "It was called . . ."

"A Bucky," we both said at the same time.

I reeled. First Karim and now him? How was it possible I had never heard of either of them? Mom told me everything about her life—she overshared in most people's opinion, to be sure, but she had never mentioned ever being anyone's "Fi-fi."

And what did that even mean? My mother had hardly been a "Fi-fi" by any measure. I felt like Alice from Wonderland and I was certain that tomorrow morning I'd wake up a different person than the one I woke up as today.

Suddenly, I was yanked from my delirium as I heard the old woman from the couple cry out, "Help! Please, someone help us!" The ashen grey face of her husband and the bluish hand on his chest signaled an emergency. I lunged from my seat and caught her beloved as he careened toward the floor.

Chapter 6

The Coast Starlight screeched into the Sacramento train station. At the break of dawn, the noise was an assault even if you were already awake. Packed up and ready to go, I was feeling nervous and exhilarated. I could barely contain my excitement at the astounding circumstances that had just turned my cross-country journey into a full-fledged adventure.

With ten minutes to get my things off the train and meet up with my new traveling companions, I reread the letter my father would see in days. It seemed antiquated and cruel to communicate via snail mail when life could change entirely in a moment. In this case though, the letter was going to offer me a convenient excuse if he didn't approve of my decision. Satisfied I had shared with him my new itinerary without divulging too much to cause him worry, I proofread my letter. You can take the kid out of the home, but not the homeschooling out of the kid.

Hey Dad   *August 21, 2013*

Traveling by train was the right choice. I am having an adventure I could not have ever imagined for myself. And I can feel Mom's presence with me in a way that I never have before.

Speaking of Mom. You know how we were both so sad that she didn't finish her final piece from her Crypto Chaos series, which she affectionately called "Blackjack"? Well, Dad, I think she did.

I am including a rough sketch of what I believe was her final one. I didn't tell you about it when I found the sketch because scrolled across the top of her drawings, in bold letters, was written: "DON'T SHOW JOHN!" I figured Mom must have had her reasons.

However, you have already seen part of it. I noticed when I looked in the mirror while getting ready for dinner, that the beautiful pendant you gave me is the same one as is in the drawing.

Did you actually know about the sculpture, Dad?

Things are a little confusing and I am going to try to sort it all out. I am going to make a slight detour in my route to enable me to meet with someone from her past whose son I came across quite by chance. I do feel like you have some explaining to do.

Love,
F@r!3L

I refolded the letter and stuffed it into my pocket, hoping he'd have the good sense to talk to Jan or Ng if he didn't understand my signature. Snail mail, what a hassle. It was going to serve me in this case, however, as it would give me a few days before he would start to worry or want answers.

With no sign of my fellow travelers, I headed to the dining car. Karim had assured me I'd be able to get a quick bite, even though breakfast did not start until 6:30 a.m. It was now 6:28.

As if they'd all felt a migratory call, the blue hairs had all congregated in the same place, filling the seats and tables. Some had newspapers in one hand, with the other protectively wrapped around the handle of a coffee mug. Others were chatting to each other while still maintaining their grips upon their drug of choice. Nobody seemed to notice me as I slipped in, so I headed straight for the kitchen, where I hoped to grab a couple of hard-boiled eggs, some oatmeal, and a few bananas and oranges.

I hadn't made it halfway through the room when I heard, then saw, a woman call out, "There she is! That is the girl I was telling you about." I could feel all eyes turn upon me, including the left one that belonged to Patch. She had missed out on the previous night's dramatic unfolding, after apparently deciding not to return for dessert. Patch was cloistered together with three others, including the woman pointing a finger at me. I felt obligated to stop and make some sort of remark.

"Good morning, Ms. Foster. We missed you last evening," I said, with a slight pinch at my own willful insincerity.

"I doubt that," she responded icily. I shivered. "I was just informed of your heroic efforts to save Mr. Smith's wedding ring."

"And she was successful!" chimed in my herald, who was now making me regret not listening to my own voice that had told me to get breakfast in town. I made a mental note to growl at Karim later, as well as to listen better to my instincts.

"We were, in fact, able to save Mr. Smith's ring," I said, unwilling to be baited by the old coot. "He was a bit overindulgent on the sodium and together with his meds, it caused his hands to swell. But all's well that ends well, right?" I smiled at her one good eye and wished my admirers a pleasant day. Thinking that was sufficient, I turned to go, only to have my hand jerked abruptly.

"Please, Phariel," said Ms. Foster, "indulge me, if you would."

Extracting my hand from her grip, I stepped far enough away so she'd not be able to do that again, and I looked at her narrowly. "What did you say?"

"Do tell us how you ever thought to use dental floss to remove his ring, Phalaen," she replied.

I could have sworn she had said "Phariel." Wow, did I need to get out of my head! I needed a bike ride. I inhaled and exhaled slowly.

"I had a very handy mother who taught me a lot of little tricks like that," I said. "And she happened to get this ring I'm wearing stuck on her finger once, while trying it on prior to bestowing it to me."

I held up my right hand and showed them all the star ring that had been a treasure of my mom's when she was a young girl. I always wore it, but had taken it off to wash my hands before dinner and had left it on the vanity in my compartment. "So I just did as my momma taught me."

"Aren't you a clever girl?" Ms. Foster asked with a tone that sounded more like an accusation than a compliment. "Why don't you sit down and join us," she said rather bristly. "You can tell us more stories about your mother's home remedies and anecdotal wisdom."

Hearing Ms. Foster, who by now I was convinced was a real witch, mention my mother set my teeth on edge. However, it also gave me an out. "Oh, well, that is so very thoughtful of you to offer," I said, "but I must decline." Bounding with exuberance, I informed them all that I would be disembarking in moments and would not be continuing on with them to San Francisco.

"Isn't that rather irresponsible of you, Miss Lundgren? You did say that you were on your way to school, didn't you?" Disdain dripped from her lips like pitch from a tree. Slow, dark, and thick. She seemed to find me guilty of something.

"I am not scheduled for classes for another week," I said. How had I let myself be drawn into this uncomfortable conversation? I found my ability to remain civil disintegrating each time the woman said a single thing to me. "Get a grip, Phalaen!" I could hear my head say. Only it wasn't my voice telling me this; it was my mother's.

To the sweet old lady who was excitedly repeating her version of last night's events, I said with a genuine smile upon my lips, "I had quite a surprise land in my lap and I am seeing where it takes me."

"Oooh, a real adventure, dearie!" exclaimed the woman who had outed me.

"Yes, it is!" Inhale one, two, three . . . Exhale one, two, three. Composed and ignoring my nemesis, I happily shared my plans, feeling like any sign of optimism or joy would surely be like pouring water upon the Wicked Witch.

"I have a full day ahead of me. I am headed out to ride my bike along the American River trail, then to a gem store, where I am going to research the significance of this stone." I pointed to the pendant that I was wearing. "It is a clue to the last sculpture my mother ever completed, which neither my father nor I have seen." I felt a surge of triumphant pride.

"You say the pendant is part of a sculpture?" I watched Ms. Foster looking intensely at my neck and I could have sworn her pupil dilated like a focusing camera lens. She gave me the creeps. Thank God we had reached a fork in the road and would be taking different paths.

I heard Karim say, "Phalaen, girl, grab your brekkie and let's go. We've got two minutes to get off the train." His timing was once again impeccable.

Richard came dragging himself in behind Karim, looking as though he'd not slept a wink since his and Karim's midnight visit to my room when Richard told me stories about my mother. If they had not been substantiated by facts that were indisputable, I'd have called bullshit.

Like about the origin of the ring on my hand . . . a gumball machine version of it had been a gift from Richard to my mother when he was six. He had proposed to her. She later found an exact replica of it while on vacation in Hawaii and wore it until pregnancy had fattened her fingers for good. Nobody knew that story except my father and me. And the person who had given her the ring, of course.

"So all three of you are going?" Patch inquired with presumed authority. Or perhaps she was just as relieved to be getting rid of us as we were of her.

"Oh, hello there, Mrs. Foster," Richard mumbled grimly.

"It's 'Ms.'" I piped up, unable to help myself. Blame it on my youth.

He passed by the table, making a beeline for the coffee, tossing out casually that we had discovered a connection. "Phalaen's mother was my babysitter growing up. Isn't that remarkable?" It seemed odd that he didn't say "sister" or even "first love."

"You don't say? What are the odds?" The sweet old lady started in on a story about a friend of her cousin's twice removed, which gave me a chance to slip away.

Karim must have called ahead because, as I pushed myself through the swinging doors, the chef handed me a white sack and told me to have a great ride. "Make sure to check out the rope swing, which should still be hanging at a good turnaround spot."

I gave him a hygienically accepted handshake by way of a fist pump and thanked him for the food and the tip. A rope swing was just what I needed, assuming it was high enough to get a little adrenaline shock to reset my brain.

The three of us then made it past the table of ladies, where they were telling the story of so-and-so who knew so-and-so, who was related to someone's cousin twice removed. Ms. Foster looked bored and irritated. We didn't bother with a final farewell. We hopped off the train like hobos and it pulled away, taking the witch with it.

"Has anyone ever told you that you have a big mouth, Richard?" Karim barked at him like an interrogator. Richard responded with a grimace. He had been duly scolded.

We caught up to the Smiths, who would not stop thanking us. Mr. Smith had hardly been at risk of dying, but he was very grateful to have kept his ring . . . and his finger. The couple had taken a shine to Richard, who reminded them of their own boy. They explained their son had been a ranger in Afghanistan until he died in 2004.

I spoke up. "So here are my thoughts. Richard takes the Smiths to see the doctor and then makes sure all prescriptions are filled; Karim will change over our tickets; and I'm going on a bike ride and then to visit a gemologist. We will all meet back here at 11:15 a.m. sharp." I looked at them and quite honestly expected someone to argue. After all, I was just a kid. But they didn't. Everyone was suited up and ready for action.

"Hey, Richard," I said. As I had requested, he had already downloaded Red Phone and Text Secure, two cell phone apps that were evidence of open-source brilliance and a commitment to privacy by security experts. "Let's exchange encryption keys now." I watched him navigate his smartphone enthusiastically, like I'd imagine grandparents would do.

My father, the only father he'd ever known, was a computer scientist, so Richard was used to the vernacular and jargon. It made it much easier for him than it had been for me with my history. My dad would probably call me from a landline. With the exchange of keys done, Richard turned and walked off with his two elderly fans, who waved to me enthusiastically. "I guess that is what grandparents look like," I thought.

Karim gave me a hug as I slipped the letter into his pocket. "Mail this to my dad please, in care of Jan." He nodded, then took the group's luggage and hauled it away on a steward's cart. Cool. I felt relieved that more words were not required. I had done more talking in the last twenty-four hours than I usually did in a week, and I was ready for the sound of silence.

I rode away while I reached into my white sack to see what the chef had packed for me to eat. I was hoping for a hard-boiled egg and a piece of fruit. Instead, I was stoked to find a breakfast burrito wrapped in foil, some banana bread shmeared with cream cheese, and an orange. Nice! Maybe on second thought, I shouldn't scold Karim for insisting I grab something before leaving.

Pedaling toward the trail while eating my breakfast, I chewed on the events of the last twenty-four hours. The familiarity of my bike felt good. Consistently cycling through subtle positions—adjusting every fifteen seconds or so to relieve my discomfort, with one hand on the bar, and the other shoveling food into my mouth—I felt a much needed sense of normalcy.

I would have to discard my top layer before too long, but right now my dad's favorite blue flannel, which I had snagged from the laundry basket and now wore over my jersey, brought a feeling of home. The acrid stench of the workshop, mixed with the warm, amber-scented perfume he dabbed on his heart every day to remind him of his beloved wife, comforted me.

The bike trail was nearly as flat as an ice rink as it meandered along the American River. I was used to descending and climbing, but these flats made it easy to eat. I put the foil from my burrito into my breast pocket and grabbed my earbuds.

"*I took my love and I took it down,*" sang Stevie. This mix I made for Mom did for my mind what Dad's shirt did for my heart. I turned it up. I could finally zone out and maybe something would come to me so I could make sense of it all.

How different the landscape was from home. The grass wasn't green. Not on this side of the river, nor the other. Rather it was yellow straw begging to be set afire. This was the dried-up Sacramento Valley.

A few bathers snuck a dip before hikers and bikers made privacy impossible. They did not look like campers or typical homeless people you wished would bathe. These were most likely victims of the subprime lending debacle I'd read about, who lived under the bridges and overpasses.

I nodded to them. They didn't nod back. A sign outlawed bathing in the river. Maybe I was supposed to treat them as though they were invisible.

A sign also outlawed skateboards. I felt overjoyed as I whizzed past three boys about my age cruising on longboards. They must have heard me coming, because they moved to the right. I waved and called out thanks.

California postcards and TV shows always displayed lush abundance and flowing water, or crashing waves. But the whole state is a desert. And the inside of my nose felt it. To be a pioneer or early settler would certainly have required one to be a rugged individual. The West was wild and the people must have been too.

To leave all that was familiar and everyone you knew to move to a strange land seemed so foreign to me. Even leaving my home and family to go to school would be challenging, but hardly required risk. What kind of a person would venture to do something so extreme?

The image of Karim flashed in my mind. The kind of person who has nothing to lose was the answer that came to me. It must have been so lonely for him. And he must have really trusted my mom.

Listening to Richard talk about her was like listening to stories about a different person than the one I had always known. Karim was a polite listener, but not once did he mention our previous conversation or that he had known her. It seemed odd.

He did pick up the Moroccan wedding blanket I had brought and he held it tenderly. I almost hadn't brought it, but then had run back to the house to get it, along with a photo. Missing Q and the Harrisons at my going-away party sent me after the photo I had stashed in the secret compartment of my jewelry box. Only it wasn't there, but the drawing was. It was as though Mom had wanted me to find it.

Watching Karim as he held the blanket to his face reminded me of how I too would try to soak up memories from it. His eyes glistened with tears as he set it down. Richard had been so busy talking that he didn't seem to notice. He was a talker.

The sun started to heat up the ground and my tires were getting sticky, which made nice, fast turns safe and easy. I was lucky to have the trail all to myself, except for the boarders who were probably on their way home to bed after a night of illegal riding. They definitely did not wear their helmets for compliance reasons, nor their gloves and pads because they thought they might biff on a flat surface. They looked like serious downhill riders.

These thoughts barely had time to leave my head, when I caught the sight of a dark blue figure standing

71

tall on something and waving his hands. Was the figure motioning to me? As I continued, the motioning became more furious.

It was hard to make him out from a distance, with the sun in my eyes, but as I got closer, I could see it was a cop. On a Segway. The image was farcical. I came to a stop before him, as he was directly in my way, with his hand held up like a traffic cop.

I raised mine and said, "Hau!" thinking myself terribly funny.

"What do you think you are doing?" he barked at me, as though I had done something wrong.

"Excuse me?" I was honestly confused and had no idea why he had stopped me. And with his shocking orange hair, I was pretty sure he wasn't Native American, easily offended by silly things.

Officer A. Diddle pulled out a notepad and began scribbling on it with hands so tense that his knuckles were white. I started to pedal again and he screamed at me, demanding that I stop. "Do you want me to arrest you?" I always thought that a funny question. Does anyone ever say yes?

"Of course I don't want to be arrested. But you are asking me as if I have done something wrong. And as I have done nothing wrong, I can't imagine why you have stopped me, much less why you are yelling at me."

"Do you think you are funny?" His face was contorted with hostility. I felt alarms going off in my head and listened. He had one hand on his gun as he stepped off his toy and motioned for me to get off of my bike. He told me to take out my earbuds and give him my name and address.

72

I did so and wished I wasn't alone. The skaters were several miles behind me. It didn't feel right and I was not sure what to do. I decided quickly not to inform him that yes, I thought that I was extremely funny. Somehow I was pretty sure he wasn't like the cops back home.

There were only two police officers in the town I lived in and they held the unique distinction of never having handcuffed anyone, much less arrested them. The closest they had come to a real crime was when one of them had gotten bleary-eyed drunk after learning his son was coming home from Iraq without legs. The officer had run over several mailboxes, passing out after hitting his head on the steering wheel.

Jan had found him on her way home from the tavern, after taking everyone's money, and she claimed responsibility, saying she had lost control of her mail truck. While letting him sober up at her and Misty's place, she took all the mailboxes to my dad's shop and repaired them, while my dad fixed the front end and bumper of the officer's car. The cop hadn't had a drink since. Though everyone knew what had really happened—because of course Jan told everyone, as she was prone to do—nobody judged him.

Clearly I was a long way from home, I thought, as the Segway cop handed me three separate tickets, all of which included a court summons to appear before a judge in a municipal court. He then informed me I'd have to walk my bike, since I did not have a helmet.

"Oh, okay." I walked away laughing. Was this guy for real?

"You had better take this matter seriously," he said. "If you do not appear in court, the judge will issue a bench warrant and you will be found and arrested. You will remain in jail until your court appearance, at which time your fines will be assessed."

What happened next came out of nowhere. Whether it was teenage angst, extreme stress and fatigue, or an overwhelming sense of my own humanity, I was done taking this guy's shit. "Hey, Diddle, Diddle, why don't you go find yourself a cat and a fiddle and go jump over the moon." I tore up the tickets. "I have done nothing wrong."

Without a moment's hesitation, the cop leaned into his walkie-talkie and called in a disorderly conduct. He pulled out his handcuffs and informed me I was under arrest.

"Oh, fuck that!" I flipped my bike around and hopped on it in one movement. I had never had the opportunity to try to outride a cop, but I had escaped the jaws of several dogs. The key was to not look back and to not slow down.

I was very grateful that my legs were warmed up, that I had fuel in me, and that the cop had the reflexes of a dead cat. Odds were, had he risked eating shit, he could have lunged for me and made contact, potentially taking me down. It was a measured risk. And I won.

I was upon the skater boys in a flash, and shouted, "Pig!"

They shouted back, "We got you girl! Make a right at the dead fountain!"

Did they say "dead fountain"?

Although I had never experienced being chased by law enforcement or code enforcers, I had plenty of experience—for as long as I could remember—playing chase. The familiar tightness in my belly poured into me with a gush. I felt like I was going to pee.

Changing gears, I labored and grunted until I found that place in me when sound ceased and all I could hear was the beating of my heart. "THUMP THUMP!" I didn't see any of the tall grasses thirsting, or the lights dancing upon the water with disco-esque flare, that had captivated my attention earlier.

The cop didn't even have my correct name. What proof did he have of anything? And what did I care? I carried no ID on me. I had told him my name was Alia Atreides and that I lived at 1 Melange, Arrakis, Oregon and I offered the zip code for Florence.

I had hoped he would laugh. Nope. That would have required him to be familiar with *Dune*. No sense of humor and not well read. He was not of my tribe.

Chapter 7

The viewing window revealed a girl with long auburn hair draped about her like a veil. She sat cross-legged on the floor. If you were of average height, you could peer into the room, which had concrete walls painted the color of a faded daffodil. It was as though the mental hospital was intentionally being ironic, and the result was most depressing. However, the serenity with which she held herself defied her circumstances. She didn't live within the walls; she lived somewhere else. And in that place, she appeared more alive than anyone I had ever seen. I was instantly captivated.

"I think you can reach her, Diane," Milan, my former shrink said, almost desperately.

I had agreed to come meet with him, because, quite honestly, I was horny and thought he was going to tell me that he'd left his overweight, whining, weak-willed wife once and for all. No such luck.

And really, I hadn't wanted him to leave her; I just wanted to have sex with him. Why did that have to be such a bad thing? A two-day-long romance at a conference for war widows six months ago didn't quite cut the mustard.

But instead of a plea to get into my panties, he had pulled out a file from his briefcase and set it on the table of a diner café, leaving his thick-fingered hand to rest upon it. A girl with silk flowers in her hair, who seemed to twirl as she moved across the floor, approached us to take our order.

Milan requested the chili cheese dog with extra onions, and I opted for the Reuben. As if he had read my thoughts about him, he told me his wife had been diagnosed with cancer . . . because being a transport nurse who had witnessed the brutality of war just wasn't enough pain. Thanks, God.

Smack! Right upside the head. Nice going, Diane. Shit, I didn't even know anything about her, but I had projected so many rude thoughts onto her just to make myself feel better about what I wanted to do to her husband.

"Sorry to hear that, Milan. That's a tough blow," I said. Without asking, I knew the prognosis was bleak. I sipped my ice water and realized it was the same temperature as my heart. War is brutal and kills more than just the dead.

"Thank you," he said. He must have said that several times, to so many different people by now, but he still sounded like he meant it. I wondered how long I sounded sincere when people told me how sorry they were about my loss of Jim.

"Let's just see if we can help this girl, okay?" he asked. I expected to see a vacant look that I'd witnessed so often before in the eyes of the wounded, but instead I saw hope and kindness.

I was moved, and he could see it in my face. "She touched me, Diane," he said, as if confessing. "There is something about her. But she is definitely broken right now and I think she needs you. To be honest, I think you need each other."

As a twenty-six-year-old, I felt like I needed no one. As a widow with three fatherless children, I felt like the hole in my life—caused by a war nearly 7,000 miles away and created by a single landmine—had left a vacuous space that threatened to suck me into an abyss. I ached for a man to fill both me and the void.

In the meantime, I did need more money, as the military was not taking care of us—Uncle Sam was a shitty uncle. Teaching art classes at the VA and the local college was enabling me to make ends meet. But participating in the professional world as an art therapist was really what I wanted to be doing with my life.

"Show me what you have. I am not sure how a twelve-year-old could possibly help me, other than as a babysitter, but I'll take a look," I said. He pushed the file toward me and told me to take a breath.

"Is there anything in here that is going to cause me to lose my appetite?" I asked. "I am awfully hungry and would hate to miss out on my pastrami on rye." I knew I sounded like a tough, old broad and that my voice was tainted with anger and resentment. I was angry and I was resentful.

"Yes." He said this matter-of-factly.

Something deep within me called out a warning: "Tread lightly, Diane." I chose to listen. Rain beat against the windows. But all I could hear was the clanking of dishware being dumped into bins, and the rude, but affectionate, banter between line cooks and waitresses. The rain continued to pelt against the panes of glass.

"My heart has become like these windows. Life beats against me and my being is immune to the penetrating blows. I am indeed insulated from the discomfort and inconvenience of life's storms. But I also feel nothing; just the chill of numb." I looked away from the windows into his warm eyes.

"I don't believe that you even believe you are as tough as you act, Di."

Our waitress returned and huskily purred, "Your lunch will be right up. Would you like some more iced tea with lemon?" I nodded and she smiled back.

I said to her, "You have a very interesting sounding voice. Has anyone ever told you that before?" She beamed at both of us and nodded, then walked off, looking happy, to get our drinks.

I found Milan looking at me with a slight grin and crinkled eyes. He said, "It is really quite a gift you have." He just kept sitting there looking at me. He didn't offer to elaborate. And I didn't ask him to.

"And here you go!" said the waitress when she returned. I licked my lips at the sight of the Reuben, which had sauerkraut clinging to the edges of toasted rye bread, hanging on by melted cheese. "The pickles are really good. Irene's husband makes them." She set our plates down in front of us and promised to come right back to refill our glasses.

Across the table, Milan turned his lunch into a volcanic inferno as he pelted hot sauce on top of the heap of meat and cheese. Bits of tomato and onion poked through, looking like molten rock and white hot ash. A big toothy grin stretched across Milan's face, from ear to ear.

"This is going to taste as good as it looks. Let me make sure it's not poisonous and then I'll offer you a bite." He sliced right through and the chili oozed like a lava flow. I watched in awe as he opened his mouth wide and engulfed an unfathomably large bite.

"Okay, anaconda, you may be successful in digesting that, but you might still have a heart attack!" His joy could not be deterred. I cut into my own sandwich and dipped it into the ramekin of mustard. I was not disappointed.

The layered meat had a rich peppery flavor that was wonderfully complimented by the sour of the pickled cabbage and the crunch of the rye kernels. Whoever had made this sandwich knew how to fill a mouth with pleasure. "Delicious! Wanna swap?"

We traded plates. Meat-filled richness filled my mouth with savory, pungent onion flavoring, perfuming each bite as I crunched into the little bits. The flavor finished with melted cheese and remained as I chewed through the hot dog. It was a mouthful of tasty.

It reminded me of the county fair, when my Jim and I had shared a plate and a cob of corn before going on the tilt-a-whirl. I threw up afterwards. And I kept on throwing up for three months. Tracy and Jan were born six months after the vomiting stopped. I never could eat another chili dog after that . . . until now.

"God, I miss him!" I blurted out, barely having swallowed when tears erupted. "I can't take it. Night after night, I tuck the kids in after a full day of extraordinary bliss, and for one second, I feel content. And then the realization that he is never going to walk through the door again and demand his woman come

80

give him a smoochie. It was my favorite moment and what I looked forward to most."

Milan grasped my hands between his, after handing me one of his famed, monogrammed handkerchiefs, tatted by his doting wife. The same wife I had willed him to cheat on and give me one moment of escape not even fifteen minutes ago. I was an awful person. I wiped tears away and blew.

"What happened to your beautiful family wasn't fair," Milan said. "You are a lovely woman inside and out; and those kids need and deserve a father."

I looked at him pleadingly, my eyes begging him to tell me everything was going to be okay. He didn't. He did give me back my sandwich after admitting that mine was better. They were both so yummy. There was something comforting about good diner food.

I took a deep breath and exhaled slowly, pushing the last bit of air from the bottom of my lungs until I felt tightness grip me. And then I took another breath and reminded myself to just keep doing that over and over, hoping eventually it wouldn't take so much effort to want to take another one.

"You have mustard on the side of your lips," I told him. He tried to lick at it and looked absolutely ridiculous doing so. I couldn't help myself and laughed before reaching over, in that motherly way we women do, dabbing it away with my napkin.

"So let's see what we've got here," I said. I ran my tongue through my mouth, sucking out pieces of bread and bits of seed, swallowing the remnants as I prepared myself to face what lie inside the file set before me.

Page one was a fact sheet on young Vivienne Lane, age 12, born March 14, 1962. Only child, father deceased—military, killed in the line of duty. Mother living. There was an addendum regarding her drug and alcohol abuse.

A paper clipped to the page showed a photo of a young girl holding a bird in her hands. She had flowers in her hair and wore a purple, tied-dyed T-shirt and faded jeans with patches of peace signs and rainbows on them. I think I had a pair just like them somewhere in the back of my closet. She had freckles sprinkled across her nose. She looked happy and sweet.

The next several pages showed photos of a crime scene and blood-splatter reports. The only apparent weapon was a Louisville Slugger that had been bleached clean, but it fit the pattern of the wounds to the deceased. Male, white, early twenties. Died as a result of a blunt force trauma to his left temporal lobe.

The photos here showed a man who seemed to have been unsuspecting. There was the close-up of the death blow, but pictures supported the forensic report that showed there was an initial strike at the back of his head. There were more photos of his hands; they were beaten to bloody stumps. Lab reports indicated those injuries were inflicted postmortem.

"Why his hands?" I inquired before turning the page.

"Hard to say. She hasn't spoken a word since the incident."

"Seriously? The file here says that it took place three weeks ago."

He nodded affirmatively.

"A twelve-year-old girl hasn't spoken a word for three weeks?" I said, "I find that hard to believe." I looked at him wondering how he might imagine I could be of help if he hadn't even had a conversation with her.

"She is very smart. If she isn't talking," he said, "it's because she doesn't want to, not because she cannot."

"So smart that she murdered a man, and yet she has said nothing in her own defense about it? That doesn't sound very smart to me."

Waiting for his response, I took a bite of my sandwich, appreciating the care that had gone into making it. It was a gluttonous masterpiece and my taste buds were dancing. What did it mean that I could enjoy eating a meal while looking at photos of a body that looked like the meat I was eating? Minus the mustard.

"She was found in the kitchen doing dishes as if nothing had happened," said Milan. "The first cop who arrived said it could have been his daughter—that it looked like a scene he'd walked into at his own home a thousand times. Except that this girl was naked, with a rope tied around her neck and two others around her ankles, with lash marks on the backs of her thighs and buttocks. And she was splattered with his blood."

My throat tightened and I had to take a drink in order to help down the bite I chewed. "Was she raped?"

"It is unclear whether there was penal penetration, but she was definitely sexually assaulted and abused."

"Poor lamb," I murmured as I came to the photos taken of her the night of the murder. It was obvious from them that she was angry at being photographed. She certainly didn't have the same look in her eyes as in the photo that had been taken of her with the bird only the summer before.

"I don't think she did it, Diane."

I looked up at him, confused. Obviously, she did it.

"I'm serious." He lifted up his hands, palms facing me, as if to ward off any protests I might offer. "There were no prints on the murder weapon — a baseball bat that definitely belonged to the victim."

"But you said she was found washing dishes. I presume she was wearing gloves? And the bat was bleached, you said."

"But this guy was a 6'2", 220-pound college defenseman who, by the looks of things, had managed to tie her up and whip her. She is maybe 5'2" and all of 100 pounds."

An involuntary shudder ran through me. She was basically my size, and twenty pounds lighter. "I can't imagine warding off a man that size, even with a bat."

Milan waited a few seconds before adding, "He had apparently used a towel for some of those marks. The cop who found it vomited on the spot."

"Like a locker towel snap? Are you kidding me? So he enjoyed it."

I covered my face with my hands. As I pulled them down, I hoped that as my fingertips passed over my eyes I would find I was imagining this conversation, just as I had imagined so many conversations with Jim. Even the thought of hallucinating seemed better than the reality of sheer horror. No such luck.

"What did the police say?" I asked.

"The two cops who first arrived initially said they did not think she did it. However, their testimony was thrown out because one was heard saying he thought the guy got what he deserved, and that he hoped she had done it."

"So it is not okay now to offer one's opinion during a breakroom chat?" I asked incredulously. He said nothing to deny or confirm.

"The judge has a history of serving harsh sentences to kids like her," Milan said as he looked down at his plate. "I am ashamed to say that some of my psychiatric assessments have helped him put kids away who, in my opinion, were totally treatable. In fact, in many cases, good food and a parent at home to look over school work would have made all the difference."

"What exactly do you mean, 'kids like her'?" I asked. Milan knew this was a trigger for me. I knew all too well what people meant when they said that.

Growing up, I had been completely oblivious to any judgements about my family's lack of means. I was a happy kid and my brother and I always started the school year with a new pair of gym sneakers and everyday school shoes.

Early in Jim's and my relationship, I attended his younger sister's sweet-sixteen party. I was all gussied up like the other guests and I felt very pretty. I overheard three mothers discussing my dress, and I beamed.

I had been so excited when my mother brought it home for me. It wasn't new, but it was new to me. She transformed it into a real holiday party dress. She even took apart her inherited fur stole to make a beautiful collar and wrist cuffs for it. I thought it was spectacular.

Apparently, the dress had belonged to one of the women's daughters. The women weren't admiring; they were snickering, I soon realized. It had been given to the cleaning lady. That is how they referred to my mother. My mother! The woman who took care of my father who was crippled by polio, and who had recently started cleaning a couple of homes to pay my college tuition.

Those spoiled, self-centered, entitled women had referred to me as "kids like her," as if I was somehow less of a person because they had more stuff!

The real tragedy, though, was my response. I left the party and went home, where I proceeded to yell at my mother about how she had humiliated me. I took the dress off and hung it up in the closet, where it remained for four years. At my father's request before he died, I put it on again for his funeral. He wrote that he'd never seen me prettier, other than on my wedding day.

After the service, I was approached by a young woman, who told me how envious she had been to see me in the dress that had once belonged to her. She threw a fit when her mother bought it because it was "too old-looking" for her. She was very tall and hadn't fit into children's clothes, but at age fourteen, it would not have suited her. She told her mother after the party that she hated her and wished that she was more like my mother.

I had looked across the room at my once-beautiful mom, who was leaning against a wall wearily, so frail and tired. She must have felt me because her head lifted; she straightened a bit, and then smiled at me with such joy and glowing pride. I excused myself and walked straight into her arms. I could feel the bones of her back as I held her, whispering into her ear how much I loved her and that she would come home with me. Jim and I would take care of her.

With a burst of energy and renewed vigor, Mom sold the house. She gave my brother and me the things we wanted, and made everything tidy and organized. She lived with us for nearly a year, sewing curtains, making baby clothes, and cooking all of Jim's favorite dishes when he was home on leave.

On the anniversary of my father's death, we sprinkled his ashes at Shore Acres, where they had visited on their honeymoon. Afterwards, we had a family dinner with my brother, his wife, and Jim, who had been able to come home for the memorial — the military do like their memorials. It was a beautiful day.

Mom died in her sleep that night. I found her the next morning, smiling and clutching a photo. It was taken the day of the party, and I was wearing the dress she had made. And I looked radiant, as did she.

Wiping away tears that were falling down my cheeks, I thought of how pictures were often dishonest constructions of the photographer's making. I held the two photos of Vivienne in my hand. The second one did not even resemble the first. The before picture showed a young girl filled with wonder and hope; the after one did not.

In that moment, I understood what my mother had done. She had covered up the shame of us being poor, using all of her skills and talents so I would not feel ashamed. I wanted more than anything to honor my mother by being a cover for this girl. If she was guilty of anything, it was of being neglected.

"I will do it." I said, "I will see her and help her in any way I can. You have my word."

I felt I had just sworn a blood oath. And at that moment, I knew I held his heart in the palm of my hand. The impact this girl had made upon him was significant. Any debt I owed him for pulling me out of the abyss I had plummeted into after the death of my beloved husband would be paid in full by the efforts I put forth to save Vivienne.

Little did I know at the time that it would be me who would be truly saved.

The waitress returned to our table with fresh drinks, a slice of apple pie, and two new forks. She said, "Dessert is on me." We had no chance to protest, even if we had been rude enough to do so. She set the pie down between us and smiled tenderly. "My daddy always says a little sugar will cut the bitter taste of sorrow."

"You have a unique way of putting things—quite poetic," I told her, feeling endeared to her. She reminded me of what I was once—a free spirit, dancing through life.

"Thank you, ma'am. Truth be told, I am a singer-songwriter." She smiled bashfully, the way people do when their humility is surpassed only by their talent or ability. "I'm from Arizona, but have been playing with bands here and there. I'm sort of a gypsy, I guess, so I haven't yet settled down with one."

"Is that right?" I said. "Well tell us your name and I'll be sure to keep my ear out for you on the radio."

"Really?" Her face lit up and she told us her name was Stephanie. "But I go by Stevie."

"Well, Stevie, thank you for your service and your kind attention." I cut into a bite of the pie as more tears welled up in my eyes. "I look forward to seeing you on a big stage someday." Taking a bite and tasting the tart apples enveloped in sugary syrup, I had to agree that it was exactly what I needed to cut the gall that filled my mouth.

An hour later, with a fresh piece of pie in my hand as an offering, I hoped to be able to coax a bit of conversation from Vivienne. Milan seemed to think it was not going to do the trick. And now, looking at her through the viewing window, I felt ridiculous. Pie was hardly what someone who'd not eaten for three days needed.

I had barely finished the thought when she looked over her shoulder and straight at me, as if she had been aware of my presence the entire time. She was fierce in a way I was not prepared for.

I tried not to flinch at the sight of her swollen and bruised face. Even bloody, she was stunning. I stared back at her, and then lifted a hand, hating myself at the same time. What was I? A movie version of an Indian?

Her lips curved up into smile. She moved very slowly and rose to her feet, facing me proudly and in no way like a victim. She lifted her hand. At that moment, I was sure we were from the same tribe.

Chapter 8

The clay spun around the wheel and from it emerged an Aphrodite. The artist's hands were an instrument molding what was being born of heart, not of rational thought. It was like magic.

I watched in amazement at the effortlessness with which Vivienne worked the clay. In that moment, I understood the difference between someone who creates art and someone who is an artist. I couldn't be jealous; I was too busy being in awe.

Milan had been correct: apple pie was insufficient to tempt the alleged murderess into talking. But he could not have possibly anticipated the condition in which we would find her upon our arrival at the mental hospital.

It was beyond anything I could have ever imagined. I now not only had a project to add to my do-gooder list; I was a woman on a mission. And God help anyone who got in my way.

It had been two months since I had first met Vivienne. She still had yet to utter a single word. Once the hospital staff realized she was immune to their carrots and sticks, they happily relinquished her to my care, washing their hands of her.

When she wasn't studying her academics, we did art projects. And then there was Milan. They played games together and went on daily walks to his office, where they fed his two Yellow Hawaiian Tang. Rather unoriginal, he had named them Mr. and Mrs. Lemon. As far as I knew, Vivienne was alone on the weekends.

I had never witnessed anyone frustrate people the way she could. She was neither compliant nor disobedient. She did what she wanted, and if what others wanted her to do did not jive, she just stood there looking at them with her soft brown eyes remaining expressionless.

The staff was accustomed to controlling people with promises of rewards or threats of punishment, but they had been unable to identify a single thing they could offer her or take away from her that they could use as a tool of manipulation.

The delusion of control the staff suffered from was challenged by her absolute indifference to it. She made them lose their minds. Pretty ironic considering she was the patient.

Only once had she resorted to violence since being admitted for a stay that was not to exceed beyond the date of her trial. That is what her involuntary confinement was called — "a stay" — as if the mental hospital were a hotel with plush linens and turndown service.

None of the staff or other patients could exactly say what had provoked Vivienne to be violent, only that she had been, and that she must have done something wrong. The incident had occurred at 2 a.m. Saturday morning, two days before we met. The episode happened to be the catalyst for her solitary confinement.

Vivienne had apparently bit the hand of the male nurse on duty hard enough to cause him to call her a bitch before punching her in the face, breaking her nose.

It had taken eight people to restrain her, including three other nurses and four men whose jobs seemed to be to act like gorillas more than people. Each member of the staff had written up their version of what had happened. Interestingly enough, not one of them had bothered to question what his hand had been doing near her mouth in the first place. Nor was there a mention of her shattered septum.

It was purely by chance that Milan had reached out to me on the very same weekend as Vivienne's "violent outburst," as it was described. Protocol required that a patient's psychiatrist be contacted immediately, in the event of a crisis. The administrative and healthcare staff had not contacted Milan, and had therefore broken their own rules. So when we arrived for his regularly scheduled five o'clock session with her, he heard of the "violent outburst" for the first time.

For three days, they held her in a bricked room without food or the use of bathroom facilities. She also did not receive medical attention. Breaking all the rules of doctor-patient protocol, Milan insisted he take her to the hospital. Instead, we took her to his house, where his wife Delores, an army nurse, could tend to her injuries.

When we arrived, Delores greeted us at the door. I was taken aback. Not only was she not fat and whiny, she was quite lovely. But disfigured. Milan had told me she had been sent home injured, but not that half of her face was covered with a burn scar. She noticed my surprise, took it in stride, and immediately assumed command of the situation.

She handed her patient two pills, ignoring the furrow in her husband's brow; she was in charge now and she was going to execute her duties faithfully. Addressing the pain seemed to be a priority.

Vivienne shook her head no. It was only the second obvious sign of communication I had seen from her. Delores put the pain killers at a place setting and suggested we all sit down. Milan and I followed orders. Vivienne remained standing, looking at her host.

Besides the obvious displaced nose and bruising and swelling in the upper half of her face, we had no idea whether there were any other injuries. Delores explained to Vivienne that she was a nurse and had served as a medevac in Vietnam. She offered to attend to any wounds Vivienne wanted addressed.

It was odd to me that this woman asked, as if there was an option to refuse treatment. Maybe it was because she wasn't a mother, so she was unaccustomed to telling children what to do.

I had miscalculated again. Vivienne moved her gaze to Milan, stared for a moment and then looked back at Delores, who then asked her husband to go pour bowls of soup for all of us. He did as he was asked.

Milan and Delores were a good balance for each other. Although I was sorry for the circumstances, I was glad to see them together like this. Any desire for Milan as anything other than a friend was replaced by a deep compassion. His wife was obviously a remarkable woman. I realized his momentary indiscretion had been as a result of his own human weakness, not a lack of love and respect for his wife, nor any romantic feelings for me. I was humbled.

Once Milan had stepped away from the table, Vivienne raised her pajama top. I was glad that I was sitting down. There were bruises where fingers had pressed into her delicate skin, as though she had been grabbed and clawed at. Worse though was a red swelling on her rib cage. Dark purple and blue traveled where someone had struck a blow. The bruise covered most of the side of her body. Delores asked if there were any other spots that she would like to show her. Vivienne lifted her pant legs. More bruises.

And then I noticed the scab marks where the rope had dug into her ankles. It had been almost three weeks since she had been tied up. The pictures had not shown the story I could so obviously see now. She must have struggled violently for some time against the ropes to have them leave such marks.

I excused myself to help Milan, who was doing a bit of crashing around in the kitchen. He was "shaking that tree," as Cool Hand Luke would say.

I said nothing to him in the kitchen, afraid that I might burst into tears if I opened my mouth to speak. I couldn't even make eye contact with him. The soup smelled delicious and I focused my attention on stirring it. I felt useless to both Vivienne and Delores, but I could stir a pot of broth.

After a few minutes, Delores came into the kitchen. She grabbed several jars of dried herbs and crushed them in a bowl, then poured hot water over them from the kettle. She retrieved a few bags of frozen peas and told us as she exited the kitchen that we could bring in the soup.

The two of them were sitting down at the table when we returned. It had been only a few hours since I had woofed down a gluttonous sandwich, but I was already hungry. The aroma wafted to my nose. I thanked my host and tilted my bowl away from me as I let my spoon fill. I lifted the soup to my mouth at the perfect ninety-degree angle like my mother-in-law had insisted was the proper way to ingest soup. Milan did the same.

After swallowing a few spoonfuls, I noticed that neither Vivienne nor Delores had touched their soup. Vivienne had lifted the bowl to her face but didn't drink it. She just sat there still.

The girl had to be starving. I resisted the temptation to tell her to eat what was offered, if not because she needed the nourishment, then to be polite. I also did not correct her etiquette. I hated it that my in-laws did that; apparently I gave them plenty of opportunity, as they seemed to do it often.

I felt rude, but could not take my eyes away from the unmoving girl. She just sat there with the bowl cradled in her palms and held it under her face. I doubt she could smell the aroma through her blood soaked nostrils. Maybe that was the problem. I set my spoon down and waited.

After about ten minutes and without a word, Delores lifted her bowl. She mimicked her guest, cradling the dish in her hands. Vivienne peaked with blood-filled eyes over the edge of her bowl and watched while her host took a small sip. Then and only then did Vivienne drink. She had two more bowlfuls after she finished that one. Then she popped the pills into her mouth and swallowed them.

Stupefied, I realized that in judging her, I had heaped judgement upon myself. Milan smiled at me with that look of "I told you so." I promised myself then and there to never underestimate her again. It really came as no surprise to me that she caused me to break that promise repeatedly.

As a result of her "acts of violence," which none of the staff proposed were committed in self-defense, she was to have new restrictions imposed. As Vivienne sipped soup, Milan described these to her. She occasionally acknowledged with a glance, that she was listening.

She was prohibited from attending group; she was no longer allowed to go on field trips or attend movie night; and she would also have to do school alone. Milan agreed to the new rules only after he gave prescribed orders that Vivienne was never to be touched, put in solitary, nor disciplined — whether in punishment or reward — without his consent and in his presence.

This last requirement was allowed only because, as fate would have it, he had been granted temporary custodianship over Vivienne while her mom was in a treatment facility. That was some silver lining; she finally had somebody to watch out for her.

Although I considered isolation to be a form of torture, I imagined the consequences, meant to be punishments, were really rewards for someone who refused to speak and just seemed to want to be left alone. But I still could not understand what made her such a threat. It couldn't be her table manners.

"What I would like to do is get you settled in the spare bedroom for the night," Delores said. No protests from Milan. Technically, patients were not allowed to leave, but as Vivienne had been voluntarily committed by her mom to the better choice of two facilities — the other being juvenile detention — she could be checked out overnight by her guardian.

Delores told Vivienne, "There are clean towels in the bathroom, so you can wash up whatever you are comfortable cleaning, but avoid rubbing where it is tender. I have some remedies to make a poultice to place on those areas to help heal all the marks." Delores winked at Vivienne and smiled impishly. "The doc thinks I am more witch than nurse." Vivienne did not take her eyes from her.

Delores's voice became grave, while still maintaining a very calm and soothing tone. "You are very dehydrated. The pain killer I gave you is also a sedative, so you should be getting sleepy pretty soon. I would really like to hook an IV up to your arm." Milan, who had been letting his wife do her thing, agreed and assured their patient that she would feel a whole lot better when she woke up, if she allowed it.

Delores added that of course she would attend to Vivienne's nose, but a doctor would need to reset it. Once that was done, she said she thought it would be good as new. A look of fierce resolve crossed the girl's face. She slowly shook her head from side to side before following Milan toward the hallway.

Of course her response was no. It would be twenty years before she would have surgery to repair it. By then, she taught us all about her World of No.

Finished with the shaping, Vivienne carved *Primum non nocere* at the base of the sculpture. There was a graceful fluidity about it. As I looked closer, I realized it did indeed portray the shape of a beautiful woman, but not Aphrodite.

The statue represented Panacea, the goddess of universal health . . . with flowers emerging from what looked like a burn scar on the side of her face. Milan was the one who told me what the Latin phrase carved at the bottom meant. *First, do no harm.*

—

Chapter 9

Minors who were institutionalized during the school year were required by law to attend classes and do regular coursework. Regular is hardly the word I would use to describe what I observed to be the hospital's excessively low expectations for teenaged people, whose minds were still sponges, able to absorb gobs of information. Despite being prohibited from attending classes with the others, Vivienne still had to complete math, literature, science, and history requirements, even if at a boringly intolerable level. Once again, fate stepped in and gave her the last laugh.

With nobody to talk to, nor anything to do, she had plenty of time to read. And so she did. She read everything she could get her hands on. That was fine with everyone because it kept her occupied.

But when she handed in an essay on *Le Petit Prince*, the man overseeing the kids' schoolwork took it as a personal affront that she had written it in French—a language he could neither read, nor write, nor speak. So he brought it to the attention of the administration. As a result, they labeled Vivienne's behavior "subversive" and punished her by taking away her library privileges.

Within a few short hours, both Milan and I became aware of the situation. We went looking for her and found her in pj's, lying on her bed, staring straight up at the ceiling, expressionless. The hospital staff had finally found something to take away from her that would crush her spirit. By all appearances, that was the objective.

The paper trail required by the institution led to two people: the male nurse whose hand she had bitten the month before, and the head nurse whose responsibilities were in administration. I felt enraged and wanted to punch the sadistic bitch right in the face. But when I saw her lazy right eye drifting off as she tried to look at me, I laughed instead.

Her nostrils flared as she continued to insist Vivienne must be punished for not following protocol. "She must learn to obey authority and to follow the rules of society," said the nurse. "The rules are there for the good of everyone."

"Are you fucking kidding me?" I blurted out. "You are honestly going to try and justify removing her access to books, and therefore education, as punishment? For what? Being smarter and more capable than you and your so-called teacher?" Her one good eye stared straight at me as she seethed. I was positive I detected a hiss.

"She does not respect authority. And it was intentionally rude to write the essay in French," the woman said. The harder she tried to appear menacing, the more her eye drifted away. It was almost comical.

"It is written in very basic language, but is grammatically spot-on," Milan declared admirably. He spoke Russian, French, and English. The head nurse only spoke English.

100

I said, "She does respect authority. And she is respectful. She demonstrated that by honoring Saint-Expuréy, who is French, and the story he wrote . . . in French." I ought to have stopped there but could not resist the low-hanging fruit. What could I say? I was hungry. "You might want to be asking the person assigning her work why he would select a French classic for an American lit class."

Milan must have sensed things were heating up and he stepped in between us. "I am on the board of this hospital and with a single phone call, I can have you removed and replaced." There was no question in anyone's mind that he meant it as a threat.

I was absolutely overjoyed. He had championed Vivienne. We both had. We were going to save this girl. Or at least we were going to give her a fighting chance at having an environment in which to heal from whatever had happened to her. Until, of course, the State decided what was to be done with her.

As a result of our intervention, Vivienne spent her days undisturbed. She had three meals a day prepared for her, which gave her better nutrition than what she had gotten at home; she had the luxury of a very large bedroom to herself, and even better—her own bathroom. And since the teacher had refused to work with her any longer, I was able to use a loophole to bring in tutors from the college to oversee and encourage her education.

If there was one thing I wanted to impart to Vivienne Lane, it was the idea that she could take her brokenness and make something beautiful out of it. I had never believed that about anyone at any time more so than about her and now.

The tutors were TAs who worked for peers of mine whom I trusted. They found Vivienne fascinating. And teaching her was a joy, since she devoured everything, making it a habit to do more work than what they had given her. Secretly, I think the college kids, all of whom were sick of the war and therefore the government, considered their role in her education to be an act of disestablishmentarianism. I was thrilled; she now had an army of advocates.

She exchanged books with a couple of them, which must have given her a sense of comradery. She still didn't speak to anyone. She was a very good listener, though, and followed along until she couldn't, and then it was quite easy to see her mind stop. She wasn't reactive; she was responsive.

One of the students pulled me aside one day to offer anecdotal encouragement. He told me Vivienne communicated plenty but the key was learning her language. Of course, a math and computer science student would be the one to offer me that cryptic tidbit.

It was then that I decided to pick up two copies of a few different books and offer her one of each, suggesting she pick the order in which we would read them. She seemed to really like that. She chose to start with *Alice in Wonderland*.

Like Alice, young Vivienne would manage to disrupt the entire system. Only Miss Lane would do it without a single utterance. I later wondered whether she had masterminded the whole thing from the day we met, but then I brushed the thought off as preposterous.

The State must have believed Vivienne to be that powerful as well. Speaking on the state's behalf, the head nurse argued that "the patient," as she referred to her, was a manipulative subversive, and recommended that Vivienne remain in custody until she was of legal age. That was horrific! The nurse basically called for five years of institutionalization.

I listened to this woman and felt appalled at her outrageous misrepresentation of the events and interactions that even I myself had witnessed. No mention was made of Vivienne's academic or artistic accomplishments. Not a single word of praise was given. The nurse really had it out for the girl.

The courtroom seemed stuffy and too warm until the retched shrew had taken the stand. Now a chill filled the room and I shivered. Vivienne offered me her coat and I took it. Sitting and listening to vicious lies was bad enough, but it was made worse by the fact that the judge nodded in agreement, as if the woman was the voice of God.

I stuffed my hands into the coat's pockets to keep myself from strangling one or both of them. There was something inside the right pocket. I kept my hands where they were while I carefully felt around. It was the same size and shape as a playing card.

I could not believe I had not figured it out before. The answer had been right in front of my face the whole time. Frozen, but with my senses heightened, I knew exactly what needed to happen. But how?

Vivienne sat between Milan and me at the hearing, with her eyes following whoever spoke. The only response she had throughout the proceedings was when her mother testified that the neighbor had been a nice boy, trimming her hedges and caring for her yard when she needed it. I felt Vivienne's entire calf press gently against mine as though she were leaning upon me. She continued to look at her mother, expressionless. I gently pressed back until, through the resistance, we both found support.

I had concluded up to this point that Mrs. Lane wasn't a bad woman, just a weak one. She believed she loved her daughter, but she knew she was ill-prepared for the responsibilities of motherhood. I agreed with the second part.

From what I had gathered from the information Milan had shared with me, Mrs. Lane had been spoiled as a girl and remained as such. She simply stopped growing up when she stopped growing taller.

Listening to Mrs. Lane express grief for the loss of the person who had abused and tortured her daughter was beyond reprehensible to me. To her credit, she did say she thought her daughter incapable of hurting anyone. But she then agreed that Vivienne was obviously troubled and she felt unable to handle her.

Her mother just gave her up without a fight. Vivienne pressed harder. I pressed back.

Discussing Vivienne's fate as if she was both deaf and dumb, the judge asked if anyone had heard her speak or demonstrate any sign of verbal communication. I kept my mouth shut. Milan said, "No." Vivienne stared at the judge.

For whatever reason, I had not told Milan about the outburst of laughter I had both seen and heard from Vivienne. In fact, I had not even told him that she had a visitor. I also saw to it that nobody else would learn of him.

I remembered that day like it was yesterday. It was a game changer. After watching the two teenagers play cards without ever speaking to one another for what seemed like an hour, I exited my car. She would have been expecting me to arrive in a few minutes. Maybe she wanted me to meet her guest.

The weekend receptionist had her eyes glued to a portable TV. I asked her if there had been any visitors for Vivienne Lane. She glared at me, annoyed that I was distracting her from *The Autobiography of Miss Jane Pittman*. She poked at the clipboard with a lacquered, hot pink nail and told me to look for myself.

I did. SIGN IN WITH BLACK PEN ONLY was typed in bold and all caps across the top of the page. There was even a pen provided, attached to the clipboard by a string tied around a chewed cap. It had blue ink.

About halfway down the page and written in pencil was the name "Brother Jack." But no visitors had been signed in for Vivienne. This person had come to see Nichelle Nichols. I gulped hard and tried not to let out a squeal. What a clever, clever boy he was. I was both flummoxed and wildly impressed.

"Brother Jack" was a main character from Ralph Ellison's award-winning novel about social and intellectual issues facing African-Americans in the early part of the century. The book was titled *Invisible Man*. I knew this because it was the third book that Vivienne and I had read together.

And Nichelle Nichols played communications officer Lieutenant Uhura aboard the *USS Enterprise*. Her character was one of the most powerful in the entire *Star Trek* series, with some novels even stating that she was promoted to commander of the *Starfleet*. Vivienne and I had watched an episode together the night she stayed at Milan and Delores's. Delores and I commented on how much we both liked Nichelle's character. Milan teased us for being Trekkies.

"Now, do you mind if I get back to my show?" asked the receptionist. "I realize it ain't important to you white women, but it is to my people." She raised her eyebrows and crossed her arms as if to dare me to challenge her. I didn't.

"That Cicely Tyson sure is a good actress," I said, trying to endear myself as I thought of my next move. "I watched the first two parts but I got stuck having to work today."

"Yeah, she is. The best. If it wasn't for all them damn Jews in Hollywood, she'd be more famous than that Zsa Zsa Gabor."

"I know what you mean," I said, nodding my head and leaning in to watch the box with her. I knew I had her when, after a few minutes, she moved it a smidge so I could have a better view. My mind raced. There was something I was missing. Something I needed to do . . . but it just wasn't coming to me.

And then it did—like a splash of cold water in my face. The young man wanted me to erase his name. I never came on Saturdays. Today had been an exception that I had prearranged with Vivienne. Or that she had prearranged with me actually.

I was taking her to an art exhibit featuring "Industrial Objects," a piece by a local artist she had come across. It would be her first outing with me alone and we had planned it a few weeks back. So Vivienne knew I would be here, and when.

My gift to the young man for making Vivienne smile, and for that hour that I had been able to see her as a typical, healthy, happy teenage girl, would be to help him remain invisible. I owed him that.

Noticing a side-by-side frame with pictures of two young children taken in front of the same JC Penney backdrop that every other low-income parent used to commemorate their child's first birthday, I let out that "Oh shit!" that is common to all working parents who run late, again, to pick up their kids. "I gotta hurry up so I can pick up my kids from the sitter's, or she is going to charge me extra." Bingo! The receptionist gave me a look, indicating that as single, working mothers, we shared the same plight.

"But first," I said, holding up the clipboard, "I have to get a copy of this sign-in sheet to show my boss that I was here, or I won't be paid." I was amazed at my own acting ability, which would have given both Cicely and Zsa Zsa a run for their money. She looked at me sympathetically, as she heaved herself from the chair where her ass had been stuck since she had arrived an hour before.

With the most ingratiating voice I could muster, I offered to take the paperwork to the business center to copy it myself. The frown on her face told me she was not going to go for it. After all, she did have a job to do.

"I would hate for you to miss any part of the show just to help me placate the Man," I said. Leaning on the desk, wearily, I continued, "No sense in both of us missing it."

She smiled at me like I was a sister and waved me off. I thanked her and offered to bring the sign-in sheet right back."Coffee?" I asked and smiled."Well, yeah, I'll take a coffee. Light and sweet. Extra sweet . . . like me," she hollered, louder than necessary, as if shouting it somehow made it true. She let out a chuckle, then settled her wide ass right back into the chair and returned to staring at the box.

It never bothered my conscience in the slightest that I erased the penciled-in names, writing Vivienne's and my own over them. I made three copies: one with the penciled names, one without, and one with my name and Vivienne's.

I returned with the clipboard, along with the coffee, and I was again waved away by the receptionist, who was now talking to the box. Indeed this place was filled with crazy people, I thought. They just mostly happened to be the employees.

The young man was not around when I found Vivienne ten minutes later. She still sat where I had observed the two of them; her hands were folded and resting on the table alongside the playing cards. Next to them was a pack of Marlboros, in a red box, and a lighter.

I could not get past the idea that smoking cigarettes was allowed and even encouraged by the staff. Patients were encouraged to take a break from what they were doing, and to go outside for a cigarette at any time between breakfast and lights out. If a kid didn't smoke when they arrived, they soon started.

I had never seen Vivienne light up and I had to admit, I was really disappointed. But I didn't want to take the chance of pushing too hard, so I simply laid the three pieces of paper down on the table in front of her. She glanced at them without expression.

Her face had fully healed, with just the slightest bend to her nose. Now that her eyes were not filled with blood, you could tell that the color of them matched her reddish shade of hair.

She emptied the deck of cards into her hand and shuffled them expertly. Then she fanned the cards out and waited for me to pick one. I did, looked at it, and slid it back into the stack. She reshuffled the cards and held out the deck to me. Sure enough, the top card was my card. It was the four of hearts. After gently removing it from the top, she tapped the card three times before sliding it in front of me.

She then pulled out the jack of diamonds and set that where her friend had been sitting, leaving her hand upon it and looking at me until I asked, "Brother Jack?" She giggled. My heart nearly burst.

Moving on, she placed the queen of spades directly between me and the last card that she placed, facedown, in front of herself. She set the deck down, folded her arms, and rested them on the table. She looked at me, expressionless, but with a penetrating look of focused intensity. It was unnerving.

Tentatively, because I was afraid if I made a mistake, I'd lose our momentum, I asked her if the cards each represented a person. She continued looking at me. "Am I the four of hearts?" She nodded and turned my card facedown.

Though I had not seen her mother as someone who was an actual nemesis or all that calculating, I had to assume that the queen of spades was her. But when I said so, just a blank stare was my answer.

I was crushed but did not let it show. My propensity to quit when things got hard the last few years was now a habit of my past. I had figured out her game thus far.

"I believe she is a woman and that I must know who she is." There weren't many women around with whom Vivienne interacted. A few nurses and cooks. And certainly not anyone powerful enough to warrant the title, Queen of Spades, the Dark Witch!

I knew that I was reaching, but just could not think of who this woman could be. "Did one of the cooks do something to your food?" Vivienne made no facial expression. There was the one card in front of her facedown; there was mine placed directly in front of me; and the queen was set right in between the two.

"I am getting the metaphor that there is a woman between us somehow, but I assure you that there isn't. Nobody can keep me from you, Vivienne. I will always stand by you." I reached across the table and ran my hand down her soft, sleek hair and told her I was sorry, but I just did not know who the woman could be. I covered my face and felt creases on my forehead and around my eyes. It was as if my whole body was straining for the answer.

"Maybe if I knew what yours was, I would be able to figure out what the other one was," I said cleverly to her, as though I could somehow get her to reveal more to me than she wanted. She leaned back, giving me permission to turn her card over. I did and it was the four of hearts. "Oh no, we can't both be the same thing, honey! That will totally confuse me." Shit! I wish she would just say something!

A little frustrated, I picked up my card, and slapped it down. And then I gasped. It was the Joker.

She had even made discovering who she was a fun game. I laughed harder than I had in years. "So you are the Joker?" She exhaled heavily as if she had been holding her breath. I hated to admit it, but I still had no clue who the last person could be. I told her so.

110

Without a smidge of disappointment, she put the cards all back into their box, and put them in the breast pocket of the flannel she was wearing. She rolled up the papers, grabbed the cigarettes and lighter, and climbed off the bench seat.

So I got up too and followed her. She led me over to the smoking area where there was a large, free-standing trash can with the top serving as a giant ash tray. I found it revolting.

I watched as Vivienne pulled out a cigarette, held it between her teeth and lit it like it was nothing. Later I learned it was the one and only cigarette she would ever smoke. She inhaled like a pro, exhaling the foul-smelling smoke, almost as though she was performing a ritual.

With the cigarette hanging from her lips, she took the roll of papers and set them afire with the lighter. She stood by her post, leaving them to burn in the ashtray until there was nothing left but a charred secret. She watched it, took one last slow inhale and blew a cloud, popping her jaw to form a perfect smoke ring, and then she stubbed out the butt, tossing the rest of the pack into the trash.

Recalling that day now, holding what I was certain was the queen of spades in my hand, I felt confident of two things: I was responsible for Vivienne, and I knew who the enemy was. If the judge believed Vivienne guilty, he would remand Vivienne to custody for her to await sentencing or, if feeling generous, would make her a ward of the State and put her in the system, which meant foster care. She needed a miracle.

And so I wished for one, not considering the expense of it. That is how it is — we want what we want and then we want some more. Rarely do we count the cost. I knew all this and yet still hoped with all my might for a way for this girl to escape the system. And like magic, my wish was granted.

Into the courtroom walked Delores and a half dozen federal agents. Apparently, the judge had been running a scam with the help of the nurse. The mental hospital received money from the State for each child kept at the facility, much the way public schools get paid to have students in the seats, whether they were being taught anything, or not. So the judge was taking bribes to send so-called delinquents there.

It was unclear what was in it for the administrative nurse, because evidence would show that the only money skimmed went directly to the judge. Without motive, the charges against her did not stick.

While the agents read him his rights, the judge, who upon standing was shown to be quite diminutive, flailed about with his robe flying, claiming that he was the law, and that they were all in contempt. They handcuffed him anyway.

I leaned over and whispered into Vivienne's ear, "I know who the witch is." And then she hugged me. We remained like that while we watched the nurse get handcuffed as she maintained a look of utter disdain.

"Everything I have done has been for the betterment of society. One cannot be blamed for doing what one knows is the best for the good of all," she said. Hubris was her most prominent quality. I stared at her, completely ignoring the comical appearance of her wandering eye. She stared back. I had won. And she knew it.

Just like that, we had pivoted. Delores smiled and hugged Vivienne and me. As usual, the truth was stranger than fiction. None of us could have seen this coming. Except maybe Vivienne.

Apparently, a deal separate from the proceedings had been worked out. A young man had offered a confession. He was charged with involuntary manslaughter and remanded to Pecconi Boys Ranch. Nobody wanted to see anyone punished for the murder of Vivienne's abuser, but the State required that someone pay.

Delores handed Milan a signed and notarized document from the head of family court, which granted Milan custodianship of Vivienne. He and I were actually joint custodians because Delores was not doing well. I would be the primary caregiver.

So, on March 14, 1975, on Vivienne's thirteenth birthday and nearly three months after being put into a psychiatric facility for a crime none believed her to have committed, she came home to live with my family. I introduced her as, "Vivi" on account of it meaning "alive." She didn't object.

Jan and Tracy, were excited to have a big sister the same size as Mom, but cooler. Richard thought her a goddess, anointing her with a crown of daisies. He was three and unable to make a "v" sound so Vivi was replaced by "Phi-Phi."

My heart was filled with joy. Milan had been right; I needed her.

Chapter 10

What had that skater said? "Hang a right after the water fountain"? I still did not see a water fountain. The anxiety I felt at coming up to the police brigade that awaited me, if the sirens I heard were any indication, replaced the feelings of elation I'd momentarily enjoyed. Fuck-a-doodle!

Had I not been searching for it, I'd have cruised right by. It was aesthetically boring, with its base constructed from sandstone blocks that were stacked like Tetris pieces. A plaque on the front read, "To the Outdoor Enthusiasts of Sacramento, from the Mayor's Office." It had been paid for by the city.

Attached with blue painter's tape on the spout was an official sign that read: "Do not drink the water, by orders of the City of Sacramento." Next to the water fountain, an oversized trash can filled with plastic water bottles was near capacity. It and the plastic bottles were made by the same US plastics company.

I recognized the name from a lawsuit I'd studied as part of Mom's "business ethics challenge." The corporation had been sued by the City of Folsom for contaminating the water, which was its only source for drinking, bathing, and agriculture. The town was offered a settlement and it accepted. So, essentially, it lost.

There was now a plant to clean the water that flowed into the town. The people felt the jobs the plant brought were worth the cost of putting water filters on the mains of their homes. Someone had neglected to consider that water seeps down into the ground.

Nothing grew there anymore, not even weeds. People were still diagnosed with cancer disproportionately to anywhere else in the state. But . . . the plant had really good health benefits.

I took a sip of water from the canteen Mom had bought me two years ago; I never drank water from a plastic water bottle. I snapped a photo as a testament to government collusion and the financial waste of tax dollars. Maybe it would come in handy for a class discussion. I tried to imagine the campus replete of plastic waste.

I hopped off of my bike, my dad's flannel went into the backpack, and the banana bread went into my mouth. Karim had told me the chef was known for his baking. He was an exceptional baker, but it was his secret ingredient for which he was famous.

I could barely suppress a smile, listening to Karim and Richard reference the dark net website I had developed—Panacea—where they bought medicine with cryptocoin. My mother came up with the name, which was perfect for a free-market, open-source, cure-all for the economic woes and clear violations of individual freedoms that plagued modern America.

So the chef's secret ingredient was cannabis butter made by none other than my Aunt DeeDee. She had developed it years ago after she had been diagnosed with terminal cancer. The terminal diagnosis actually saved her. She and the Vet quit their jobs and traveled for a year to all the places they'd dreamed of going. Apparently daily dosing on a little weed and a lotta joy does wonders.

Hopefully, a little bit of cannabis in the baked-in goodness would help me to chill the fuck out. Though I didn't use it often, I knew from experience that in about fifteen minutes, I would be buzzing. That gave me time to get somewhere safe to pass the next couple of hours before heading back to the train station.

Floating my arms overhead, I let my eyes follow them upward until I stared at my outstretched fingers, set against the backdrop of cornflower-blue skies streaked with white. I was certain some chemtrail conspiracist was pitching a fit and pointing with indignation toward the heavens. Once I looked up though, I understood why Karim laughed when I asked him if the smoke would be hard to see. It wasn't exactly billowing plumes, but there was a clear and distinct, steady rise of smoke wafting up like prayer incense.

Rolling through the streets slow enough to feel like I had just sauntered into town on my horse, I marveled at how I had seemingly just time-traveled. The juxtaposition was enormous between the saloon-style buildings—reminiscent of barroom brawls and duels fought over honor—and the cement bike trail with its Segway-riding, pasty, and mentally flaccid cop.

Despite the desert landscape, the buildings—with their ornate carvings like lace tatted to the collar of a dress—made the street feel feminine and inviting. Were women to stroll out onto the balconies wearing costumes resembling the plumage of peacocks, I would only ask where the whisky-drinking, card-playing, horse-riding cowboys were. Not why the women were dressed like that.

It was one of the few places I had visited in the United States where the setting invoked a nostalgia that seemed to still fit more than a century later. Even when visiting Boston in years prior, I never had the feeling that a white-wigged, flamboyantly-dressed couple would walk out of a pub on their way to infecting each other with syphilis.

History is told by those who survive. And we all tell it according to our own point of view. Memory has that clever way of deceiving us. Sometimes it is all too much for us to process what we see, hear, observe, feel, or experience, so we tell ourselves it was something different. We rarely describe our heroes as they really are — with all the grittiness required to actually be a hero.

Had I done that? Had I remembered my childhood as something different than it was? My head pounded as I shook it from side to side. I was certain that it was the most idyllic anyone could ever imagine. So why were memories gnawing and clawing at me?

Reminding myself that I had just gotten stoned, I tried to quiet the paranoia. Hurry, I told myself, think of something ridiculous. But I couldn't.

Coming to a stop at a spot on K Street, where I would hopefully uncover another clue to my mother's twenty-first sculpture in her *Crypto Chaos* series, I realized that I had the munchies. Was that chicken soup I smelled? So what if it was barely nine o'clock. Chicken soup sounded good. Wait. No, those were chicken coops and I smelled chicken poop! Okay, I was definitely high.

117

The front door was unhinged and resting against an otherwise lovely and well-maintained house. The place offered no indication it was a business besides the hand-painted mailbox sign that read "Maison de Merlin." If it was my home, my mother would have removed the entrance as a metaphor for something. It could mean that all are welcome to enter, or that the whole place had gone cuckoo for Cocoa Puffs. Or both.

A request to remove outdoor shoes was taped to a bin filled with rubber slippers. Maybe that was how the store owners protected themselves against thieves. Where is one to go without shoes? Or maybe they just liked clean floors.

Next to the bin was a five-gallon water jug, with maybe two dollars in change laying uncrowded on the bottom of it like coins tossed into a fountain. I had a fiver. I figured it would cover the cost of the flip-flops if I had to make off with them. Or if I forgot to return them. I was high after all. My bike shoes went into my bag and a pair of size eight flip-flops replaced them on my feet.

Walking over the threshold, I indeed felt like I was entering the wizard's den. "Come in, dearie," crooned an eerie voice from a cage in the corner of the salon. A stuffed bird sat perched atop a coat rack and stared at me pointedly with an eye of judgement. It reminded me of Patch. Despite being a fake, I felt like I was being watched and judged. It did say that I was welcome. But where was everyone? I seriously needed to pee.

From behind a heavy, gold-threaded tapestry emerged a woman with thick, snow-white hair cascading over her shoulders. Smiling at me with glistening, pearl-white teeth between delicate pink lips, she told me that my five-dollar donation was twice as much as the cost of

118

the slippers, so I had a store credit. I had barely walked into the place and they already owed me.

"I am far from home and would really appreciate the use of a bathroom to freshen up, if you could spare it," I said. I had never used these exact words in a sentence before, but I had rehearsed them plenty with my mom, who told me they were like "open sesame" to those who provide shelter to nomads and fugitives. I wasn't sure which I was at the moment.

It worked. The stunning crone's smile broadened as she stood aside, granting me safe passage. She said, "You are just in time for tea if you'd like to join me."

"A bathroom would be great first, thanks," I said. I was very close to doing the pee-pee dance. With a curled finger, the woman motioned for me to follow her.

This was a place used to welcoming visitors. So early in the morning for most, yet Madame already lit candles in the loo. I felt bad that I had not introduced myself to the woman. She must be the owner.

How should I do introduce myself? Awkwardness was something with which I was not accustomed simply because I avoided the situations that would spawn it. I wanted my comfort zone back.

The smell of something savory filled my nose as I heard the whistle of a tea kettle. The gorgeous crone, if there could actually be such a thing, was laying out plates on a kitchen table with chairs around it for four, though she appeared to be the only one here.

"Is this your shop, Madame?" I asked her.

Her head bent, focusing on the task of setting about tea. I could see she heard me by the way her eyes crinkled. "How did you know I was a Madame?" she asked, with thinly veiled amusement. I was completely befuddled.

"Oh, I am so sorry! I didn't mean to imply . . ." My voice trailed off as she looked up at me, mirth on her mouth and a gleam in her eyes. "I just hadn't introduced myself before and . . ." Her eyebrows raised and I stood there feeling like a jackass until she released me. She erupted in a cacophony of laughter.

"Oh, honey, I am playing with you. I knew what you meant," she said, giving me a little wink. "Besides, that was a long time ago."

I swallowed hard. I wasn't sure how to navigate this conversation. Funny, but it sort of felt the same as when my mom used wordplay with me, until I begged her to stop. If I were more familiar with Madame, I might ask her the same. But something about her assured me that nobody told her what to do, ever.

"Please, dear," she said, "sit down and tell me all about what has you so upset." She sat in the chair closest to the stove and asked me if milk was fine, just like a grandma might if I'd come home from school in a huff. I think, anyway. Never having had a grandma around, or the experience of coming home from school, I was just guessing.

The events of the last twenty hours had taken their toll and I was desperate to share my thoughts with someone, but there was really only one person whom I could trust. And she was not here. I really needed Q.

"It's silly, really," I began, accepting sugar, and then a bit more. And then a bit more. I looked up as I hesitated with the spoon hovering above my teacup. She smiled and nodded to me to go for it. A little tea in my milk and sugar, my mom would say.

I continued, "I am traveling back east via Amtrak to go to school. I just boarded last evening, but due to unforeseen circumstances, I hopped off here. I thought I needed a bike ride to clear my head and get some fresh air." Looking around and appreciating why Karim would have enjoyed this place so much, I added, "Your shop came highly recommended. I would like to learn about this stone." I pulled the pendant out from behind my jersey and watched her eyes grow wide.

"That is beautiful! Where did you get that?" she asked. She pulled her glasses up and affixed them on the end of her nose, leaving a chain to dangle in an arc. Everything about her seemed elegant and soft, her movements made with swooping grace. She held the stone in her hand and mumbled, "Inca Rose, the state mineral of Colorado."

"My mother made it," I said. I didn't volunteer any more than that. I was telling the truth. And thinking of all that was in Colorado.

"Well, she was quite talented and creative, wasn't she?" Madame released the pendant and let it fall gently back onto my chest. "You miss her a great deal, but you are unhappy with her right now and are feeling guilty about being mad. Why is that?" I wasn't sure which felt weirder to me: that she had read me so well, or that I didn't find it odd that she did.

"Yes, she was talented," I said. I lifted the stone and gripped it in my hands. "And I am not unhappy with her; she died in a car crash. I am just confused about some things." Fortunately the woman didn't push me. "You said 'Inca Rose.' Is that what this stone is called?" I asked her.

"Indeed it is, dear. It is rhodochrosite and it is known as the stone of love and balance. The Incans believed it is the blood of their former kings and queens turned to stone. It's quite special and very powerful." She sipped her tea and dabbed away the crumbs of coffee cake from her mouth.

Although I was a scientist of sorts, accustomed to relying upon verifiable data for establishing facts and beliefs, it was impossible not to embrace the magical musings of this mystic. She really was a fantastic character. I realized that had my mother lived another twenty-five years, she would probably resemble this woman.

She said, "It is said to be the stone of freedom because of the helping it does to resolve inner conflicts." She paused and looked at me intensely, as though she was looking into my soul. Wait. It wasn't my mother whom she reminded me of. . . . She was exactly like a grown up Q!

Pouring my heart out to her—a very unlikely thing for me to do with anyone—I told her how I had just discovered my mom had not been who I thought she was, and that I felt like the foundation of my existence was shaken. "I met a man on the train, just by coincidence, who knew my mother from the time he was a toddler. And he's old now!" She chuckled when I said this. I added, "Well not as old as you. I'm sorry. You know what I mean."

"Do you mean to tell me, young lady, that you are disappointed because there is more to your mother than you thought?" Even though her tone was as sweet as could be, I felt like I was being scolded a bit.

122

Madame continued, "Everyone has a past. And it seems to me that she may have been trying to reconcile hers. I bet you this pendant you have is the key to whatever secrets she had, and that by giving it to you, she was trying to tell them to you."

She looked away for a moment. Her eyes were bright and so full of life. It seemed like the two tears that welled up in them could birth all the wisdom of the ages. She said, "There are some secrets that are just too horrible to tell anyone. They are the kind of secrets that change who you are forever. I am sure that if your mother kept things from you, it was to protect you. I am certain of it."

"The thing is," I responded, "I am starting to have these flashes of memories that now seem to be different than I remembered them." I realized there was a difference between being daring and being brave. I had never been challenged in such a way that I had to be courageous. And considering my mom might not be the person I had thought scared me like nothing else ever had.

"Be still and quiet your mind. The presence of your mother is all around you. If you had not told me she was deceased, I would have thought she was just absent. I don't get the sense that she has gone on to the spirit world." She got up from the table and walked to the kitchen door. Holding it ajar, she invited me to join her.

Everyone I knew was aware my mother had been burned in the fire caused by the car crash. Nothing remained of her body or that of my dog. My father had always been bothered that there had been no remains to bury. I didn't see the difference. . . . Dead is dead. Spirits probably didn't care where their discarded vessels were laid to rest.

The backyard was a wonderland of junkyard artifacts. A claw-foot bathtub made of porcelain sat in the yard, along with a mannequin posed and reclining. The mannequin looked toward her hand, which had a large, colorful, pressed-metal butterfly resting upon it. Flowers grew all around the base, with morning glories climbing over the edge. The scene was comical, but made almost scandalous in its execution. It was delightful. Mom would have been thrilled at the humor.

Various birdhouses were stationed about, in no particular order, with seed spilling out of them. Two sparrows landed upon a birdbath and sang to Madame and me while preening. It was hard to feel sad or confused listening to them when the woman joined in as though they were all having an intimate repartee. It was all very comforting in the way hot chocolate was on a snowy day; it just felt right.

The famed cauldron that was built in the traditional fashion hung from a spit over a fire. As we walked around the yard, the woman selected branches of herbs and added them to the boiling pot, which she reached by climbing a ladder. It seemed pretty sketchy, but she had a handle on it. I was very impressed by her agility and independence. The smells that rose along with the steam perfumed the air.

"I'm sorry, but what exactly are you trying to do?" It didn't appear she had a purpose for the boiling and toiling, and the risk of an accident seemed high, though calculated.

"I am not trying to do anything," she said. "I am healing the world. I am adding health from the earth to

124

absorb the illness that is created by the waste of industry, which does not work in harmony with life." She used a ladle, reached her arm into the enormous pot, and drew out liquid in a way that I had seen vintners do at wine tastings. "It's very hot, so be careful," she said to me as she bent down to pass me the long handle.

"It smells amazing!" I said and inhaled the aroma deep into my head, the way I used to when Q and I made potions to go with our mud pies. The scent of sage and frankincense filled my head. I sipped slowly. There was an initial bitter flavor, which was instantly replaced by an earthy sweet taste that filled my mouth with such deliciousness.

"It is said that, psychically and spiritually, the Inca Rose is used to ease issues of past lives and to help bring those issues to resolution. I think the answer to your questions lies with whatever it is that your key opens."

At some point in everyone's life, they ought to experience an old but radiant and ravishing woman standing upon a ladder, stirring a cauldron, and pouring out doses of wisdom like nectar from the gods. I could hardly wait to tell the aunts.

"Oh no, this isn't a key. It's just a necklace. It was meant to be a Christmas gift to me from my mom. She died just before, so we sort of skipped the whole present thing. Dad gave it to me yesterday as I was leaving."

The pendant weighed heavy on me. Knowing the meaning of the stone brought a sense of soundness, while also irritating my thoughts. Yesterday, I thought I knew everything there was to know about my mom, and now I was filled with questions.

Climbing down, the woman assured me that it is in fact a key. "Do you mind taking it off for a minute and I will show you."

Clearly this sweet lady was off her rocker, but not in a bad way. She was eccentric like Q in that she had her own way of seeing the world and it was very imaginative. I could appreciate that. Einstein did say that it is imagination and not reason that makes someone a genius. I unclasped the necklace and handed it to her.

She smiled with absolute delight. "Yes! You see here," she said, pointing to the groove on the back of what resembled a dagger beneath the inch-wide stone. Because my father had placed it upon my neck, I had not looked at it closely. There was a cryptographical etching on the back on either side of the groove. Another piece goes with this pendant and it slides into this space. I am sure this is a key to something."

The excitement I felt upon discovering another clue to my mom's piece gave me a renewed sense of adventure. Dispelled, for the time, were any feelings of frustration or betrayal. After all, it was true—we all have secrets.

I had not told my parents about Dookie or Gizmo, that I wrote code for CryptoCoin, or that I had handed over control of Panacea to Ng. It's not that I didn't think they would understand; I just liked keeping some things to myself.

"I wonder where the other piece could be," I said to myself, not realizing that I had spoken out loud.

Madame heard me and said, "Let your mind be still and pay attention to the signs. I have a sense it is all right in front of you. Trust yourself, little bird." The two sparrows flew off from the birdbath and the yard fell quiet except for the sound of the fire crackling.

I closed my eyes and tried to quiet the voices in my head. Well one voice—mine. But it voiced lots of questions. I felt the woman clasp my hand, and she began to hum the sound of familiar melody that filled my ears and warmed my soul. The voices were silenced. We stood like that until the heat from the fire became too intense. We gave each other a hand squeeze at the same time, as we backed away.

"Did you build this fire yourself? It's very impressive."

"Oh, no dear, one of my twin grandsons lives in the basement apartment. He helps me in the mornings and evenings when he has returned from the hospital. He's going to become a doctor." She sounded so proud.

Without saying anything else, we walked back inside and went straight to the front door. I was very grateful for her time and the pearls of wisdom she had so graciously bestowed upon me. I was not certain how to thank her—five dollars was certainly not a fair trade for her hospitality and insight.

She excused herself while I put on my bike shoes, and she returned within a minute or so. Handing me a business card that was covered with symbols, she asked that I write to her when I discover what the key opens, encouraging me to not stop searching until I knew. I looked at the back of the card and saw a photo of her with her name beside it. Rose. Rose Wilder.

"Rose Wilder." That was the name of the daughter of Laura Ingalls, the author of *Little House on the Prairie*. "She was an anarchist."

"Yes, She was the daughter of Laura Ingalls Wilder. My mother named me Rose and used to say I was 'wilder than all get out,' so after my third divorce, I decided that I didn't need a man's name; I needed my own. I chose Wilder out of love for my mom and out of respect for the prominent thinker with the same name."

She laughed to herself as if she had been caught with her hand in the cookie jar. "Wouldn't you know it, but as soon as I did that, I met the love of my life and have been happily with him ever since." Her already bright eyes lit up at the mention of her beloved. "He insisted I keep the name, since it was the wild in me he was drawn to." She blushed.

What a sweet thought that after three failed marriages, one could still find true love, and at such an advanced age. I wondered though if people that old even had sex. The thought made me embarrassed.

"Well, Rose Wilder," I said, "it's been very nice to meet you. Thank you for welcoming me into your home here." It was clear to me by now that it was definitely her home and she conducted business as an extension of her hospitality. She accepted my outstretched hand, and I told her my mom was also an anarchist and that my mom had named me after a flower too. "Phalaenopsis is my name. Phalaenopsis Ariel Lundgren."

"So we are both flower children," she said. I held up my fingers in a peace sign, which she returned before taking me into her arms and hugging me tight. "I have a feeling we will be meeting again, Phalaen. You don't mind if I call you that, do you?" A lump formed in my throat.

"No, please do. My mom called me that and I miss hearing it. Everyone else pretty much calls me Ariel."

Mom and Q always called me Phalaen and they were who I wanted with me right now.

Life had such a strange way of working out. This woman reminded me of what I valued, and over tea and cake she had set me back on track. And all because Mr. Smith ate too much salt.

"Well, Phalaenopsis Ariel Lundgren, you may be called by many names but you will only ever have one that was given to you by your mother. Find the key and you will uncover the answers to questions you don't even have yet. Don't stay away long; you have a store credit, don't forget."

And just like the old couple, she stood and waved to me as I rode away.

Chapter 11

The public library was not far from Maison du Merlin or the train station. Even if I did not find any answers to my questions, I knew that within the book-lined walls I would find my sanctuary. And maybe a quick nap. Nothing like opening a book to close my eyes.

The roll-o-cop was far from my thoughts until I rode past an ugly billboard that reminded drivers to buckle up. Splayed across the top of it in red was the ominous warning: "It's the law!" Just then a yellow school bus passed by; only the driver wore a seat belt.

I only once had ridden a bus similar to the one passing by. It had been my dad's idea to have me stay over at one of the girl's homes after dance class because Mom was having a moment. I went to school with her the next day—that was something you could do then and we rode the bus.

I had no idea that it wasn't normal for moms to have moments that could sometimes last for days. Her normally bright eyes and sunny disposition were replaced with dark circles under her eyes and an exhaustion that seemed to engulf her.

It really wasn't a big deal. She would play video games and take a bath, after which Dad would massage her ankles. She was always self-conscious about her ankles and wore socks or boots to cover them. Except for those days. They seemed to correspond to when she was preparing to create something.

I always figured it was on account of her being an artist. Van Gogh cut off his ear. And Yoshiro Nakamatsu, inventor of the floppy disc, uses near drowning experiences for inspiration. Playing *Resident Evil,* soaking in a tub, and getting a foot massage hardly seemed strange. That she wouldn't say a single word to anyone during these spells was hardly what one could call an "awkward silence." I loved being quiet.

But on that bus ride, my friend told me it was unhealthy. She knew this because she had been seeing a therapist for three years. She suggested Mom take antianxiety and antidepressant medication because it had worked for her mom and sister. She then poured vodka and orange juice from her thermos into a cup and offered it to me, assuring me it was the best way to get through the school day.

As the bus farted black smoke at me, I wondered how many of the unbuckled teens were breaking the law, swigging swill from a flask. A law against bringing lunches from home had made thermos containers obsolete.

Energized and inspired, I thought about my visit with the old woman. Although Rose was probably just a well-practiced fortune-teller who loved to charm and give hope to people who had become derailed by life, her point about my pendant being part of a key was an interesting one. It's not like she was defrauding me by suggesting the pendant was more than a trinket, albeit an artistic and sentimentally valuable one.

Strangely, nothing in Mom's sketch lead me to believe the pendant was a key, nor that there was any component of the sculpture that was a lock. As a rule, she was precise in drawing everything out in advance. She was committed to her clichés, one of which was, "Measure twice, cut once."

There had to be answers to some of my questions, and the internet was sure to have them. Dad had requested, and I had agreed, that I not get online while I was on the train. But he said nothing about doing so while not on the train. Mom would not have missed that detail.

Locked up near the front entrance was an array of bikes, and my candy-colored one fit right into the spectrum. The library would be a safe spot to hide out for the remaining time before meeting my group to reboard. I had to laugh at myself. Even a roll-o-cop had better things to do than try to track down a runaway, non-helmet-wearing cyclist.

I needed to get my bearings. In less than twenty-four hours, I had been tricked by Dad — which I thought him incapable of doing; I had discovered that Mom had indeed finished her twenty-first sculpture; the people in my life had actually known me all of my life; and my mother had a life before me that was a total mystery to me, right up until a fortuitous train excursion and coincidental encounter with an average Joe.

Although the library had been remodeled, it still had traces of old-book musk that comforted me the way the back of my parent's closet did. The closet had been my favorite place to read on rainy afternoons as a little girl. I would tuck in behind Mom's floor-length, flowy hippie dresses that she assured me would someday come back in style. They did, though avocado green and harvest orange did not.

A tidy-haired librarian who worked beneath her pay grade, meticulously wiping around the shelved books, brought a sense of authenticity to the otherwise sterile environment. The smell of Murphy's Oil Soap scented the voluminous room and reminded me of the smell of my parent's workshop. My heart rate slowed to a normal rhythm.

Smiling at me over the top of my stickered laptop, she paused with the rag in her hand and asked if I needed the login information to get online. Her smile broadened as she studied my stickers for a moment, before she pointed to a sign, then returned to the painstaking task of dusting her books' home. The library password was: "MindYourPsAndQs." Cute.

Using Panacea's VPN to browse without snoopers, I hoped to find a picture and maybe send it to Dad to help me make some sense of all this. Even though Richard might not like having me hack into his life, I did it anyway, figuring I could ask for forgiveness instead of permission. Hackers hack. We are curious.

"Be careful how you justify what you do, Phalaen," I heard my mother say. "Using the ends to justify the means is a slippery slope that can easily become an avalanche of ethical destruction. Be intentional and be ready to live with the consequences." My mother lived in my head.

Richard had shown himself to be at least acquainted with technology, but he hardly seemed like a security expert, or even concerned about identity protection. He surely had to have a Facebook account, where he undoubtedly posted evidence of his life that

133

could help me engineer some semblance of a connection between the girl he described and my mom.

I guessed his password on the third try. I had to give him credit for not using his son's birthday but "veggieeatingowllover" was pretty obvious. He hadn't even bothered to use numbers to increase difficulty. It's like he was asking to be hacked.

Scrolling through his timeline, I laughed out loud a few times. He really was witty; his caustic humor was slightly more tolerable because he was quite dashing for an old guy. His "friends" seemed to like him and be actual friends.

I was disappointed at the lack of cat videos, but the ones of screeching owls made up for it. He had a pretty cool job, it seemed. I was always a bit envious of Harry's pet owl.

Then suddenly, there it was. Richard had posted a photo to mark the anniversary of his tenth birthday. It revealed more than I had hoped.

Standing behind a young boy with front teeth too big for his mouth was a girl who could have been me, except she had purple dreads and was almost as tiny as a child. Seeing the two of them together confirmed what Richard had claimed: he definitely knew my mother. However, the other people in the photo left me unable to move.

With muscled and tanned arms wrapped around my diminutive mother, my father was tall and built like an athlete. She looked like a fairy. Together, the two of them made an unlikely, though strangely enough, perfect couple.

On the other side of him stood their best friend, Uncle Peter. Next to Mom was a teenage girl who looked familiar. She was tall and blonde, with a lanky body bathed in sunlight. For the first time I realized Richard and Jan had a strong family resemblance. I recognized her smile and freckled nose, but she was hardly the flannel-wearing, cargo-pants-sporting dyke I knew and loved.

A woman who must have been Richard's mother stood next to the girl whom I was certain was Jan. The arm of a man was draped around her shoulders. He had a shaggy thatch of hair and wore dark sunglasses. He smiled widely, displaying slightly yellowed teeth, evidence of a Coke and cigarette addiction. He had to be a nerd. There was something about him that gnawed at me, but I couldn't place it. A girl who looked nearly identical to Jan crouched next to their little brother. The girl posed kissing the boy's cheek.

Last were two people whom I didn't recognize. They stood at the edge of the group, next to Peter. The man held a leash to a tethered husky whose tongue hung from its mouth. He was the only member of the group dressed in a suit and tie. The woman was hard to make out on account of the scarf covering her head and tied under her chin, and she wore big sunglasses that covered half her face.

I tried to recall in the recesses of my brain whether either one of my parents had ever mentioned having known these people before they moved to our little town in Oregon. Why had I always thought my parents and the people in the picture had met each other when I was a little girl? Clearly that was not the truth.

I squeezed my eyes shut and tried to think of when I had first seen these two people. Nothing came to mind. Clicking on the photo and zooming in, I searched for something that might trigger a memory. And then it hit me. That was my mom's dog, Sadie. And the couple were the Vet and Aunt Deedee, only he was much chubbier in the photograph and her scar was hidden by the camera angle. I had never seen him wear a suit. Or a tie.

As I allowed the smiling faces of the people in the photograph to become animated in my mind's eye, I recalled exactly when I had last seen all these people together, minus Richard and the twin girls. They had been at my seventh birthday party when I received my puppy from my Uncle Peter and Aunt Jenny and the jewelry box from Jacob. That was the last time I had seen my best friend and her family.

The man with the yellowish teeth gave me a computer kit that Uncle Peter helped me put together. It was an Altair 8800. Mom started to cry when I opened it, and the ladies all huddled around her. It was a weird thing to remember, but maybe even a stranger thing to forget. It was my first computer; and it was the only time I ever saw my mother cry.

I slammed down the lid of my laptop as a shudder ran through my body. It struck me that I had never before considered that my parents had a life prior to having me. The self-centeredness of youth had left a backdoor vulnerability. I felt so exposed, like I was waking from a dream and unsure whether what I had dreamt was real, or the state of being wake was.

Looking up, I caught the librarian looking at me. Her face registered more concern than irritation. I smiled meekly. She had just witnessed me confronting the brutal reality that my life as I had known it, and life as it really was, were colliding. I started to sweat.

I needed to talk with my dad. Maybe I was overreacting. My mind was spinning and I felt my throat constrict, making it hard to swallow everything I was taking in.

"Excuse me, please. Is there somewhere I can go to make a private phone call?" I whispered loudly.

Climbing down from the stepladder, the woman approached me. "You are not supposed to talk so loudly in the library, young lady. I expect you to honor the rules." She spoke to me tersely, as she wrote something on a notepad she pulled from her skirt pocket. She set the notepad down next to me as she redid a French twist held in place by the pencil she had used to write: "Third floor, women's bathroom."

"I apologize and will be quieter. Thank you," I said, grateful for the stealthy note. The cameras poised every ten feet had not gone unnoticed by me.

Gathering up my things, I smiled at how clever the woman was . . . like Mr. Coreander with Bastian, only I wasn't stealing a book; I was stealing a moment of privacy.

The third story had been the first area to be renovated. But in the far corner of the building, the women's bathroom had either been overlooked or forgotten. Romantically, I hoped it had been left alone at the request of the librarians. The faded shades of tile and the coordinating baby-blue stalls and toilets were a reminder of the poor taste that plagued institutions. I liked the honesty of it.

However, unlike the public bathrooms permitted today, this one had French doors that opened out to Juliet balconies on each of the two adjacent walls. To be able to step out from the ladies' room and feel the breeze or get some fresh air seemed genteel.

Even now, one of the doors was held ajar by a heavy iron similar to the game piece in Monopoly. There was a race car, a thimble, and an equestrian near the corners of the other doors as well. How fun!

Down below, I could just make out the edge of the bike rack on one side, and the main street entrance on the other side. Handy view! There was my Pink Lady in the bike rack.

The hot and cold handles were actual handles, not those silly things you run your hand in front of to automatically turn water on. There was a dish with a large bar of lilac-scented soap, and the towel bar held real linens. This had to have been where the librarians maintained a semblance of the past before everything was made illegal for their own protection. I was convinced that romance had won out.

"One point to Slytherin!" I said this aloud to the wall, as I stuck out my tongue and looked at its reflection in the gilded-frame mirror hanging over the basin. The piece had a Mexican feel to it, like the buildings on the street I had rolled down earlier. Call it Mexico or call it California. It didn't change the fact that it was dry as dirt here. I was covered in dust!

Chapter 12

Every ladies bathroom should have a cozy couch.
Did women actually ever faint upon them? I wondered if
it had occurred to anyone back in the day to simply
loosen women's corsets or feed them a sandwich.

For my purposes, it was the perfect spot for a nap.
Naps make everything better and I needed nothing more.
Maybe sleep would lessen the pain I felt, or increase the
logic of my parents.

Why would my dad lie to me about how long he
had known the Vet and the aunts? They had been in my
life as long as I could remember—obviously even before
that. And why was there never any mention of Richard
and his family, when they were such an integral part of
their lives, or at least Mom's?

Dad sounded so chipper when he first heard my
voice. Not accustomed to having to be sneaky with my
parents, I asked bluntly why nobody had ever told me
about Richard, Mom's brother. He actually said he had
no idea what I was talking about. Which meant that he
lied to me. Straight up lied.

Neither one of us was sure where to go with the
conversation. The lull allowed me to lie and say I needed
to reboard. Well, it wasn't exactly a lie, as my train was

boarding . . . in an hour. But it wasn't like honesty was as big a priority as my parents had raised me to believe.

I was determined to get to the bottom of this no matter what! There was a disconnect and it seemed to have occurred on my seventh birthday. I had always just accepted whatever my parents had said or done as truth. My eyelids fell over my eyes as my mind chased after memories to find one true thing. The couch was comfy.

"Hey, Q, are you awake?" I asked.

Baby's tongue kisses upon my face had woke me. He needed to go potty and I wanted chocolate cake. Q didn't stir. She always slept like she was dead, with her arms crossed over her chest and her body still.

"Come on, Baby. Mommy will take you out. I am so proud of you for waking me up." He was squiggly in my arms, making whimpering sounds of affection. I knew he understood me. "Thank you for not peeing on my blanket," I said. "You get a treat! But not chocolate cake." His little body fit against my chest and tummy, while his face snuggled into my neck. I loved him more than anything.

I was going to have to relearn how to sneak downstairs without making the stairs creak. Having a baby was throwing off my balance. I said, "Sshhh. We have to be quiet, Baby."

It didn't matter how quiet I was or was not. Nobody was around to hear me, except the boys and they were all camped out on the living room floor, as dead to the world as Q was. I snuck a piece of pink-frosted, chocolate cake and crept outside.

Light came from the workroom. It was bright like a TV, not like the warm glow of the fire I was used to seeing escape through the glass windows. "Mommy and

Daddy must be out there with the grown-ups," I said. "You go potty and then we will spy on them together!"

Pallets were stacked alongside the building, high enough for me to peer into a window once I climbed on top of them. Mommy and Uncle Peter stood on either side of a table while Sato sat in front of it. They were so excited they were shouting.

"Look, Baby, they are playing with my 'puter!" I said. "Sshhh, stop wiggling. You have to be quiet or we'll get caught. And we don't want that, Baby." Puppy breath filled my nostrils and I let him lick my face.

"Whenever Mommy or Daddy are about to catch me, I run to the big tree," I told Baby. 'That's where you'll go if you need to be safe. Tomorrow, I will ask Jacob to carve our names in it."

Then Mommy screamed, "I said noooo!" Mommy never screamed. Mommy never raised her voice except when she was laughing. She looked so mad. And so mean.

Even Sato stood up and reached out to her, trying to calm her.

"I can't do it!" She pulled away from his hands, practically knocking his sunglasses off his face.

"Vivienne, why don't you just try?" Uncle Peter begged.

"Because I don't want to, that's why," her red eyes glared at both of them.

"Nobody ever calls Mommy 'Vivienne,' Baby. They must be serious."

"But what about Phalaen," he began. . . .

"Phalaen will never know!" my mother said. "Never! That is non-negotiable. This is mine to carry and she will never know. Do you understand me? Do all of you understand me?"

What did they not want me to know? I squeezed Baby too tight and he yelped. Everyone in the workroom turned their faces to me. The last thing I saw before I fell was Mommy looking straight at me, crying, "Phalaen!" And then everything went black.

Sirens blaring below the window woke me with a start. I bolted up and was at the window in one move. It was a helluva wake-up from a crazy dream.

Drifting sideways around the corner entrance, one right after the other, were three black Dodge Chargers, souped-up presumably in preparation for a chase scene from Mad Max. They all parked at an angle with their noses pointed toward the main entrance, joining an all-black SUV. Someone was in trouble! They were obviously in hot pursuit of a dangerous criminal.

Feeling like a spy, peering from my proverbial bell tower, I watched men in blue scramble around, hollering and pointing. "Oh brother," I thought. "Don't let there be a shooter hiding out in the encyclopedia section; that is where the sweet librarian is." Against my better judgment, I had to leave my perch and have a look. Suddenly, alarms went off inside my head.

"Phalaen Ariel Lundgren! What did you just say young lady?" I heard Mom's voice inside my head scolding me.

"I said, 'I know, but I just want to'."

How many times had some version of that question and answer set the stage for one of Mom's oracles? What had I just thought? "Against my better judgment. . . ." It was almost as if I had been programmed to not act on whatever it was I wanted to do. Fuck! I am so paranoid!

No one was in sight as I made my way to the elevator. Only the faint buzz of the fluorescent lights and the sound of my flip-flops shuffling along the wood floors disturbed the eerie quiet. The third floor felt like a tomb. What a contrast to the grating pitch of sirens.

The bright orange hair that peeked out of the roll-o-cop's helmet was now displayed in its entirety as he stood with his back toward me. He pointed and gestured to the librarian and another cop. Even from behind, he looked wimpy.

I stood back far enough from the window so they would not be able to see me. This could not be real. All of the drama and theatrics could not possibly be about me and my bike! The two cops turned for the front door. The librarian must have detected I was watching as she looked straight up at me and headed toward the elevator.

Shit! Running back to the ladies room, I dialed Richard, crossed my fingers, and hoped he would answer.

"Hello, Phalaen, what's wrong?" Karim, not Richard, answered the call.

"I am at the central library, third floor women's bathroom, and a dozen or so cops are here looking for me. Three sedans and one SUV are parked next to where my bike is locked."

Dead air.

"Hello! Karim? Did you hear me? There are cops here looking for me and I am stuck on the third floor."

"Yes, I heard you. I am headed toward a cab now. I will be there in four minutes," he said. I heard him say something in Arabic and a muffled voice responded, then a final "yalla yalla" from Karim. I knew that meant "hurry up."

The bathroom door opened behind me. "They are all about to enter this building to search for you." The librarian said this without asking me what I had done, which I found very odd. I stared at her as she climbed up on one of the toilets and removed a panel from the ceiling. Feeling around for only a second before her hand found what she was looking for, she replaced the panel and hopped down with the agility of a teenager.

"Give me your bike lock key. I will call you on this phone when they are gone and I'll meet you with your bike, though I will probably cover it in duct tape." She laughed when she said this. She had that tone the aunts had when I'd done something sneaky I'd likely get in trouble for, but from which they'd help me escape anyway. She seemed almost to be enjoying herself.

The phone in my hand yelled at me. "Phalaen, are you listening?"

I told Karim I was.

"I am three and a half minutes away. I am in a yellow cab and I will meet you at the corner of Improv Alley and 8th Avenue." He paused. "You are going to have to get yourself there. Can you do it?" The librarian nodded to me affirmatively.

"Yes. I will be there. I am hanging up now." I stuffed both phones into my backpack, along with the flip-flops, while the librarian waited patiently.

"I am not going to be here later," I told her. Taking a chance that she was indeed on my side, I told her I was catching the train to Colorado.

"Well then, when you get to where you are going, I will get your bike to you. It's a nice bike and I don't imagine you want to give it up." She smiled as if this was all nothing. "All you have to do is dial one on the speed dial."

My brain felt like a tunnel with my heartbeat pounding in it. A bead of sweat formed on my upper lip. "Why are you helping me?" I asked.

Walking toward the French doors and peaking at the scene downstairs, she said, "I have worked at this library for forty years and I have enjoyed everything about it. I have never had to work, but I do it because I love it." Turning around and looking me squarely in the eyes, she leveled her gaze and said with a rigid coldness, "I do not tolerate bullying tyrants. And those people out there are just that."

"Whoa, you sound like my mom," I said.

She gave me a wink and said, "She is obviously a brilliant woman."

"Yes, she was." I swallowed hard. I missed Mom so much in that moment, but I could not think about it. I needed to get downstairs, past the cops, and to the street. I handed the key to my helper.

"Stay along this wall until the end and you will reach the service elevator. It goes all the way down to the parking garage. When you exit, you will go up the stairs, turn right, and go one block." She gave me a hug and told me to run.

"I just want you to know that I really didn't do anything wrong," I said. I wanted her to know that she was helping someone who was not a criminal.

"Oh, honey, I know you didn't." She held my arms with a surprisingly strong grip. "I am counting on the smart people to win. Now go!"

And I did. I sprinted the length of the hallway and found the service elevator. It bellowed and squeaked — all the sounds seemed much louder than normal as it sank me beneath the building. I could hear my heart beating inside my ears. My mouth was dry and my palms sweaty.

The door opened to more noise. The screeching of tires reverberated throughout the hollow space. Glowing in the corner was an exit sign. It might as well have said "freedom."

Bursting through, I could feel the now hot sun beating down from the sky and emanating from the sidewalk. A right turn, a fifty-yard run, and there the car was like a chariot. Karim bounced from the front seat, holding open the driver's-side back door for me. It felt safe, like The Big Tree.

Chapter 13

Looking back at me, Karim smiled. "We will make it. Inshallah!" I knew he meant it. I also knew he meant he was standing in for God, so the driver better get us to the train station in six minutes. The driver seemed to understand perfectly.

Neither one flinched at abetting a young girl in escaping the throes of tyranny, either. I started laughing uncontrollably and said, "Well, I did wish for a grand adventure."

The driver looked into the rearview mirror and made eye contact with me. "Be careful what you wish for," he said. Karim told him to focus on the road.

"So Karim, why did you answer Richard's cell phone, anyway?" I asked. "Don't get me wrong; I am very glad that you did. Shukran."

"Afwan, habibi." He replied. He told the driver to make a left and continued scanning for police.

The driver caught my eye again in the rearview mirror and smiled. "You have a good accent. Where did you learn to speak Arabic?" he asked. He was quite pleased and maintained the Middle Eastern commitment to etiquette in any circumstances.

"From her mother. Didn't I say to focus on the road?" This Karim was a little scary.

He then turned to me and firmly but tenderly gave me instructions in French. "Êtes-vous prêt? Vos sacs sont mis sur le train et j'avoir votre billet. Cependant, je vous emmène à travers la voiture de la cuisine. Suivez-moi et ne rien dire!"

Karim pointed to the exit of the parking lot, where he told the driver to leave us, and he tied a hundred-dollar bill to an all-seeing eye that dangled from the rearview mirror.

Before the car came to a complete stop, Karim already had my door open and he whisked me out. He noticed I was barefoot and scooped me up like a doll. I could hardly believe this was the same man who less than twenty-four hours earlier sashayed and giggled with overt effeminate stylings.

Setting me down, he turned and — as if he was preparing me to walk onto a stage — took a breath, brushed the hair out of my face, and gave my cheeks a little pinch. "Remember what I told you: do not say a word," he said. Without waiting for a response, he pivoted and led the way. I followed without questioning. What choice did I have?

It was impressive how abruptly his demeanor changed, moving in and out of gender roles with as much fluidity as he had shown when juggling three languages. Placing a hand on his hip, he swayed his way toward the train platform. Not even my magenta-fringed hair was splashy enough to detract attention from this peacock.

We managed to board, walk through the kitchen — where he either blew kisses at or air-smooched

148

each and every person—and exit to the dining car without a single person objecting to me being there. Kitchen staff, doormen, and housekeeping personnel were the real eyes and ears of the service industry. I was glad to have Karim and his Spidey senses in my corner.

Richard and the Smiths sat having a cup of tea and they called to me as soon as I came through the door. "Yooo-hooo!"

They were apparently ignorant of my harrowing escape because they continued right on talking about how rude the nurse had been, scolding Mr. Smith for not being more careful about his sodium intake. "She was a pushy broad," he grumbled. Everyone laughed. Except for me; I felt confused.

The events of the day were catching up, and adrenaline filled my body. Fear and stress came out of my pores. I could smell it. I needed to get into a shower and let the water pour over me.

"I would love to stay and chat," I said, "but I really need to freshen up." Nobody disagreed.

"Karim and I are sharing a semiprivate, and you are staying across from us with a room to yourself." Richard said this to me while sliding out of his seat and shaking Mr. Smith's hand. He stooped down and delivered a peck on the cheek of a very charmed Mrs. Smith.

"Let me show you to your room, Phalaen. Your bags are in there already, thanks to a very organized and hospitable dining steward extraordinaire." He tipped his head to the beaming sissy turned badass turned sissy again.

My head reeled. I was going to throw up. But I couldn't just yet. Willing myself to talk to myself, I focused: "Breathe in and hold your breath. Exhale slowly. Think about the woods."

"Honey, are you okay?" asked Mrs. Smith. "You look a little peaked." She dabbed a fresh paper napkin with water from her untouched glass. "Put this on the back of your neck. You need a little sugar is all." Her fussing was nice, if a bit overkill. But I let her coddle me.

The icy cold compress felt good. I felt better already. Sweet old lady.

Out of her purse appeared a baggie of assorted chocolates that were wrapped in individual sizes. "I just love Almond Joys," she said, "but since I had my bridge work done, I am not supposed to eat hard nuts." She winked as she opened one of the chocolate and coconut almond candy bars, took a bite, and savored it like she must have done for fifty years. "I am not supposed to have my other favorite, caramel, so I trade off and just don't ever have them together."

She was delightful. Like Rose, but a little ditsier.

Reaching into the Ziploc, I found a Reese's Peanut Butter Cup. I unwrapped it like it was a present, undoing each fold. Once I had the candy out, I concentrated on nibbling at the edge and eating only the chocolate. The chocolate melted in my mouth and gave it something to do, along with an excuse to say nothing.

"Honey, sit down. It's not good to stand and eat," said Mrs. Smith. Her husband grunted. "Wellllll! Even if there is no scientific reason that says it isn't, it doesn't mean that it's good." Sitting up a bit taller and gracefully pointing her hands, without actually pointing any of her ringed fingers at any of us, she shared her views on the role of etiquette in digestion.

150

Once she started, she forgot any of us were there and went into a sort of reverie. I was fine with it, as was everyone else. Five of us together in multiple conversations, and the only one any of us listened to was the one in our own head.

A glass of fresh-squeezed orange juice was placed in front of me. I drank it.

I wanted an adventure. I wanted to learn about my mom's sculpture. And here I was traveling across country to a dream of an opportunity — to attend MIT.

Well, right on, Mom. You left me quite a treasure hunt.

And because of her, even though she was gone, I was certainly living an adventure. I was going to be just fine.

Mom had accomplished a goal that spanned over twenty years in execution, after almost as many years of learning and training. I felt a duty to find that twenty-first piece. Not just for me, but for my dad. He always supported her and me. They deserved to have me see it through.

Who cares if my parents weren't perfect? So they said and did things that weren't honest all the time. And didn't tell me things. I didn't tell them everything either. I just wanted to learn the truth about my mom.

The face of the taxi driver danced before me, with his melodic voice warning me to be careful what I wished for. He seemed a bit mystical. It had been that kind of trip.

I wished for Q. My heart called out to her. Q, I miss you so much; I want to see you.

"Phalaen. Phalaen, dear, would you like another candy to take back to your room?" Mrs. Smith asked me.

She had not stopped talking. Her voice had been hypnotic with its pleasant hum.

"Yes, Mrs. Smith, I would, thanks." I reached in the bag and after ascertaining that there was more than one, I selected an Almond Joy. Her face lit up. It seemed like me wanting to have one of her favorites made her happy.

It reminded me of a debate among my parents and their dinner guests regarding artificial intelligence. Could AI ever replace humans, and would we even be able to distinguish them from us?

One side of the argument was that no, AI would never replace humans because we operate on fear and hope most of the time. Pleasure is not measured through reason. The other side claimed that the emotional component in decision-making was at the root of unevolved thought, and therefore AI was the next generation. Both sides agreed we could distinguish between us and them.

Leaning now toward the former, the nonrational component led me to Mrs. Smith's joy. One could reason I should not have taken her favorite candy, but should have left it for her. I didn't know she would be pleased, and I didn't really feel it either because you can't feel anything about something that hasn't happened — you can only suppose and imagine. Maybe it's intuition.

Richard sounded perplexed more than horrified that I was barefoot. "Phalaen, where are your shoes?" The filth from the day had embedded into my soles, wandered up the sides of my feet, and in between my toes. Dirt has a way of getting into the cracks.

"I, uh, took them off." A circle of blank faces prompted me to explain, but I forced myself to resist. "I

152

have a blister," I said, as I dug into my backpack for my flip-flops.

I hated to lie; it was so unoriginal. Mom used to say that lying is for those who lack the ability to be creative. "Try again, Phalaen," I heard Mom urging.

"Not actually a blister. More like a splinter. It was bugging me all morning." That seemed to satisfy them and me as well. The cop really could be considered a thorn.

"Oh no! Would you like some help getting it out?" Mrs. Smith asked and went rummaging through her bag again, promptly appearing with a sewing travel kit. "I have a needle right here!"

"You are so kind, but I think I have it taken care of. At least for now." I smiled as wide as I could. It seemed the wider I smiled, the more convinced she became of my well-being, while at the same time she was disappointed that she wasn't needed. "I promise to ask for help though if it starts to bug me again."

Her eyes twinkled in a way that reminded me of my dog, Baby. He had gotten so old and had begun to look sad. However, he would still spark up when I cried, nuzzling his nose in between my tear-stained cheeks and my hands as I held them to my face to cover the tears. It was as if being needed was what gave Mrs. Smith and my dog life-force.

I wish I still had Baby. But I was glad to know he had been with Mom. Maybe they were able to comfort each other, though we were assured they had died on impact.

Hard to know how that could be true when the fire had left no remains. Mom always took Baby on her road trips. Mom said Baby was the best tracker. Thinking about Baby reminded me of the Vet and the photo, and I suddenly remembered my dream. It had seemed so real.

"Thank you so much for the chocolate and the orange juice," I said. "I do feel better. Will I see you all back here for dinner?"

A round of nods confirmed so, and the word "dinner" tipped off Mrs. Smith to remind her husband of the restrictions to his diet. She was busy tuning him, and he was busy tuning her out.

Karim whispered into my ear, "Now is your chance to get away. You'd better take it." He smiled at me with understanding. Of course he understood. The guy was a PR genius. "I will bring you lunch, if you'd like. We stop in Truckee for a few minutes and I always pick up lunch-to-go from a fantastic restaurant near the station."

"Thanks a lot; that would be great." I reached into my wallet to get some money and the closer I got to it, the further Karim got from me. He almost cringed as I tried to hand him a twenty dollar bill. "For my lunch," I said, feeling as though we were speaking a different language.

"No, please, put your money away." He folded my hand over the bill inside his hand, which I now realized was very large, and his hands had scars all over the backs of them like burn scars. "I insist on treating."

Considering this was my first major outing "on my own," people were sure offering me a lot of help. "Okay," I said. "Thanks a lot. But at least let me offer you something in return for all you've done. Tonight, at dinner, I will set you up with a wallet and give you some 'magic internet money'." I was rewarded with a deep and hearty laugh.

154

I swung my backpack up onto my shoulder, nodded, and smiled to the Smiths who were busy arguing over whether the salt in the broccoli soufflé was zeroed out by the wine, or whether Mr. Smith should go with the garden salad and chicken so he could have a beer. It seemed more like negotiating than navigating. It made me glad I had no interest in boys.

"Karim, why don't you give me a hand so we can get Phalaen set up in her room?" Richard said. He seemed ready for a break too.

"Give me one second. . . . We should have pulled away from the station ten minutes ago." Karim's face clouded as his eyes narrowed at the view outside the window.

Looking in the direction of his intense focus, I saw the reason for his concern. There were three police officers, including one from a K9 unit, as well as the carrot top. Standing next to them was the conductor. And the taxi cab driver.

"Oh, you have got to be kidding me!" I could not take it anymore. What a complete joke this was becoming.

"What's wrong, honey?" said Mrs. Smith. Her wrinkles all came together, knitting her brows and pursing her lips.

"The city wastes money on trivial things like hall monitors, instead of getting rid of the trash, is what is wrong," I said. I would have been laughing if I did not think they were here for me. They could only be here for me.

Staring out the tinted windows, we could see out but nobody could see in. Had they been able to, the cops would have seen eight faces staring at them like the cops were curiosities.

"Phalaen, would you like to fill us in?" Richard said as he rolled up his shirt sleeves.

Thinking this must be what it was like to be sent to the principal's office, I decided to just be honest. "Okay, so here it is. I took off this morning, on my bike, as you know. It was a beautiful day and the sun was sparkling. . . ."

"Get to the point, dear. Do the cops want to arrest you?" asked Mr. Smith. He was all business now. "I was in law enforcement for thirty years. We used to serve and protect. But that is not what I see cops doing anymore and it pisses me off!"

"Well, yes, I believe they do. The one with orange hair and holding a helmet is that thorn I mentioned. You see, I was riding my bicycle 'too fast' and not wearing a helmet, so he stopped me to give me a citation. Oh, and then I ran over his boot. On accident." I didn't mention the escape because I did not want to implicate Karim, though it seemed apparent that the taxi driver had already done that.

"Oh, for Christ's sake!" said Mr. Smith. "You must be kidding me! And for that, they are willing to hold up a train and bring out the K9s?" He was fuming now.

He looked about and motioned to a trio of college-age guys who had come into the dining car and were also staring out the window. "You dudes smoke dope, right?" They looked at each other and me and then back at him. "Oh, come on! I smelled it on you the second you walked in. Just give me some."

A guy wearing an ill-fitting letterman's jacket shrugged and pulled out a joint from his pack of

American Spirits. Mr. Smith smelled it and gave him a thumbs-up.

Wanting to reassure us, Mrs. Smith clarified, "He had cancer. The marijuana helped. He has a prescription, so it's okay."

"Ha! I'd be dead without it!" He motioned for a light. He was going to hit it right there on the train. The tallest guy pulled out a lighter and offered to light it for him. "Oh no, no, I'll light it out there in front of them. Show them what's what." Mr. Smith reached for the lighter held out to him, while the other two guys practically drooled in awe.

Richard assumed command. I was too bewildered and shocked to think.

The six guys made gestures and hand signals, while Mrs. Smith handed me more chocolate and a bottle of water. "Stay hydrated, honey."

Suddenly, I was whisked off. I turned to say good-bye, only to see the couple once again waving at me, sending me off with big smiles. "We've got ya covered, Phalaen. See you at dinner, honey." What was it with old people waving good-bye like they were seeing me off to board the Queen Mary?

Chapter 14

"Let's do this!" Karim clucked. Marching us in single file, he led us through three doors and hallways, away from the dining car. Each door we closed behind us provided distance from the cops. So why did it feel like I was walking into danger, and not away from it?

"You have only two real choices, Phalaen. You can lean into what you fear, or you can avoid it and hope it avoids you." Oh good; Mom was back. If she were actually here and not just in my head, she would be able to make all of this go away with some charming explanation that would have the roll-o-cop offering her a ride on the back of his toy.

"Honey, do you have any makeup?" Karim asked. "Huh?"

"Oh, never you mind. I will just grab mine." Of course, Karim had makeup. I wonder what he would think if he saw my glam bag. Lip balm and sunscreen were the extent of it. Oh, and an old toothbrush to keep my brows tidy.

I felt like a child, wanting to be back sitting on the bathroom counter while my dad shaved his face with a straight razor and I shaved mine with an old toothbrush.

Our last conversation had not ended well and suddenly I felt very mad at him. I couldn't even miss him properly.

Why was there such an emphasis on truth telling when I was growing up? My parents had so obviously deceived me my whole life about who my mom was and what their relationship was to the people I knew as extended family. This feeling of confusion regarding my parents was so foreign to me.

"Here we are!" said Karim. I must have missed some part of the planning, because his proclamation brought us to a halt, with all eyes suddenly on me. I had not the slightest idea why, nor what I was supposed to do.

The hunkiest of the three college guys looked straight at me. He had greenish-yellow eyes and bronzed skin. He had to be a swimmer, the way his hair was streaked almost translucent from sun and chlorine. Maybe he played water polo.

"Here, let me help you," he said. He lifted the hair up off the nape of my neck and tucked it into a baseball cap that he took from the weed donor's head. Then he slid a way-too-big jacket around my shoulders, coaxing my arms into the sleeves. Not since I was six years old had anyone dressed me. It made me feel even more like a child.

"Stop!" I said.

Five sets of eyes stared back at me as if they were waiting for my head to spin. But that was just it—my head was spinning and I needed to get a grip.

"Look," I said. "I appreciate all of you and the fact that you are trying to help me, but I didn't do anything to warrant being chased by the police. This has to be a misunderstanding."

"This is 'Merica, girl," said Richard, "and not since before October 26, 2001 has there been any such thing as a 'misunderstanding,' where law enforcement didn't have the authority to kill first and get a month's paid leave after." Richard had barely spoken a word that wasn't laced with sarcasm or charm, so his forceful anti-state declaration had a chilling effect.

"Okay, okay. I got it," I said. I snatched my backpack from Green Eyes, who had slipped it out of my hand after helping to conceal my hair. He smiled with obnoxiously perfect lips and teeth.

The cleanest cut of the three guys, who had remained silent until now, spoke up. "What happened on October 26, 2001?" He was rewarded with a slug to his arm and a unanimous outcry from the rest of us.

"The USA PATRIOT Act!" we all said together.

You could have heard a pin drop. Nobody called that heinous piece of legislation by its actual acronym, not even the politicians who voted for it, nor the journalists who wrote about it. And yet, five of us just did, in unison.

The "Uniting and Strengthening America by Providing Appropriate Tools Required to Intercept Terrorism Act" had actually been a topic of debate on numerous occasions at my house. Nobody welcome in our home was in favor of it. Mom contended that people were lulled into accepting it as a *fait accompli* because it had been tagged "The Patriot Act."

In the wake of 9/11, everyone was a patriot, even U2. Bono proved it by lining his jacket with a satin replica of the American flag, which he flashed to the world during his half-time show at the Super Bowl.

160

"I am sorry. It's been a really weird day. You guys obviously have a plan. What is it?" I asked, mustering up as much energy as I could to show gratitude.

It didn't matter at the moment that I could not understand what forces had brought us all together. I had to be realistic. Cops could not be chasing down a young girl for a ride-by toe-crushing and a misdemeanor ticket offense. California could not possibly need two hundred dollars that bad, despite their lack of funds to clean the water or empty the trash. Something was amiss.

Karim said things were about to get even weirder, as he opened up the cabin door to the berth he shared with Richard and stood aside to allow us entry.

"We just watched a gray-haired ex-cop demand a joint from us that he intended to smoke in front of cops, in the hopes of distracting the police from their target—a teenage jackboot-runner-overer. I can't wait for what's next!" Opi squealed with childhood delight.

His enthusiasm was annoying. "Careful what you wish for, Opi," I mumbled.

Karim looked at me and smiled with the saddest eyes I had ever seen.

Somehow his look gave me a feeling of remorse and guilt. A feeling I did not feel toward the cop, whose badge gave him the right to exact justice for his hurt feelings. What a fucking pusillanimous dirt bag! But I had other things to worry about.

"So I need to get something from my room. Would you mind giving me my key?" I asked. The berth was very cramped with six of us and I could smell the model-looking guy, he was standing so close.

His sweat smelled like pine. Like one would imagine Peter Pan smelled after an adventure. "Look,

Snow, can you back off, please?" I said. Why did this guy annoy me so? The fact that he just stood there looking at me made me even more incensed.

"Whoa, 'Snow'? Are you a gamer girl? That's hot!" Opi was absolutely oblivious. I waited to answer until I had all of their attention. I looked at each of them, rolled my eyes, and let out a deep sigh.

"Yes, Phalaen," said Karim. "I have your key and will take you next door." He had once again slid into a rather masculinized version of his former personality. I was beginning to wonder which one was the real one.

"You got this, Richard?" he asked, passing the proverbial baton.

"Yep, got it."

Richard had become so quiet, taking a back seat to Karim. All through the first dinner, he'd been talkative, carrying the conversation with Ms. Foster. And now, he too was even acting differently than how he'd first portrayed himself. Was anyone who they seemed?

Karim opened a bag and pulled out what I thought looked like an animal. But no, it was a trio of wigs with a ring that attached them to each other. With the care one would use in handing over a newborn, he placed them into Richard's hands and whispered something to him. Richard laughed.

"Are you boys ready to woman up and take one for the girl?" Richard asked and stood there holding the wigs and Karim's bag of makeup, which was nearly as big as my backpack. I guess it would take a lot of concealer to cover up a face that probably needed shaving twice a day.

Much to my surprise, the guys seemed totally willing, although the tall one said he'd have to catch up because he forgot his bag in the dining car. Before leaving the room, he asked if he could get me anything. I told him I wanted a do-over for the day. He smiled and said I just needed a fork. That made me laugh a little. Nobody else got the joke.

"Alright, sweet girl, do you want to come with me?" Karim asked. He had the key so I don't know what choice he thought I had. Unbeknownst to him, he was standing between me and what I wanted most at that very moment.

When it was just mom's drawing, I had held it to feel her close. As if the very thing could somehow bring her back. Knowing she had finished the last sculpture and her series, though, and that I was wearing a piece of it on me, filled me with a determination that I could feel growing inside me.

There was one place that I had not yet looked for answers. Not for anything related to my mom or her sculptures anyway. Why would I? The dark net was hardly her stomping grounds. After all, the only way she could turn on a computer was by taking off her clothes — her words, not mine.

Chapter 15

I focused on the sound of the wheels against the tracks and let the repetition nearly hypnotize me until I was somewhere else. It was just as I had practiced so many times before with my mom. We called it "entering the world of endless possibilities."

It was a place where one could escape the cacophony of confusion. It was always safe there, like The Big Tree, only in my mind. And I always found the answer to what I was looking for, even when I was unsure of the question.

However, that was not the case today. Today, I did know the question. But did I really want to know the answer? Would Pandora still open the jar if she could have a do-over?

It was the avatar. I had seen it before. It belonged to someone on the Panacea forum who posted a reply the same day my mother had died. Their username was "Joker," with a thumbnail of a sexy, vixen-like riddler. He or she had replied to a post left by a grieving parent, desolate at the loss of their only child. The parent had written:

Brian was such an obedient and good boy. He was going to be testing for his Eagle Scout certification and was a senior in high school. I was so proud of him!

While on a climbing expedition, he had an accident and required surgery. He was given oxycodone for the pain. He asked me whether I would mind if he used marijuana instead, because he didn't like the way the pills made him feel. But, of course, I said no because it was illegal and a gateway drug. He didn't argue with me. He never argued with me.

After a month, he started rehabilitation and asked for another prescription. The doctor said that was fine. He lost the bottle and I got him another one. Then he left that one at his dad's, so I got another bottle. I should have known there was a problem, but my son didn't even drink. And our doctor, who was a family friend, refilled the prescription and never blinked an eye.

But then Brian became so moody. He actually demanded that I get him another bottle only after a few hours of having one refilled. The doctor refused and said I should consider that my son had become addicted. I had no idea that was even possible. Why would doctors prescribe something to my teenage son that he could become addicted to? When I refused to get Brian more, he became enraged.

Our pastor said it was a phase and that I needed to use 'tough love.' He warned me that 'sparing the rod is spoiling the child.' So I told my only child that if he was going to act like that, he would have to move out. And he did.

He went to live with his dad. When I tried to explain the situation, my ex-husband told me it was normal for teenage boys to push away from their mothers. My ex-husband said I was being ridiculous and there was no way Brian could be an addict. After all, Brian didn't even smoke weed.

Meanwhile, Brian had developed some new friends. Popular ones he'd made by sharing his pills. His father was thrilled that his nerdy son was hanging out with the cool kids.

Those cool kids introduced him to heroin. They were all doing it. Like we used to smoke cigarettes in the back parking lot at school.

They paid for it by stealing from their parents or by selling sex. I found out when the police called to have me come to the station to pick up my underage son. He had been arrested for solicitation. My son wasn't even gay, but he had propositioned a male undercover cop, who explained to me that it was common behavior for drug addicts. I didn't even think he'd ever had sex before!

I picked Brian up and brought him home. He smelled horrible! He said nothing, ate nothing, and went straight to bed. He didn't even shower, nor say a word to me. All I could think of was how ungrateful he was, and what had I done to deserve this?

We went to court the next day and he was let off with a warning, as long as he attended a ninety-day drug treatment program. The facility was private, but our insurance would cover it after a $2,000 deductible. There went my savings! But the program came highly recommended by the judge and meant that Brian wouldn't have to go to juvenile detention or a boy's home until he turned eighteen.

He would miss high school graduation, but that didn't matter because he had missed enough days that he was going to have to attend summer school anyway. He would not be going to college in the fall either, as he had not completed any of the applications.

He went through the program and became sober. But he was not the same boy. He had become thin and very sick.

He was diagnosed with HIV – an epidemic in New Jersey among teenage drug users. Nobody was *talking about it. My pastor said the HIV was the result of my son's sin. He offered to pray for him.*

The day before Brian was to be released, my baby hung himself. He wrapped his neck with his favorite T-shirt so as not to leave marks from the rope. He left a letter telling me how sorry he was that he had disappointed me.

He died thinking that he had disappointed me. Me? When it was I who had failed him. And now he was dead. Because I didn't want him to become a pothead.

And sick because of his sin? What about my sin?

I will forever pay for the sin of abandoning my child. I will suffer every moment of my life because I abdicated responsibility for my son's welfare to the authorities — the State and the Church and then a father who had never cared about him in the first place!

If I could do it all over again, I would listen to my boy, who had actually studied up on cannabis and its use for pain. I would have used Panacea to purchase it for him. I would not have listened to those who claimed to know, with absolute certainty, what was best for my son. I would have taken responsibility. And he would be alive today.

Do you know, after Brian died, I looked for the scripture about 'sparing the rod,' and it is nowhere to be found in the Bible? It actually comes from a seventeenth-century poem written by Samuel Butler, a British poet who mocked religious extremists and hypocrites. Isn't that something?

Her guilt weighed so heavily that even as I had read her words, my shoulders slouched. How could one assuage her sorrow?

She went on to praise the site, claiming we were doing "God's work." Methadone was free to anyone who asked for it, and we offered an anonymous hotline so people could seek help or have someone to talk to in crisis.

Yes, she and I both had suffered a loss, but somehow I felt this woman deserved pity more than I. As hard as it was for me to lose my mother, I could not help but think it would have been worse for my mother to have lost me. And no words would have consoled her.

Even so, the words offered to her by the Joker felt like they were words for me. Simply, they were a few lines from *Purgatorio*, the second book in Dante's trilogy, and one of my mother's favorites.

[Virgil to Dante]: *This mountain's of such sort that climbing it is hardest at the start; but as we rise, the slope grows less unkind. Therefore, when this slope seems to you so gentle that climbing farther up will be as restful as traveling downstream by boat, you will be where this pathway ends, and there you can expect to put your weariness to rest.* (Purg. IV 88–95)

It was a lovely way to say: this too shall pass; the sun will rise tomorrow; it's always darkest before the dawn. People keep inventing new ways to offer consolation to the inconsolable.

I pulled up the letter for Karim, wanting to show him the mother's heartfelt words, before looking for answers to questions about my own mom. Karim made no objection to me using his laptop or logging into the deep-web site. As an employee, he was able to access Amtrak's secure WiFi.

He reminded me that my mother had saved him from the same plight that the young man in the letter experienced. Boys like him who were homeless often turned to drugs and prostitution, with many of them dying of AIDS or suicide. The difference for him was that someone had loved him and owned up to the responsibility.

After we hugged it out, I had an absurd idea to check Panacea's "for sale" items to see whether Mom might have thought to sell her final sculpture within the agorist marketplace I had designed. It would be like her to leave a "fuck you" finale that incorporated a hat tip to me. After all, I was her greatest creation, as she was fond of saying.

And then there it was: a post with the lyrics to "The Mock Turtle's Song" from *Alice's Adventures in Wonderland*. With the familiar Joker avatar profile smiling coyly. I felt like I was being laughed at. I clicked on the post without hesitating. The lyrics turned to snow.

"What the heck?" I said. I had never seen anything like this. It was described by Neal Stephenson in his book, *Snow Crash,* but I had not seen it myself. Of course I had read the book; it was like a textbook for crypto anarchists. But analog is a relic, so how? . . .

I immediately pressed Alt F4, but nothing happened. Alt Ctrl Del. Still nothing. I turned over the Toshiba laptop and yanked out the battery. Finally, the screen went dark.

"What was that about?" Karim asked, from where he stood shaving his face.

"Nothing. Just a reboot." The truth was I had no idea. I used a VPN so Karim's IP address was hidden, but to be safe, I was going to need to scrub the hard drive.

He just looked at me and shrugged, then returned to preening.

This hiccup was outside my area of expertise, but I was pretty sure I knew who could help me: Dookie and Gizmo. They were into the old-school cypherpunks and would love a crack at this. It would have to wait, though, until I was able to log into Panacea on my own computer, and that meant waiting until I was somewhere with privacy and a secure connection.

"Are you almost finished? I am starving!" I said.

"Yep! Just one more thing and we can go." Karim removed the cover from the fluorescent light and taped something to the inside.

"What's that?"

"It's a microphone. And if you would please step aside, I am going to place a camera right here," he said, nudging me out of the way from the sitting area reading light. "I hope you don't mind, but I just like to be cautious." He replaced the light cover and turned to me with a look as though he'd done something as mundane, but necessary, as changing out old vase water.

"Why did you put a microphone and a camera in my room? Wait. Don't answer that." I could feel my face scrunch up like a shar-pei. "What I would really like to know is why you travel with surveillance equipment, like one might carry dental floss or a penknife?"

He laughed at me. "How about you come and stay with Karl and me for a couple days and I will tell you all about it? Colorado seems to be calling to you, Phalaen."

It was true. I wanted to see Q more than I wanted to see anyone else. And it would be fun to hunt for Inca Rose and imagine my mother doing that very thing while searching for the perfect stone for my pendant . . . the key to her greatest creation. But was staying at a stranger's house really a good idea?

As if reading my thoughts, Karim said we could give the aunts a call. I gave him a little grin. He smiled broadly in return, proclaiming, "Trust, but verify!"

That was exactly what my mom would say. And just like that, like a dam bursting, tears flowed from my eyes. Unable to stand anymore, my body went limp, and I was once again scooped up by this gentle giant.

"Ssshhh, it's okay. Oh, habibi," said Karim. "I'm here. I've got you."

And he did. I was weightless in his arms, as all of my fears and doubts flooded my mind and overcame me in waves. With each surge, another threat of drowning met with his embrace. He whispered words of assurance in so many languages, all of which spoke right to my heart.

"Oh, Karim, I want my Mommy. Pleeeease! I want my Moooomm." The pain engulfed me and I got lost in a world without sound. I stayed like that until I caught my breath, cradled against his chest like a little girl. His shirt was wet from my ocean of tears.

"How about some dinner, cherie? You will feel much better after you eat something." Karim was just old enough that he could be my dad and he cared for me like I was his child, but it felt different. He felt like a guardian angel sent to me.

I said, "Yes, I think that is a good idea." It was hard to get the words out with the soreness in my throat caused by the anguish that had escaped my lips. My throat felt parched once the well had run dry. If it hadn't, I was sure I'd still be crying.

"That's a good girl. Now splash some water on your face and put on a bit of lip gloss, and nobody will be the wiser." I did so and I couldn't help but feel a laugh rise up as I heard him mumble something about the envy he felt toward me.

"You know that you won't always be able to cry that hard and still look pretty. My eyes would blow up like a puffer fish, with my face splotched like a Pollack painting!" Karim could change roles faster than a Broadway actor could change costumes.

"It's quite obvious why my mother would be so drawn to you," I said. "You are absolutely ridiculous and fantastically lovable. If the offer still stands, I would very much like to stay with you and Karl."

For about two seconds, he was without words. The moment passed, though, and once again he was his effusive and demonstrative self. "That pleases me greatly! You will just love our place. We are in the mountains, surrounded by Aspen groves. And you know something? That stone in your pendant can be found everywhere there."

If I had needed a sign, that was it. "It's settled then. I will get off the train with you. But if you don't mind, let's not tell the others." There was no particular reason for the secrecy, other than the fact that being the center of attention of so many strangers made me feel uncomfortable.

"No worries, though I am fairly certain the boys and Richard are also departing for there. But we don't need to tell them you'll be my guest, if you prefer it that way."

"I do, thanks," I said.

"Pas de problème!"

"Merci bien."

"Good! And we will work on your accent. You sound American," said Karim. He winked at me, knowing I understood the irony. When he was my age, there was nothing one could hope for more than to be American, but that had changed.

Chapter 16

"You have to follow the money. It's always about the money," insisted Opi. "It is the root of all evil. Like the song goes, *Money, money, money, money, money . . . money . . .*" He reached the high notes, and his friends asked if his balls had dropped.

"I appreciate what you are saying, son," said Mr. Smith, "particularly your appreciation for the O'Jays; but really it's about power. Consider the myths that explain the struggle between good and evil. They are about the ability and authority to dominate and subdue. Someone is always on top."

"First of all, Opi," I said, "the song is about 'the love of money'. It is 'the love of money' that is the root of all kinds of evil. It's from 1 Timothy 6:10. Why does everyone always get that wrong?"

"The girl knows her Scripture! And her tunes." said Snow.

I stuck my tongue out at him. Like a child. He grinned. I flipped my hair.

"And Mr. Smith," I said, "I would argue that money and power are simply tools. The struggle is always between good and evil. But of course, having a meaningful debate about that would require that we

174

actually be able to agree upon definitions of 'good' and 'evil.' Not since 1998 have we, here in the United States, been able to agree on what the definition of 'is' is thanks to Bill Clinton and the media, so I am not hopeful that collectively we can agree on anything."

The Smiths and the Three Amigos all turned to look at me. I heard Opi whisper in Snow's ear, "She's a gamer girl and she is really smart. That is so hot!" The weed donor just stared at me, with a wad of chew barely concealed in his slack-opened jaw.

I tossed Snow the hat and jacket without saying a word and spun around to sit at the table next to them, wishing that either Karim or Richard were sitting with me.

"Oh now come on. Don't be like that." Snow said and gave me a look I didn't recognize. "You can be smart and hot."

I sat down and glared at him. Everything about him irritated me. It even irritated me that he irritated me. That, too, was irritating.

Mr. Smith laughed. "That was quite an impressive retort, young lady. So tell me, if you are not hopeful that we can collectively agree upon anything, what keeps you from ending it all? If there is no hope, then what do you got?"

I appreciated that Mr. Smith was even considering these questions. And I was encouraged to see two generations bridged by discussing first-cause principles. But he still demonstrated the limits of binary thinking, as if there are only two options: open the door or close the door. Rose would have something to say about that for sure!

"I said I didn't have hope that we would collectively agree upon anything; I didn't say that I don't have hope. I have hope in myself and my ability to determine good from bad, execute decisions, and live with the consequences."

"I'm with you, Phalaen," Snow said. "But to address what you two said about money and power, the great thing about cryptocoin is that its peer-to-peer transactions bypass third-party regulators, promoting the decentralization of power. Without that artificial struggle, people are free to act." He looked straight at me and added, "Good or bad." It was my turn to be impressed. Snow was smarter than I had given him credit for.

Mrs. Smith had been sitting there quietly, hands placed elegantly on the edge of the table, her nails freshly polished. With her wedding rings clean and sparkling, she reached over and gently laid her hand upon her husband's, as if to indicate that it was now her turn to talk.

"That sounds well and good for you, kids, but you are all healthy, smart, and capable. What about those who aren't? Are you just going to let them fall by the wayside? People left to their own devices will just look out for themselves."

I had heard this argument so many times before on forums and social media. My parents had insulated me from people whose line of reasoning was such, but I knew it well. The same people would inevitably ask, "What about the roads?" if I, or any other independent thinker suggested eliminating the State.

"Do you mean like the elderly or the sick?" I asked hoping that she would understand the implication. She didn't.

"Well, yes. Nobody is perfect," said Mr. Smith, "and sometimes we are even victims of our own bad decisions and we need help." He sat looking at me, anticipating what I might say. It seemed absurd to me that he could be clear on an issue like marijuana, but not be able to understand the fundamental truth that lay at the core of both, or of everything, really.

I was on the brink of eating my own hand. I was so hungry, kicking myself in the ass for taking a nap and foregoing lunch. As my hunger increased, my ability to be patient diminished. This is one of those times Mom would say I didn't really live in my body, so to focus my will.

"You are both correct to say that we all need help. And yes, I am healthy, smart, and capable, but look at how I have needed help from all of you," I said. They each smiled at me and I smiled back. "None of you were forced, nor did you do it because you feared punishment if you didn't help." They all nodded in agreement. "Just like I helped you two last evening."

"Touché! You got us there, you clever girl!" Mr. Smith looked pleased as punch, as one from his generation would say.

Weed dude spoke up, catching me by surprise. I had assumed he was dumb because he didn't speak. "Don't you think you ought to tell Pinky here why the cops are after her?" He spit into a Styrofoam cup. "And no, hot stuff, it's not 'cuz you're bangin'."

"Oh yes! I almost forgot. Well, actually, I did forget," Mr. Smith admitted in a way that indicated he was happy to have the attention back on him. "That joint you dudes gave me was potent!" He and Opi were the only ones to find it funny. Mrs. Smith was busy color-coordinating the sweetener packets.

"It's actually very serious and not something to joke about. But before we get into that, do you know our names?" The one I had been calling Snow spoke up sounding very stern.

"No, no I don't." I was at once embarrassed. What was wrong with me that I accepted the kindness of strangers and didn't even bother to call them by their actual name? It was so unlike me!

"Well my name is John, not Snow, and my name is spelled with an 'h,' unlike that dashing dolt Jon Snow. By the way, I do appreciate that you chose one of the most beloved and handsome of all the game characters as your pet name for me."

My first inclination was to throw something at him. But then he smiled at me, his eyes twinkled with such fun and mischief, and I realized he was teasing me. I blushed.

"And I am Andy," said weed dude, "though everyone calls me 'Zag' and you can too, if you want."

I laughed. "Is that short for Zigzag?"

"You know it!" He smiled, pulled a grinder from his pocket and rolled up a fatty, carefully placing a clutch inside the tip. It seemed a funny thing for a guy to do, who doesn't mind tobacco being in his lip.

Like a puppy wanting attention, the fresh-faced one spoke up. "My name is Mike, but I am kind of liking Opi." His two friends looked at him and laughed. "What? I've never had a nickname before."

"Well, it is nice to be formally introduced. My name is Phalaenopsis Ariel Lundgren. Some call me Phalaen, most Ari, some attach Scary in front of it, which annoys me, and my dad calls me PAL. So take your pick—I answer to all of them."

"Can I call you 'hotness,' Scary Ari?" Opi asked and put up his arms as if to defend himself from potential blows. I couldn't help laughing. He really was quite sweet and totally harmless.

"Now that we have that squared away," said John. "You should know that the cops were looking for a pink-haired girl who is wanted for questioning on a federal matter regarding the dark net website Panacea." I looked at him and froze.

"Yeah! Craziest thing thinking that a sweet girl like you could be running an online drug-trading business." Mr. Smith turned around to tell me this, so he didn't notice John's eyes burning into me. John shook his head nearly imperceptibly, but it was enough that I caught the warning.

Mr. Smith, the ex-cop, boisterously recounted the story of how he had sauntered off the train with joint in hand. "It was easy; I simply told them the truth. I said you had come to my aid and rescue, probably stopping a heart attack, and that your friend had followed up, taking me to the doc today."

He continued, "I also said I had seen you board the train, grab your bags, and drive off with a dark-skinned fella about fifteen minutes before in a dark SUV. Sorta like the ones they were driving. The cops hopped in their vehicles and squealed out of there. That was it. Oh, and I said that Richard was with us and we were headed for Colorado."

"Did I hear my name?" Richard walked through the dining car door, his arms outstretched like a used car salesman ready to give us the deal of a lifetime. I didn't care, as long as it involved food going in my mouth. I could not think on an empty stomach.

"We have got a treat waiting for you!" Richard seemed pretty thrilled with himself. Once again, I was the last to know what was going on. One by one, they each stood up from their seats in great anticipation of whatever awaited behind the green door. I was feeling a bit more skeptical.

Richard stood aside as they filed past, seemingly knowing where they were going. Given that the train had a front and a back made it easier. Yes, no, right, left, front, back, up, down. I could use some binary right about now was my thought. I followed behind them, happy to be led.

"We are having dinner in one of the cars that are empty except for the amazing spread that Karim ordered for us at our stop this afternoon. It smells and looks amazing! And I picked up some craft beers from a local shop," Richard said. He caught my sideways glance and added rather cheekily, "Apple cider for you."

"How did you know?" I did not drink alcohol other than when I toured a winery once. But I did love apple cider.

"I guessed. You mentioned loving the apple tree in your backyard and how much fruit it produced. I figured Phi-Phi must have made you cider, along with sauces and pies, no?"

"There you go again! Why do you insist on calling my mother Fi-Fi, as if she was a lapdog?" I was a little more abrasive than necessary, but everything had come

180

at me at once and I was feeling like someone waking from a coma; the questions didn't necessarily have a proper order to them.

Richard grabbed ahold of my shoulder and whirled me around. "Phalaen! Who in their right mind would ever consider giving your mother a nickname appropriate for a lapdog?"

We stood looking at each other as if wondering what on earth the other could possibly be thinking. We were both speaking English. Obviously this was, once again, a case of not defining one's terms.

"So then, what?" I asked.

"You should know. Phi . . . the Fibonacci sequence."

I looked at him and felt utterly perplexed. My head started to pound like I was under water and hearing loud booms. My mother didn't even know what Pi was, much, much less Phi. And she definitely never made pies or sauce.

"You said your dad called her Seven, her best friend called her Six, so why would you think it strange that I called her Phi? Although it started out as a condition of my speech impediment, I admit. Phi-Phi was the best I could do at age three, as the story was told to me. As I grew older, I saw it written as "Phi-Phi," and she was a math whiz, so I never questioned it.

"My mother, a math whiz? Okay, now I am thinking that maybe we are talking about two different people. My mom flunked Algebra 2 . . . three times!"

"Hey, I don't know anything about that. I do know that she loved math, she was really good at it, and that everyone knew her as my Phi-Phi. . . . NOT Fi-Fi. Okay?"

I was about to start crying again, and Richard got a look on his face like it was his mission not to allow it.

"Oh no! No, no, no. . . . Don't cry, don't cry. Please don't cry. I didn't mean to upset you, Phalaen, and I am sure it must be quite shocking to hear that your mother has a family. Or had. But I assure you, I loved your mom, and so did my mother and sisters and father. So much."

He sounded sincere and I was happy to hear it, even if it did make me confused. I had always thought my mother's parents had both died, and that she had no family. Dad and me, we were her family. And all the crazy aunts and friends.

I said, "I am sorry. This is all so confusing. And overwhelming. And, and, and. . . ."

"No, no, no. No crying!"

I swallowed hard. "I just wish that I had known that she loved math. We could have shared that, but she always left my teachers and Dad to teach me. All she taught me was how to write cursive. And I told her that was stupid."

I didn't care that I couldn't hold back. I just cried as I spoke my feelings. I had never known I had so many of them.

His face clouded with sadness. Tears fell from his eyes. Just a few, but they emptied out like water spilling over an edge. "Oh, honey. I know what it is like to tell a parent, who taught you something that it was stupid — only to never be able to take back the words."

"You do?" I tried to sniff the tears and snot up, to no avail.

"Yes, I do. My dad knew computer languages, like you. Not my biological dad — he died before I was born —

but my adopted father who raised me and whom I consider my dad."

Richard continued, "He tried to teach me about programming and I told him that only loser nerds used computers. I went to boarding school and the opportunity passed. He has dementia now and doesn't remember that he ever knew anything about computers."

Unwrapping my cryptocoin-covered bandana from my arm, I reluctantly blew my nose into it. It had been a gift from a crypto charity that Panacea donated money to. It was either use the bandana, or my shirt.

"Hey, what is that on your arm?" Richard gently lifted the fabric square out of the way. "Is that an ace up your sleeve?"

Instinctively, my hand reached over and covered my tattoo. I wasn't embarrassed. Nobody but Mom and the tattoo artist had ever seen it. Not even my dance partner, Steven.

It had started out quite simple. Mom took me to get a tattoo on my seventeenth birthday. Afterwards we came home for a dinner party with Dad, the aunts and everyone. I wore a long-sleeve over my bandage, not to hide it, but to protect it.

Mom approached me halfway through, a little bit stoned, and asked if I had shown Dad or told anyone yet. I hadn't. She whispered to me, "Isn't it fun to be the only two people in the room who know? I wonder how long it can stay that way." She looked so mischievous. She loved games.

Her teeth were slightly stained and her tongue was darkened from the wine. So were her lips, so when she smiled, it looked like she was wearing lipstick. She had slight mascara smudges under one eye. She smelled of wine, the only perfume she ever wore, and smoke from the fire pit. I could see her and smell her like she was right here, right now.

I wrapped the bandana back around my wrist and told Richard to forget about it. Now I was back to three people knowing my secret. That was really two too many, if I expected it to remain one.

"Yeah, I bet it was Phi-Phi's idea to get that." Richard smiled at me as if we were all in on the joke, and he just rambled on. "Your mom didn't talk when she first came to live with us. I think she had been really sick, or something. And that was fine with me because talking required so much effort with my stuttering. But she still taught me things—mostly my numbers and math. Blackjack was her favorite card game."

"No, my mom never played twenty-one. That was what my dad and I called it. She liked nearly everything else—bridge, poker, hearts, but not blackjack."

"Well, maybe she got tired of playing it." Richard looked like he had just remembered something and then forgot it again.

I couldn't think of anything to say with my head so full, so I started heading back again to where the others had traipsed off. Just before I opened the sliding door where I could see the rest of our dining party, Richard said my name softly. I turned and looked at him. He looked like he was scared.

"Phalaen, do you know why your mother chose to create twenty-one pieces for her *Crypto Chaos* series?"

I bit my lip, trying to remember why and I could not think of an answer.

"You know, I am embarrassed to say that I have no idea. Maybe because it's in the Fibonacci sequence?" I
184

said. I laughed and shrugged it off, but inside my brain, the wheels were spinning. I really had no clue why she'd chosen that number.

I entered our dining car for the evening and found it decorated like a bazaar. There was even a hookah with tubes coming off it like the arms of an octopus. It sat on a coffee table with little tea cups stacked next to it.

"Isn't this something dear?" asked Mrs. Smith. "The boys did all this themselves today, while we were being lazy." She swayed to Middle Eastern music that was playing softly, and told me to taste the meatballs. I could smell mint and the sweet, nutty flavor of pine nuts as she waved a half-eaten one under my nose.

Placed on a table covered with brightly colored scarves was an array of other equally delicious-looking dishes. My mouth watered. In fact, all my senses tingled.

There were individual cups of Hariri that we could easily sip without using spoons because the tomatoes, lentils, chickpeas, and lamb had been run through a sieve. A chebakia rested on the rim of the cups. Oooh, I just loved dipping.

The Zaalouk had a little different flavor than I was used to. Opi pointed to it after delivering a huge dollop to some bread. He told me there was cannabis in it. "Eggplant that gets you high. Who wouldn't love this?" he asked.

"It's Indica, habibi. I think we could all use some chill after the day we've had, don't you?" Karim asked. He had a plate all made up for me with kefta and couscous, different salads, alongside some herb-crusted sardines. The munchies were giving me the chance to eat more than I would normally, and that was just fine with me, if it tasted as good as it smelled and looked.

185

"Shukran, Karim. This is perfect!" I said.

Colorful pillows were set about on sofas. I had not seen any of the cars set up with this configuration, but it lent well to a lounge-like setting that complimented the food, music, and now-dancing Karim. I was told to sit down on a pillow. The guys had a surprise for me.

They donned the wigs I had seen earlier and wrapped their hips with some of the fabrics that were draped over everything. Suddenly Richard set about playing a doumbek and the guys started doing what I could only imagine was an attempt at belly dancing. It reminded me of the time I had seen Dad, Uncle Peter, and the Harrison boys all try to hula hoop. It was hysterical and I had a hard time keeping food in my mouth.

"Wow! You are really good, Richard," I yelled over the music.

"Your mother gave me one of these when I graduated from high school," he yelled back.

It felt very strange to hear these things about my mother, as if she had been an entirely different person before she had me. But as I thought about it, maybe it was like she always said: You have to clear some things from your plate to make room for other things. You cannot have it all.

It occurred to me that, had she lived, maybe she would have cleared me from her plate to make room for something else. After all, it seemed apparent she had walked away from one family when she got a new one. Would she, could she, have walked away from Dad and me? And if so, for what?

186

Chapter 17

The inside of my mouth felt like I had swallowed a wad of cotton. There was no moistness for licking my lips, which I sensed were stained with the tannins from Karim's coffee. My mouth tasted awful! I reached down to unbutton my jeans, which I had not bothered to take off, so I could hold off getting up to pee just a few more minutes while I tried to wake up.

"Good morning, Scary Ari."

"Good morning." My eyes bolted open to find John's head peering over the edge of the bunk above me. "What are you doing in my room? You just nearly scared the pee right out of me, you big jerk!"

"Easy, hotness. Before you go freaking out, I need some water." John popped off the side and poured a glass for me and then proceeded to drink the remainder straight from the bottle.

He was still wearing his jeans, too. But that was all. He looked like he had been carved from butter, if butter was tan. There was a sliver of pale skin peeking out at the lower part of his stomach, with a little line of soft, golden curls that led from his pants to his belly button.

I sat up and drank the water slowly, trying not to look at him. He was as defined as the male dancers whom I had partnered with, only he had much bigger muscles. And dammit! There was that smell again.

"Richard told us you were on your way to MIT and that you were into distributed systems." He chuckled. "He called you a hacker, Scary Ari."

"Yeah? Well, Richard says a lot." I let my feet flop off the side of the bed and carry my body with them. "And stop calling me that!"

"Or what? Are you going to have me turned into a dookie ball?" he teased, barely able to contain himself.

I flipped my head up so fast that I smacked it on the upper bunk. "Shit! Ouch, that friggin' hurt." I ducked back down and rubbed my head while I looked down at my perfectly polished pink toes, afraid to look up again. "Johnny?" I asked with a bit of a whimper.

At once he was kneeling at my feet and checking my head. "Are you okay?" he asked. "That sounded like you cracked it good." He gave it a kiss and told me he'd be back in a jiff with some ice.

"No! Don't go. Is that really you?" I asked feebly.

He turned back from the door and grabbed my wrists to pull me up. "Come here, sweet girl. Awww, you have had quite a time of it, haven't you?"

He held me against him with my cheek pressed against his chest. "You got really tall," was all I could think to say, before pulling away to use the loo. "I need some breakfast and coffee."

"As you wish. . . ." Before he could add his pet name for me, I gave him one of those looks and he finished with " . . . Ariel, Queen of the Flower Fairies," then closed the door behind him.

188

As urine drained out of me, I felt a sense of relief, while at the same time experiencing a funny feeling in the pit of my stomach. It wasn't exactly an ache, but it did sort of hurt. I had no idea what it was, because I had never felt it before.

Oh no! Maybe it's an infection from wearing my bike shorts all day yesterday. I knew girls from dance who had gotten UTIs from wearing tights too long. Apparently UTIs could be quite miserable. Great! Something to add to my list of new adventures. A tingling vag and tummy ache. I needed Aunt DeeDee.

The icy cold water felt like an assault as I splashed it on my face. But the fog was thick. The more numb my hands and face got, the more sharp my brain became.

What was Johnny Harrison doing on the same train as me? I didn't know how I felt about it. One thing was for sure. He still totally got on my nerves.

My toothbrush had never tasted so good. I scrubbed away the film of debauchery from the night before, trying to remember how I had gotten back to my room. At least my pants were on. Karim's surveillance equipment may provide some answers. The thought of what I might see nearly made me laugh out loud.

As I stood looking in the mirror, resisting the urge to poke at my face, I noticed the door handle start to turn. I paused to think. It made my head hurt.

I recognized Johnny's voice saying, "Hey there, Mrs. Smith. Good morning! What brings you around so early and after such a wild night?" Was it he or she who had tried to open the door? "You sure do know how to cut a rug!"

"Well, good morning to you, too, John. It's already seven o'clock; that's late for us old fogeys. Gotta get up and have my bran muffin and coffee. Keeps me regular."

I put my hand over my mouth to stifle my laughter. Old people are so funny. I could just imagine Johnny trying not laugh.

"What about you? My son would have slept 'til noon after a wild party like we had last night. I see you got yourself a cup of coffee, too. I don't suppose you'd like to keep me company while I have my breakfast?" She sounded so darn sweet! Listening to her made me wish I had a grandmother.

"You know," said Johnny, "I would love to, but I have some catching up on reading to do. You know how it is: teachers want us to have read the material before we show up for class."

Now THAT was the Johnny I remembered. Bullshit just came out of his mouth like it was nothin'! How old was he? Twenty-six? That's a little old to still be an undergrad. Ha! He probably was on a ten-year plan, living on campus, and trying to date freshman.

"Oh, I don't know anything about all that," said Mrs. Smith. "I never did go to college. I was just a mom. But you go right ahead. You are such a good boy! Toodle-oo!"

There was a pause and then in he slipped, with a white sack in his mouth and an extra-large coffee in one hand, and his other over his eyes. "Are you dressed?"

"Yes, of course I am!" I gently removed the coffee from his hand, looking for a spare mug to pour some into for him. "There doesn't seem to be another mug, so we'll have to share this. How do you take it?" I asked. It felt completely normal to be asking him, as if it hadn't been twelve years since we last saw each other.

"Oh, not for me, thanks. I don't touch the stuff. But I would like to hop in the shower, if you don't mind. I wake up to fifty-one degree water. I like to stand under it for at least two minutes. Gets the blood pumping."

My mouth was already full with a breakfast sandwich, so I just nodded. I could not get the coffee into me fast enough. He could have his cold shower.

I sat at the window and looked out. We had to be near Colorado by now. How different the landscape was from California and from Oregon. Strange to think how different life looked from when I had departed Eugene.

"Oh, you're awake!"

I spilled the scalding coffee on me as I jumped up, startled by Mrs. Smith, who had just walked right into my room without knocking.

"Mrs. Smith, what are you doing?" I asked with scorching hostility The coffee was burning my skin but my anger at having my privacy invaded burned hotter.

"Honey, you should get that shirt off right away. Your skin is going to blister." She walked toward me with one hand outstretched, as if she actually thought I'd let someone who just barged into my room touch me.

"Mrs. Smith, explain please!" I said this loud enough that Johnny would hear my voice from the shower. At least he wasn't singing.

"Don't be cross, honey. I was just coming to see if you'd like to join me for breakfast."

"So you entered my room without knocking?"

She put her finger to her lips and motioned toward the shower. She walked closer to me and used her pointer finger to indicate that I should sit down. Why she thought she could tell me what to do, especially under the circumstances, was beyond me, but I did as she wanted.

Whispering, she said there was some sort of problem with Richard and that Karim had said I should stay close to her and Mr. Smith. "Just leave your things and we can get breakfast in the dining car. Tell your friend that you will be back in a bit." She was leaning uncomfortably close to me when the bathroom door burst open.

"Mrs. Smith! You caught us!"

Johnny stood buckass naked and dripping wet. Obviously, he was not affected by cold water the way I'd heard other men were. I closed my eyes and thought, I have just seen Johnny Harrison's penis!

It wasn't even 7:15 in the morning and I had already been awakened by a strange man in my room, who was indeed strange but, as it turned out, not a stranger. I'd spilled burning hot coffee on my boobs. A woman, who for all intents and purposes was a stranger, had entered the same room. And I had seen a grown man's penis, and not on a website. This was going to be some day!

"Here you go. Let me see you out." She stumbled backwards as he startled her. He kept her off-balance with that aggressive teasing that irked me so. I liked it now that it was directed at someone other than me. Funny how that works.

"Phalaen is just fine. You run along now. I am sure that Mr. Smith will be wanting that bran and coffee. Gotta keep him regular. Be a good girl and fetch it for him, okay?"

Johnny literally moved her along with the threat of his naked body bumping up against her. She was nearly beside herself, using her right hand to ward off his advancing, while her left reached out behind her. She didn't even talk; she just sputtered.

He closed the door behind her, locked it, and stood still, with his hand against it and his body acting as a barricade. He bent down and picked something up off the floor. Scanning the room, his eyes rested on my cell, still on its charger. He held his finger to his lips.

Taking a pen and paper from my backpack side pocket, he wrote me a note telling me to write down my emergency contacts, delete my pictures, and remove my SD card from my phone.

I looked at him like he was on crack. He looked at me like he wanted to ring my neck. "I am serious, Phalaen. Get dressed. Do as I say. We have to go!" He had never called me Phalaen before.

He didn't bother to dry off before putting back on the clothes he'd discarded in the bathroom, and putting whatever he had found on the floor into his front pocket. He looked at me, still sitting down in front of my partially devoured breakfast, and told me that he would dress me if he had to.

I pulled on my socks and boots, then rubbed on some deodorant before changing into a fresh T-shirt. I had spent the whole day yesterday stinking; I wasn't going to today. My bags were basically all good to go, since I had not bothered to unpack. I tossed in the few toiletries I had, put my hair up in a bun, and reached for my coffee.

Johnny knocked it out of my hand. "Don't drink that!" He took what was in his pocket out. It was a tiny liquid dropper. He whispered into my ear with his lips brushing up against it, "I bet you anything that I am going to test this and find that it is toxic. Take only the things you absolutely need. Karim will get the rest later. We want it to look like you are still on the train."

I stood stunned, my hand holding empty space where the cup had been, while he removed the camera and microphone out from where Karim had placed them the evening before. I asked how he knew.

"Karim showed me last night. He was the one who tucked you in, and we agreed I should stay." He finished and turned toward the door. He must have assumed I was following him because when he stepped out into the hall and I didn't, he turned and looked at me with frustration. "Come on, we've gotta go."

"No. How did you know that she, that. . . . Johnny, what is that? Why would Mrs. Smith want to poison me?" There had to be a mistake. "She gave me chocolates and wanted me to stay hydrated only yesterday."

Johnny stepped back into the room. He stood directly in front of me, placing his large hands on either side of my face. His voice was barely audible. His breath smelled like an orange grove.

"Sweet Scary Ari, I will tell you everything as soon as I have you somewhere safe. When I saw Uncle Kimo ushering you onto the train, looking like you'd seen a ghost . . . yes, that is what we call Karim; I knew things had progressed. You are in danger; we need to go. Now!"

"Should we go check on Richard? What if she was being serious and he is in trouble or ill?" I mouthed back.

"Nope. I gave him a sedative. He'll be fine."

"But what about Karim and your friends?" I asked. "Surely we should go see if they are okay, and they can come with us." Johnny started walking. "Johnny!"

He swung around and looked at me with a look that terrified me. "Do you understand what no means? If not, now is a good time to learn."

I stared at him and stomped my foot. Like I was five. "Don't call me Scary Ari! I hate it."

I grabbed my retro tees from my suitcase and extra panties and stuffed then into my backpack, checking to make sure I still had Mom's drawing safe, and I began to follow him. Nobody had ever really told me no before. I shut my mouth, but on the inside I was screaming, "Noooooo!"

Chapter 18

Johnny's movements seemed familiar as I watched him tie a figure eight. He even kept his pointer fingers rigid the way Mom did. But still, he didn't look like I remembered. For one thing, he didn't have pimples.

"Look, I am not even sure you are who you say," I told him. "I don't remember you looking like you do. I think maybe you should verify your identity before I attach myself to you then jump off a moving train. Although that does seem like something the Harrison brothers would have done, as I recall."

He gave me that look again. "You haven't become any less feisty, have you?"

I stared at him with my hands on my hips.

"If I prove to you that I am John Harrison, are you going to be easier to deal with?" I must have paused too long because he mumbled, "Probably not," as he started to untie the improvised harness he'd configured. I was using the only one he had in his climbing bag.

"What are you doing now?"

"I am showing you proof." He removed his shirt; once again, he was standing half naked in front of me.

What was it with this guy? "Sorry, but your naked body does very little for me, thank you."

He laughed, "Is that so? Well I am not naked; I am half naked. Just like I was the summer you visited and got stuck in the cellar of that abandoned house."

I vaguely remembered adventuring with Q, but I did not recall Johnny being there. I think it was when she thought she saw a ghost. Still not good enough. "I am not saying anything until I have proof."

"If you would be quiet, I am going to give it to you."

God, he was infuriating!

"I was coming back from fishing when I saw the dilapidated shack on fire at the edge of the neighbor's property. I walked up for a closer look and that was when I heard you singing your repertoire of spider songs to Q," he said.

I didn't remember a fire, but I did have a thing for spiders and I did know a lot of songs and poems about them. There were alarms going off inside my head, and I didn't want to hear any more. I told him, "That's enough. I believe you."

"Oh no, I am going to prove it to you. By the time I located you two, the whole place was in flames. I found a little window to the basement cellar and tried to coax you out. But you wouldn't leave Q. So I had to climb in to get you. I pushed you out first and then Q. While hoisting myself up, my back caught a piece of rebar and it ripped into my flesh. See?" He bent down enough so that I could see the white scar. It looked like a sword.

"I called it your sword of courage," I said. I had forgotten about that. But now it was all coming back to me.

"That is the day I started calling you Scary Ari. By the time I had pulled myself out, you had dragged my

197

sister safely away. You took off running for help, yelling at me to not be scared. My lungs were so filled with smoke that it took all I had just to crawl over to her. You ran all the way to our house and brought back our dads."

"So you called me Scary?"

"Well, yeah. You were only six years old. It was pretty amazing that you could keep it together, with my sister having one of her moments, in a house on fire, then go for help, and make your way back." He was smiling at me again with those sea-green eyes and that perfect mouth. "Heroic Ari doesn't have quite the same ring to it."

We stood there for a moment in silence. Five minutes before, I would not have been able to recount that story. But now, I could smell the acrid smoke and fear gripped me. "I was so scared, Johnny."

"I know, sweet girl. But being brave isn't about not being scared; it's about pushing through when you are. Like right now. You have to trust yourself. You did that; you can do this." He gripped my wrists and held them tight against his chest.

Too many feelings stirred in me, and the tears just seemed to boil over. "Mrs. Smith said I am strong, healthy, and capable."

"Oh, fuck that hag! You are badass, Phalaen Lundgren. Look at who raised you! There is no way that you couldn't be a force to reckon with, having a mother like Aunt V. Did you know that she is the one who taught me to climb?"

"She did? She was really cool like that." And for the third time in twenty-four hours, I was blubbering like a baby.

"Aww, come on now!" said Johnny. "Forget why we are here for now and let's just have an adventure together, okay? Doesn't that sound fun?"

I had to admit that an adventure with Johnny did sound like fun. Besides, I had always wanted to jump off of a train. It seemed so romantic. Although I was not interested in a romance with him.

I started to braid my hair. It was go time. "You say we are going to wait for the train to pull out of the station and then jump?" I asked.

"Yes. We don't want anyone to know we have gotten off. It will be a while before the next stop, so nobody will notice ropes hanging off the side until then."

He continued, "Now, you said you had a cell phone that the librarian gave you. That's good. We will use that to make calls. Tell me, who do you trust without hesitation?"

"To tell you the truth, the only person I have wanted to talk to is Q."

"You have to think about who would be an asset that you could trust in this circumstance."

Any of the people who had for years been my extended family would have fit in that category until yesterday. Now I didn't know. Johnny saw me hesitating and told me to go with my first response.

"Who is the first person that you would go to if you were hurt or in trouble at home?" he asked.

"Well, before yesterday, I would have said the Vet and Aunt DeeDee."

"Does the Vet still have his plane?" I nodded though I wasn't sure how Johnny would know about that. "And she is a nurse. They are perfect! Attagirl, Phalaen."

I had done enough risky things that were potentially life threatening, so I knew I had to get out of my head, or I'd be dead. All of my questions about the people in the photograph would have to wait. The pettiness of it all seemed pretty ridiculous, if it was true that Mrs. Smith had gone to my room to poison me.

Johnny put his hands together and closed his eyes. I couldn't tell if he was praying or concentrating. Either one seemed appropriate.

"Okay, this is the plan," he said. We are getting off at Green River, Utah. It isn't far from Moab and I know Doc knows the area because we biked there last summer."

"Excuse me, but who is Doc?" I was totally focused and on board with whatever the plan was, but I had no idea who he was talking about, which made me hesitate. Hesitation usually results in a bad take off and I didn't want that.

"Dr. Milan is who you call Vet. You thought he was a veterinarian because he took care of Baby Harry and the nickname just took. But I know him as Doc. He is a psychiatrist."

That actually made sense now that I thought about it. The Vet was a very good listener. I used to spend a lot of time with him and Aunt DeeDee when I was quite young. Weird, though, that I never knew he was a shrink all these years.

"Your ticket is booked through to Denver, so we are hopefully good until 7:30 p.m. when the train arrives. By then Karim will have moved your stuff."

"Are you sure Karim is okay? And that he will know what to do?" I asked.

"Absolutely! We knew there was something off with the Smiths since Joe Smith lied. And for all of Kimo's silliness, no one is scarier if he has you in his sight."

I really had to pay better attention because I was missing a lot. Now was not the time to entertain the voices of doubt that clamored for attention, but it was quite chilling how vulnerable I was. It came as a surprise to me.

Johnny explained, "Yesterday, I left my climbing bag in the kitchen, as I usually do on this route. I deliver some recreationals and medicinals to the kitchen staff that way. They leave the money inside and I pick up the bag a little later." Johnny ignored my gaping mouth and he continued.

"When I ran back to get it, I saw Joe headed over to talk to the cops. You know that lighter I lent him? Well there is a mini mic in it. It comes in handy when I am making deals and haven't established trust with my buyers." He took a swig from his Nalgene bottle after offering me some, which I had declined. I didn't want to drink where his mouth had been.

"Phalaen, Joe is a fed. He works for the FBI. His comment about a pink-haired girl being wanted for questioning was bullshit. The cops were really there because you had evaded the cops, resisted arrest, and get this . . . assaulted a police officer. Joe pulled the lead in command aside and said you were a suspect in a federal investigation, and he requested some 'professional courtesy'."

"What? Is this a joke?" I said. "You can't be serious."

"About which part?"

"About all of it."

"Sorry, it's not a joke. Panacea is on their target list," said Johnny, "so that means you."

"How do you know that? And what about Mrs. Smith?"

"Her too, I am pretty sure, though not certain. Karim said you passed out about fifteen minutes after she gave you those candies and the water. Maybe that is a coincidence, but he was pretty sure you were drugged."

"And what about me saving him from a possible heart attack and all of that other stuff they said?"

"That's what feds do: they pretend to be your friend and then they fuck you. I haven't quite put it all together yet, so I don't want to speculate. Richard is still a part of the puzzle that doesn't quite fit."

Johnny said all this while getting dressed again and harnessed in. He finished and caught me lost in thought, biting my lip. "What is it?"

"Richard is Mom's brother. Or at least she lived with him when she was thirteen and he was three. See this ring? He was special enough to Mom that she bought this, a replica of the plastic gumball machine version that he had given her when he proposed at six."

"You are kidding me? Okay. Put aside that he was your mom's brother and all of that. He has to be involved in this investigation somehow. The coincidences are too extreme. Do you know that he orders his son's insulin from Panacea? What are the odds that he would be on the same train as the feds investigating you, huh?"

"Well, you're here," I said.

"That's different."

Just then, an alarm on his watch when off. "Okay, here we go. You call Doc now, while I make sure the coast is clear. We'll have about ninety seconds from the time the train starts to pull into the station. We are going to climb up the back and lie flat until the train starts to pull out."

"Tell me again why we aren't just walking off the train through an exit?" I asked.

"We have to assume the feds are going to want to keep you on the train until they can control the situation," said Johnny, "so undercover agents will be positioned."

"How do you know this?"

"Just trust me; I do. Now listen. Once we are up on the roof, I want you to affix the rope using a bowline and then pre-rig a rappel line for us."

"We are going to rappel off the train?" I asked.

"Yes. Don't worry. It will be a cinch." He was definitely a Harrison twin.

"But we have only one rappel device."

"I'm going to rappel off of a carabineer using a Munter hitch, and then you are going to follow with the tube. Easy peasy." He sounded convincing, and I was confident he knew what he was doing. My mom would not have left any detail out in her instructions.

"Now the train is going to pick up speed, so hanging off the side and jumping is going to be a little scary. Are you a pretty good sprinter?" he asked.

"Will it be like letting go of the zip line in midair?" I gave him a big, cheesy grin.

"Exactly like that!" He grabbed me close and kissed me. "For luck!"

Chapter 19

It was already eleven o'clock by the time we made it to Moab. Fortunately, hitchhiking was common enough that it was easy to get a ride. It would have been easier if Johnny had let me stick my thumb out. But he said I shouldn't draw attention to myself and that the pink hair would be hard to forget. So it stayed in braids and up under a hat and my hoody.

A car stopped, filled with college girls on their last summer adventure. They just loved Johnny's eyes. They said I should wear deodorant.

Cyclists roamed around much like you'd see skiers in parking lots at ski hills, or surfers along the streets of beach towns. Everyone was in a good mood, dressed pretty much alike, and they had a relaxed air.

There was no point in acting like you were the coolest because someone was bound to be cooler. Only city people claim to be experts at outdoorsy stuff. Nothing more worthy of an eye roll than hearing a weekend warrior talk about hittin' a double black diamond.

We asked a group where to go for the best food and it was unanimous: Quesadilla Mobilla, a food truck that served exactly what it said, quesadillas. And they used local, farm-raised meats. I was famished and that sounded perfect.

I ordered the Southern Belle and Johnny got the Enchanted Chicken. When our order was up, I asked for a Fiery Fungus too. The brown-faced, large-toothed, tatted-up man gave me a thumbs up. He may have also grunted a bit. I pretended to wave a fly away and hoped he'd understand I was dismissing his primal man noises.

Johnny laughed as he doused his quesadilla in extra green chili sauce and told me that men like women with big appetites.

"Oh really?" I asked with barely concealed irritation.

"Well, I do," he said, not bothering to look up from what he was doing.

"Eeewww, Johnny Harrison, are you flirting with me, or coming onto me, or something equally gross? We are practically siblings."

"First of all, we are not siblings and second, why is that 'eeewww'?" he said, mimicking my tone. "It's not like you are seven years old. Now THAT would be gross." He was about to plunge a triangle of tortilla-filled tasty into his mouth when he added, "You are fine, Phalaen."

I busied myself with getting the hair out of my face and the food into it.

"Think about it," said Johnny. "The start of our romantic adventure would be like *North by Northwest*. Spies, intrigue, trains, planes. Come on, it's the greatest movie ever after *Magnificent Seven*."

"While I do approve of your taste in films," I said, "I think you are quite full of yourself to imagine that you are Cary Grant. Besides, everyone knows that I am going to marry Jacob."

I was quite pleased with my recollection of my birthday when Johnny had teased me so and Jacob had been my rescuer. I smiled and licked my fingers, lost in my moment of self-adulation.

"Phalaen."

"Yeah?" I asked, not bothering to swallow my food first.

"Jacob is dead." There was finality to his tone, but also uncontained heartache. He had stopped eating and was slumped a bit, legs spread on either side of the picnic bench, as though beaten. He'd not expected to have to tell me this news. "I'm sorry, but I thought you knew. He died in the car with your mom."

The food in my mouth lost all flavor and I spit it out. No, I had not known. It had been so long since I had seen Jacob that I didn't feel much of anything other than sorrow for their family's loss. It did make me wonder if that was the puzzle to Mom's death that used to stump Dad.

"I am so sorry, Johnny. Jacob was beautiful. You know Mom had a special place for all of you, but Jacob was her favorite." I wasn't sure if that was a mean thing to say or not, but everyone knew it was true.

"I think the reason that he was her favorite was because you were his," Johnny said. "There was something about you two. Pat and I had each other, and Q was always so introverted and in her own little world. When you were around, Jacob had a little buddy. We listened to him because he was the eldest; you listened because you thought that the moon rose and set at his feet. And you were his sun that everything revolved around."

"Wow. That's quite poetic." I didn't know what else to say. What I felt like doing was playing Battlefield 4 while in my flannel pajama bottoms and sports bra from the comfort of my bedroom.

"Do you like to play online games?" I asked him.

He took another bite of his lunch. "You mean like Battlefield 4?"

"I knew it! It is you! I can't believe it. You and Gizmo felt so familiar to me. Patrick is Gizmo right?" My excitement could not be contained. All this time, they were right there with me. Finally, something felt right.

He laughed. "We wanted to tell you so bad but Aunt V. forbade it."

"Mom knew? How? And . . . wait. You said Jacob was in the car with Mom. You mean you saw her? After my birthday?" He nodded, looking like he felt guilty for something. "But how? I didn't get to see Q."

Dad had tried to comfort me saying that sometimes people, even friends, part ways when they come to a fork in the road. I told him forks were stupid and that we should just spoon instead of parting ways. He had smiled and said he agreed.

"There has been so much loss," I said. "Nobody asked me what I wanted. They just made the decision for me. For us."

"There are things that I cannot tell you," he said. I glared at him, and had my eyes been lasers, he may have died right there. "I'm sorry, but I can't. Not yet anyway."

I felt if I said another word, he would remind me of my need to learn the concept of no, and I did not want to hear that word again from his mouth. So I ate in silence, swallowing my sorrow.

"And to answer your question, Pat used to be Gizmo, but Q took the account over. She liked being close to you. She missed you too, Phalaen. A lot. She never forgave us for keeping you two from each other."

He had already said he wouldn't tell me why, so I was not going to beg. Instead I got up to get my other quesadilla. I had completely lost my appetite, but I was not going to give him the satisfaction of knowing I was so upset. If he didn't want to tell me, I would figure it out myself.

"You know, now that you mention it, the personality of Gizmo did seem to change. Why did Patrick stop playing? Did he tire of children's games?" I asked with dripping sarcasm. Adults always talked about kids being addicted to video games, when, in fact, more adults played them. The average player age was thirty-one.

Johnny paused and kicked pebbles at his feet. "Nah. Pat went on to play a more childish sort of game." He looked at me in silence but his thoughts seemed to be shouting at him to continue.

"You see, your mom and Jacob were working on a project with somebody. I don't know who, so don't ask; and it had them completely obsessed. Like an 'it was going to change the world' kind of obsession. And when they were killed in the car crash, they were on their way from our house to yours to tell your dad about it."

"I have no idea what you are talking about. Was it a sculpture?" I could not imagine what else it could be because that was all Mom ever obsessed over, besides Dad and me. "Was Jacob an artist too?"

208

"He was a type of artist. Jacob was a lawyer. But I am not sure what they were working on. That is the thing. None of us knew. And nothing remained to identify the bodies or give us any clues."

"The two of them were driving with Dad and they were in a single-car accident," said Johnny. "Dad was thrown from the vehicle, knocked unconscious and woke up to see the car explode. He remembers nothing."

"How horrible for Uncle Peter!"

"Doc even hypnotized him in an effort to help him recall what happened, but Dad couldn't. He didn't even remember why they were going to see your dad. As far as he was concerned, the two of them were never going to speak again."

"Whoa. This is crazy, Johnny. I never heard any of this," I said.

"Pat had wanted to go with them, but they had said no. He always thought if he had gone, they would all be alive today. So he blamed himself. Guilt can make people do foolish things."

Without asking me, he took a bite of my mushroom-filled quesadilla, along with a swig from my water. I didn't mind.

"For months, he went over every detail of the accident and combed the whole stretch of highway like he was looking for a needle in a haystack, but he came up with nothing."

"I repeatedly asked if there was some way we could use Harry's chip," I said. "Mom always said he was a good tracker. But the Vet told me it was not possible."

"Actually, that would have been a good idea. At lease we could have been certain of his last location. Q

209

thought maybe they weren't dead and something happened to them. She got a weekend trip to the mental ward before Mom and Dad found out and rescued her. That was fucked up."

"They put her in a psych ward? For making a suggestion and questioning the official story?" I said. "That's rather Kafkaesque."

"And then one day, agents entered Pat's house that he and Jacob had shared, and the agents confiscated Pat's computer. They didn't even have a warrant."

"Wait a sec. They took Pat's computer? I don't get it."

"They said they thought maybe the car had been remotely detonated and they wanted to make sure his computer was safe from hackers."

"That is the most asinine thing I have ever heard. Did Pat say 'no, thank you'?"

"Ha-ha, no. They told him he could have it back when they were finished, but Q advised him to pick it up and then destroy it without ever turning it on, which he did. And then he applied for and was accepted to the FBI Special Agent Entry Program. Doesn't that sound fancy?"

"He what? No way!" I said. "Mom would have freaked out."

"Yeah, right?"

"So what does he do?" I asked. Somehow I couldn't imagine the tree-swinging, chicken-wing-eating contest winner as anything other than a grown-up-sized Peter Pan.

"He is a behavioral neuroscientist. So he pretty much works on gruesome cases involving serial killers and stuff. He is also an expert marksman."

"I guess that is a good thing. If he can't help them," I said, "he can always shoot them with a single kill shot. But it still doesn't sound like something I could imagine anyone in your family doing. I know my dad could never understand why your dad joined the military and stopped creating video games, especially since he was so good at it. And they had both been so antiwar in school."

"Yeah, well," Johnny said, "I was pretty surprised too. Disappointed, actually. As for Dad, he said he thought he could make a difference from the inside. Didn't quite work out like that." We finished our lunch, and without saying a word to each other, we stood up and started walking toward the airport shuttle.

"Can you keep a secret?" he asked.

I always thought it was funny when people asked that. If they could keep a secret, why were they telling it to me? I told him, "I will do one better. If you tell me your secret, I will show you mine."

"Hey, young lady, that is way too forward!" said Johnny.

I missed being teased by him. I said, "That is not what I meant, you big dummy. I am serious. I have been holding onto this and it is eating at me. I would really like to share it with someone, but not just anyone."

"Aww," he said. "I think you like me."

"Shut up."

"Okay, but you are going to have to prove to me that you don't."

"I can't prove that!" I said.

"See? I knew it." He said and started to tickle me. For a few moments I forgot that Mom and Jacob were dead, that Mrs. Smith—if that was even her name—had tried to poison me, and that my father had lied.

"Have you ever heard of Sun Tzu, the expert military strategist from sixth century BC?" asked Johnny.

"Sure. *Art of War.*"

"Well, last Christmas," said Johnny, "the family finally decided to open the gifts from Aunt V. I don't know if you know this, but she used to do our stockings. It was a thing. It had been a year since the accident and Q felt like it would give us a fresh memory."

No, I hadn't known Mom had done that; I hadn't known she was even in contact with them. But it made me feel good to know that she had connected me to the Harrisons in this way.

"Mom used to hide Dad's and my stockings like an Easter basket and we would have to hunt for them while she and Baby Harry sat on the floor playing with his new toys. She always said she loved the sound of us looking for treasure."

"That sounds like her." We both breathed a big sigh.

"Well, one of my gifts was that book. It had belonged to her, the note said. The pages were worn and there were several passages that were underlined in pencil, with beautifully handwritten notes in the margins."

I said, "Mom did have beautiful handwriting."

"So do you." He reached for my hand and held it as we walked.

"On the morning that Pat was to return to Quantico, he and I went for a climb and then we went fishing together. It was strange that he had asked me to do that; they are the two things I am better at than him.

212

We had a blast. It was like old times, when we would let nothing come between us."

I said, "You were Dookie and Gizmo."

"Exactly. So when I got out of the shower after a super day," he said, "I discovered he was gone. He hadn't even said good-bye. I was pretty bummed."

He continued, "That night, I pulled out my book and found he'd left behind a picture of the two of us and Jacob on our first big climb together. We had gotten in over our heads and we survived only by working together. We all swore on that day that we were brothers for life, in blood and in deed."

I said, "A three-cord strand is not easily broken."

"Funny you should say that, as it was something your mom drilled into our heads every time she took us climbing."

"Yeah," I said, "she loved her clichés."

"Don't you mean oracles?" He asked and we both laughed.

He continued, "On the back of the photo, there was a number that I thought at first was a date. It said: *III xviii*. I knew we had taken that photo in the summer, so it could not have been the date of our trip. But then I thought of the use of Roman numerals, which, of course, made me think of V. and I figured it had to be a riddle. And there it was."

"What? What was it?" I asked. I hung on his every word with all the anticipation of solving a great mystery. "Tell me!"

"*The Art of War* is divided into sections, as you know. *Attack by Stratagem* is section three, and the eighteenth rule reads: 'If you know the enemy and know yourself, you need not fear the result of a hundred battles. If you know yourself but not the enemy, for every victory gained you will also suffer a defeat'."

We spoke the last line together, in unison. Just like Richard and I had two days before. Just like the guys and I had only yesterday. We continued walking without talking. It seemed obvious that Mom had imprinted herself onto all of us.

The shuttle was at the stop and people were starting to board. I had the feeling that once I stepped onto it, there would be no turning back.

"So is that how you knew what the feds would do at the train station?" I asked Johnny.

"No. I knew because I am a burro."

"What's a burro?" I asked.

"Some people call it a mule," said Johnny." I transport illegal substances across state lines. It is a federal offense under the jurisdiction of the FBI."

"Did Patrick know that?"

"Yes, Pat knew. He was big on using hallucinogens to aid people in the recovery of brain trauma."

"Mom was down with that too."

He nodded as if he already knew. "I believe Pat was both warning me and telling me that, for some reason, he had chosen to enter the enemy camp and was pretending to be a friend." Johnny hip checked me and said, "Winter is coming."

"Oh, okay, Jon Snow." I gave him an affectionate sidekick and kept walking. It was a lot to take in.

"So show me yours," he said, winking at me, flirtatiously.

"That is intense, Johnny. I feel kind of silly now. My secret seems indulgent and childish compared to what you have told me."

"Why silly? If it's a secret and you want to share it with me, I feel honored."

He slowed down and now stood in front of me as he gently undid my braids. "If you should feel silly about anything," he said, "it's having pink hair."

He grabbed hold of my hands, and for the first time, I noticed how calloused his hands were from endless climbing. Yet they held me so tenderly. "Wait until you see Q's hair," he said. "She is all about the rainbow."

I pulled the drawing from my back pocket and gently unfolded it. It was too late to keep it perfectly flattened. The paper had seen more action in the last few days than a two-dollar hooker.

"Here," I said, handing him the sketch. "It's Mom's drawing of the final piece from her *Crypto Chaos* series. She started it in 2001. Dad and I had thought she had not completed the last one. But then I found this in the secret compartment of my jewelry box just before I left for Boston."

"You don't mean the one Jacob gave you?" he asked.

"You remember that?"

"Well, yeah!" said Johnny. "I remember you freaking out because you grabbed the ballerina, wanting to play with her like a Barbie, and you ended up breaking it. Then your mom showed you how you could take the inside backing out to store secrets, and you were immediately enthralled. It was a Lundson moment."

"Ha ha ha. A Lundson moment. Good one! So, anyway, I thought maybe when I got to Boston I would hit up this art dealer friend of Mom's and see if he could help me find out what happened to the piece."

"Hey!" Johnny said. "That is your necklace."

"Yes! My dad gave it to me before I boarded the train. Like your book, it was an unopened Christmas gift. Isn't that spookily serendipitous?"

He folded the paper back up and insisted I put it away and guard it. He then told me he had seen the large part of the sculpture. The box in the drawing had been in Jacob's storage unit to which Patrick and he had the only keys.

"One day," he said "Pat told me he wanted to check something out in the storage unit. To open it required both keys, so I went along with him. Sitting by itself atop a table was a beautiful and elegant metal box. We tried to open it, but couldn't figure out how to do so."

"How do you know it was a box that opened?" I asked. "Maybe it was just a hunk of metal."

"Because your mother never sculpted anything that didn't serve a multitude of purposes, and boxes hold things."

"Good point."

"There were zeroes and ones all over it, but neither of us read code, so we copied it all down to show Q."

"Why didn't you just take a picture of it?" I asked. "That would have been easier."

"Because easier is rarely better and because the NSA keeps a copy of every photo. And not just the ones sent."

"That's fucked up."

He kissed my palm and went back to holding my hand again, only this time more firmly. "So Q deciphered it," he said, "but she was not sure what V. had meant by it."

He paused and shook his head before we boarded the bus. We walked to the back where we could stand and have some privacy, and Johnny whispered in my ear, "I swear. Only your mom could make things this crazy. She did like her games, didn't she?"

"Yes she did. But we loved her games too."

"Yes we did. Yes we do," he said placing his hand over mine as I gripped the pole.

"So what did it say, Johnny?" I asked.

"It said, 'Do not change your spots. Instead, let them be a foothold for your journey'."

"That sounds exactly like something she would have said." And for the first time in a long time, I felt peaceful. Like the slope was becoming easier.

I enjoyed the ride as Johnny showed me points of interest. I had never been here and I was not much of a mountain biker, but it sure did look like fun. He said he'd bring me back.

"You know," I said, "I met this sweet, old woman yesterday, whom Karim had suggested I visit to ask about the stone in my necklace. She was like a fancy and elegant old crone, if there can be such a thing. Anyway, she told me my pendant was one half of a key to something and that I would find the answer to my questions in whatever it was that the key opens."

"Rose told you that?" Johnny asked.

The peace I had felt exploded and my knees began to buckle.

"It's okay, Phalaen. Rose is my grandmother. She is the one who told me you were on the train headed toward Colorado. She had a feeling you would need me."

I knew she had reminded me of a grown-up Q! And she said she had twin grandsons. And that she was healing the world. But fuck!

"I do need you. But this is all too much!" I said.

"Oh, come on!" said Johnny. "This is part of our adventure. Your mom has given us another game to play. Now show me that drawing again and maybe we can decipher another clue."

"Rose said you were at the hospital and working on becoming a doctor," I said rather skeptically as I pulled the paper back out.

He smiled with all the mischievousness of a Pucky boy. "She calls my lab 'the hospital'. What can I say? I'm a chemist who makes medicine to enable people to treat themselves; and she would tell you that makes me a doctor." He winked at me.

He was hard to stay mad at. And that was a little bit irritating. But only a little bit.

I gave him the drawing as we pulled into the airport parking lot. I could see a King Air C90 on the tarmac, and standing beside it were Aunt DeeDee, the Vet . . . and my dad.

"No way!" said Johnny.

"What? My dad?" I said. "Yeah, I didn't know he was coming either, and I'm not happy about it."

"I know what the other piece is," said Johnny. "And I know where it is."

"No way! Are you kidding me? What is it? Where is it?" I asked.

218

Johnny folded the drawing and gave it back to me. "I am going to take you to it," he said, with that same pleased-with-himself tone he used so often. "It will be at the meet-up tonight. I was going to take you anyway. I need to make some deliveries."

We walked off the bus. Before Dad even said hello to me, he grabbed Johnny, pulled him close, and wept.

Chapter 20

The hum of the plane and the feeling of floating put me to sleep before we reached climbing altitude. When I awoke, it was to the sound of murmuring voices discussing "Blucifer," the thirty-foot tall sculpture that was just one more thing to support the plethora of conspiracies that centered on the Denver Airport.

Drool slid from the corner of my mouth. I wiped it away and looked about to see if anyone had noticed. They hadn't. I yawned, stretched and noticed that, once again, I sort of smelled. I had run out of clean shirts, besides my two special ones. Maybe nobody had noticed.

My dad suggested, too cheerily under the circumstances, that we should all get lunch. Johnny must not have told him we had just eaten, nor that I had nearly drank poison for breakfast.

"You all go ahead. I have something to do before the cryptocurrency meet-up tonight." It was the first thing I had said to anyone and none of them had seemed bothered by my silence.

"Are you not going to tell me what is going on, PAL?" my dad asked.

Was he kidding? I was dirty, smelly, tragically off-course, and reunited "by chance" with his estranged best friend's son. How could he be so cavalier?

"No, Dad, I am not. When you are ready to explain to me why you lied about when you first became friends with Doc here and DeeDee, as well as the rest of Mom's friends and family, I will be happy to tell you what is going on."

Aunt DeeDee turned toward me. She looked tired. And sad. It made the scars on her face seem more pronounced. I had to look away.

Johnny said, "I figured we would go to my place so you could clean up. Give you time to collect yourself. Play some Battlefield 4." He acted as though nothing was going on beyond me maybe having menstrual cramps. Though his sweetness was endearing, what I appreciated most was his discretion. He quite obviously had told everyone nothing.

"Why? Do I stink that bad?" I asked. I thought the college girls who told me I needed deodorant were just being catty. It's one thing for me to be able to smell the stress hormones that were seeping through my sweat, but to have others smell them was distressing.

"No, honey," DeeDee assured me. "Let's just hit the john, wink wink, while Milan checks in the plane. I could use some freshening up myself." She was nothing if not kind. She covered human flaws and frailties like bandages covered warts and wounds.

"Okay." I waited until everyone seemed happy with the plan, then said, "Afterward, I would like to go see Diane."

It was as if the air had been sucked out of the plane. Doc was the first to speak up. He simply said, "I think it's time," and killed the engine.

There was no need for a denial or for an explanation. I was not interested in seeing life through the lens or filter of my parents, nor anyone else. If there was something from my mother's past that was so horrible that it would make me not like the woman she was, I would still have my memories and experiences of her as my mom. They were unique to me, and nobody could take that away. Not even me.

The words of the Arabic taxi driver bounced around in my head like a pinball. "Be careful what you wish for," he had said. Fables were written about how the granting of wishes comes at the expense of something held sacred. I wished it wasn't the case.

What else had I wished for? I had wished for an adventure. I had wished to see the Harrisons. I had wished to find my mother's sculpture, which I sort of had, although I knew it would be unwise for me to assume it was still in the storage unit. I had wished for a grandmother. . . . It seemed to me like I had gotten everything I had wished for.

I had wished my mom was with me. Maybe the granting of that wish meant me discovering her in a way that I never had before. "Please God," I prayed. Let it be a good thing." Did the same rules apply to prayers as to wishes?

I had not known that I wanted to go to the place my mom had called "home" — from when she was sixteen until Jacob was born four years later — until the words came out of my mouth. But I felt I needed to start with Diane, the mother of Jan — my mom and dad's best friend—and with Richard, whose role in this mystery was still unclear.

It was my first time using Uber and I was pretty impressed with the new taxi service. The driver had an assortment of cold drinks in a cooler for us. I reached for a water but then I noticed the cute, little bottles of Coke.

"There is real sugar in that one!" the driver exclaimed proudly. "I buy them in the Latin section of the grocery store. Not like the American Coke made with high fructose corn syrup." I smiled and gave him a thumbs-up.

It was clear why this free-market solution to Yellow Cab and the like could put the heavily regulated and totally outdated taxi service out of business. The only thing good about taxis, Mom had said, was the TV show. I never saw it.

We drove by a tour of McMansions, which the people who lived in them called "houses," even though they made famed Molly Brown's mansion look charming. The lawns and landscape were absent any visible signs of life. Just like the houses themselves.

Then amid brick driveways—lined with the same mix of petunias, all leading up to deep-set, wide front steps to doors that nobody used unless accepting flower deliveries or welcoming guests for once-a-year get-togethers—was the most delightful spectacle ever! I knew in an instant that my mother had lived there.

The single-story home looked the size of a guest house next to the others. It was painted Bazooka Bubble Gum pink, with white roses climbing a trellis near the front door, which you could be sure was the entrance she used. Camellia hedges separated the property on either side, as if the home and yard were embraced by a shiny-leafed bush covered with a flower that was a deeper shade of pink. Everything about the house said "Welcome."

In stark contrast to the home's softness was a feature that could only have been my mother's doing. Stained the color of shame was a humongous metal sculpture of a plate of spaghetti, the ring of noodles wrapped in a large mound. Next to it were a knife and a fork, standing maybe ten feet tall. It was covered in tomato vines.

The driver began to giggle as he pulled into the driveway, his accent becoming thicker the faster he talked, as he told us he'd never seen anything so wonderful, and that the snotty neighbors must bite their knuckles when they pass by. Denver had a new Molly Brown.

Even though I had felt confused and shattered only moments before, I could not resist the warm fuzzy feeling the whole scene invoked. I wondered what transgression had occurred to inspire my mother to create such a wonderful eye sore. The voice inside me said, "Go, Mom!"

The five of us walked up the front walkway, and as we approached the door, Doc took the lead and rang the bell. After a short time, a woman opened the door. She was short enough that I was unable to see her with his body in the way. But as soon as he said, "Hello, Diane," he stood aside, leaving me directly facing the woman who had taken in my mother.

I didn't know what to expect and hadn't even given it much thought. Diane looked like a sweet lady. She was dressed in loose-fitting clothes, a painting smock, and what would have been white Converse sneakers, if not for the splotches of paint covering them.

Before I had a chance to say anything, she grabbed me and held me tight, smothering her face into my boobs. She was as little as Mom had been and her hug felt so good.

She pulled away and began to apologize as she used the apron to dab at the tears that were streaming down her face. "I'm so sorry. I just . . . You look just like your mother," she said and then laughed, adding, "only much taller."

She kissed and hugged DeeDee and Doc as if they were her best friends and then asked Johnny if he was a Harrison. She told him she had known his father and mother and that he was the spitting image of his mom.

He grinned broadly and said he knew exactly who she was and that he loved her chocolate pie recipe. That sent her over the moon.

When she came to my dad, there was a moment of silence. She had not been at my mother's funeral. But he looked neither hurt, nor angry. Instead, my dad picked her up and swung her around, her legs dangling like a doll.

"I smell chili!" Dad said, then kicked off his shoes after he put Diane down, as if he'd done it a thousand times, and headed toward the back of the house. "Mind if I grab a beer?" he yelled. He had already popped the top off of a Stella, which he raised up and said, "Cheers!" before heading out the kitchen door, following his nose to his next meal.

I was flabbergasted. I had never seen my dad act like this. But then again, I had been too young when his parents died to know how he would be. He looked like a boy who had just run home from school to play catch with his dad.

Diane waved the driver off and welcomed us all inside. We moved toward the kitchen like people who have a feeling of home. A radio softly played classic rock and there was no TV to be seen.

I felt bad that I was probably going to blindside her, but I needed some answers. "Did my mother know how to write code?" I blurted out. Diane said nothing. Despite such an awkward moment, nobody seemed to mind.

"Honey," said Diane. "I would love to help you with whatever I can, but I don't think I can answer that question."

If this woman had raised my mother, she should be practiced at precision in her language. "You can't, or you won't?" I asked.

Dad popped his head in the door and asked Doc to bring out two more beers. DeeDee and Johnny excused themselves, too, but not before Johnny asked if he could help himself to a brownie.

"You are just like your father!" Diane laughed before waving him toward the untouched plate. "Help yourself, please. Lord knows Hiro and I don't need to eat them all!" I hoped Hiro wasn't her dog. Chocolate was toxic to them.

Diane put a pitcher of lemonade on the kitchen table, along with two glasses of ice, and sat down. I wondered if it was the same table my mother had hidden under with little Richard while Diane cooked Thanksgiving Dinner. By now, I realized that he had been the little boy from the story of my parents' first meeting.

226

She poured each of us a glass and said, "I can tell you the story of your T-shirt though." Diane nodded toward the *Rumors* vintage tee I had put on at the airport.

"I doubt that. It was a gift from my mother." My tone sounded rude in my own ears and I was glad nobody was around to hear it.

"Well that's just secondhand news," she said and cackled as if she'd said the funniest thing ever. She didn't wait for me to get the joke.

"Just before New Year's in December 1974, on a typical rainy day in Oregon, I was in a café with Milan. We were discussing one of his patients whom he thought I could help. That patient was your mother, who had been through an exceedingly horrific event. She had been in a mental hospital for almost three weeks and was not speaking to anyone."

"Why have I never been told this?" I asked. The unspoken question was, why did I feel betrayed that I wasn't told?

"It was a long time ago," said Diane. "Everyone has a past, honey. I think your mom felt like you and your father were her future; and she wanted to leave her past behind her."

I studied the beverage before taking a sip and I noticed little pieces of pulp floating to the top. It was made the way my mom had liked it.

"So what does this have to do with the T-shirt?" I asked. There was no point in digging here. And really, so what if my mom was in a loony bin. Q was too, apparently.

Diane said, "Our waitress floated through the restaurant like a dandelion after you've made a wish and blown the seeds away. When I commented on her unique voice, she told me that she was a singer-songwriter. Her name was Stephanie, but you know her as Stevie Nicks."

"Stevie Nicks was your waitress? Well, that's kind of cool. Mom loved her, which is I guess why she bought me the T-shirt."

It was hard to not be sort of excited. I was always interested in who people were before they became the people we knew them to be. Wait. Did I really just think that?

"Do you mind if I peak at the tag on your shirt, honey?" Diane asked, getting up with the agility of someone half her age.

I had never worn it before, much less washed it, and I hadn't even noticed it had a tag. I reached up and, sure enough, there was one. I lifted up my hair so Diane could see it.

"Yep, it's the very same one!" she said with great satisfaction. "I took your mother to a Fleetwood Mac concert in 1976, and afterwards we went backstage to meet the band. Stevie liked your mom's dreads," she said, shaking her head. "They totally hit it off and before we left, Stevie gave her this T-shirt, which was from their not-yet-released album, signed her initials on the tag, and put a flower outline around them."

I yanked the shirt up over my head to see for myself. Just as Diane said, "SN" was written in black Sharpie, with a flower outlined around it, like the first one Mom taught me to draw. "Oh my God. That's crazy!" I said.

"Do you know your mother wanted to have a little girl and name her Rhiannon after the song?" Diane asked.

I had never heard that, but I kept myself perfectly still. Somehow the fact that this woman knew things about my mother that were so intimate and that I didn't know made me feel scared.

"But she and Peter accepted a ridiculous bet from my son that they could not tell the difference between the calling of birds and my son's mimicking them." She seemed to be remembering as if the events had happened only the day before and not three decades ago.

"He said that if he won, they would each have to name their firstborn girls after a flower. Your mother chose Phalaen, short for Phalaenopsis, which was Richie's favorite flower, because it sounded like Rhiannon. I suppose she could have named you 'Bella Donna'." She laughed delightedly at the memory.

I myself could not see the humor in it. As far as I knew, her little Richie could be in on whatever ploy the Smiths were up to. I just smiled and reminded her that a quaking aspen is not a flower, so Peter didn't play fair.

Diane just smiled. "Yes, well, Peter was a special young man. He made his own rules. But he always took care of your mother first and foremost." She excused herself and ran off as if to pull something from a burning oven. Except we were already in the kitchen.

I could understand. This was a lot. I still wasn't sure if I was awake or asleep myself, and I had cried more in the last few days than I had since my mom died. Since I was alone, I decided to look around where she had spent time when she was my age.

I wandered into the living room and saw a sculpture on a table in the corner. It was beautiful and sad at the same time. The form was elegant, with soft lines, except for disfigurement on the face and neck. But the artist had creatively covered imperfections with flowers that grew out of them. Etched into the base was the phrase *Primum non nocere.*

I heard softly padding footsteps return and turned to see a red-nosed Diane. "That is the first sculpture your mother ever made. She called it Panacea." Diane blew into a tissue, telling me this in a muffled voice inside her hands.

"I'm sorry, but what did you say?" I was sure my ears were playing tricks on me again.

"Panacea. This was your mother's first sculpture. She made it while in the hospital. " She pointed to the Latin writing, "You see this here? It means. . . ."

"I know what it means," I said far more abruptly than she deserved. "I'm sorry, but may I use your bathroom?"

I went in and closed the door behind me just in time to get the toilet seat up and vomit. Maybe I was drugged and this was all a bad dream. I was flooded with emotions and none of them felt good to me.

Mom had been the one who suggested the name for my agorist marketplace website. She never told me it was the name of her first sculpture, or that the sculpture so obviously resembled DeeDee. Now I was certain Mom had known Doc, DeeDee, and Diane since she was at least as young as twelve years old.

"Get it together, Phalaen!" I whispered to myself through clenched teeth while staring at my reflection in the mirror. Or was that my mom's voice in my head?

"Phalaen, are you okay?" Diane asked from the other side of the door.

"Yes, Diane, I'm fine. Too much Mexican food. I'll be right out," I called back, splashing my face with cold water.

I needed to leave. I could not be in this house anymore, or around these people. I needed Q. She would never lie to me. Just like I did not leave her side when we were in the cellar, I knew she would never leave me in confusion. Together we would figure this out.

When I came out of the bathroom, Diane no longer stood in the living room. I headed out to the back with a fresh facade. Now was the time to buck up and stop being a fucking baby.

Johnny waved me over to where the group stood around a smoker and an outdoor grill with a large cast-iron pot sitting on it. They were all laughing it up and shooting the shit like it was a typical backyard barbecue.

Dad stood proudly with his chest puffed, looking at me with his eyes aglow. "Johnny was just telling us how you two decided to train hop and take a little adventure. I totally don't approve, but the one-arm pull-up you did to unsnag your sweatshirt was quite impressive."

"It wouldn't have been so if I hadn't succeeded," I said with dry morbidity. My stomach rumbled. It didn't seem to care about my mood; it was ready to eat again.

The man responsible for the wafting sweet and savory aromas had bushy, salt-and-pepper hair and stood with his back to me, brushing ribs with sauce. He could not see me as I approached from behind. When I came around in front of him, I realized he wouldn't have been able to see me regardless, because he was blind.

He was also the man with the yellow teeth from the photo, who had given me an Altair 8800 when I was seven years old. I could not identify my feelings, but I did know he was the key to me finding out the secrets to my mom.

"Phalaen, this is my husband, Hiro," said Diane.

He held out his hand and said, "Dearest Phalaen, my heart is so full to finally meet you again. Please, call me Sato; that is what your mother called me."

Chapter 21

Johnny shook his head no, and once again, I paid attention and did as he said. I was catching on to the word "no" not being such a bad thing. It was how I narrowly escaped becoming a bump under a train. But I had escaped.

"Hello, Sato. It's very nice to meet you." I took his hand and lifted it to my cheek. Mom and Dad had a dog while Dad was in graduate school that Mom had named Sato and explained that it meant "mutt." That must have been the dog with Mom in the photograph from Richard's tenth birthday and not Sadie, after all. It could be no coincidence she had called this man by that name as a girl. But he seemed to like it.

He drew his other hand up to my face and began to trace the curves. His head fell back with unabashed joy, as tears fell out of his eyes and into his wide smile. He paused briefly as his fingers traced a scar on my forehead. It was left over from when I had fallen off of a stack of pallets. He winced in pain for an instant and then it was gone; his face once again flushed with joy.

"You look just like your mother did at your age. I can remember her face as if I saw it yesterday." Somehow I knew that if this man could draw, he would be able to show the details of our faces in ways that even a seeing person could not.

"Phalaen, dear," said Diane, "I would like to show you something." She held in her hands a hand-forged picture frame like the ones that held Mom's drawings. It contained a photo taken of my mother moments after having me. Her face was red and sweaty and joyous. Around her were all of the people standing here, plus Jan and a woman who looked just like her, and the rest of the Harrisons.

Hiro said, laughing, "Vivi thought I should be there to look over her work and make sure she didn't make any mistakes." He laughed so hard and my heart melted. He was such an old-school styled nerd.

Diane slapped him affectionately on the arm. "Oh stop!" She said. "Vivi didn't make mistakes." She looked at me. "Your mother died before I ever had a chance to catch her in one. Isn't that a terrible thing of me to think?"

I couldn't be mad at these people. They had loved my mother so much. It would be selfish of me to resent that, simply because I didn't understand her choice to exclude me from parts of her life.

"Well, she did melt a pan to the stovetop," I said and everyone burst into laughter, agreeing she could not cook to save her life. "But she seemed to find a way to patch that flaw. You all are wonderful cooks, if that smell is any indication of Sato's skills." I smiled sheepishly.

Johnny beamed and said, "I just love it that you can eat, girl!"

My dad looked at him and then looked at me. And then he looked back at him. And then back at me. I just looked away. I was saved by the sound of an engine roaring down the street.

"And that would be Q and her beast!" Johnny looked at me and smiled before I ran and threw my arms around him. "I know. I know . . . You love me." I couldn't deny it.

As I ran along the side yard, under a canopy of flowers that clung willingly to an arbor, I felt like I was passing into the Secret Garden from the book by the same name. It was how I always pictured finding Q again. The book had been her gift to me and she had read it aloud from start to finish during our last visit.

But when I passed through the arbor, a child holding a lamb was hardly what I saw. Instead, stepping out of a fully restored and souped-up 1967 purple Chevelle was someone who had transformed from a fairy-like creature to a force!

"Oh my God! Q! Look at you. You are magnificent. You look like a cake!" I squealed.

Her face smiled from ear to ear; practically the only place not tattooed, and lit up like the sun. There. That's her. Radiating like a sunbeam.

"Hello, Ms. P. You've been up to things," she said, wearing that mischievous Harrison smile with twinkling eyes. "I like it! I like it a lot." She wrapped me up in her arms and whispered in my ear, "Are you ready to fuck some shit up?"

"Haven't I already?" I giggled back and hugged her until we both started to sway and dance. Just like when we were kids.

I could hear Dad say behind us, "Look at that, Johnny. It's as though no time has passed. What has your sister been up to these days, aside from decorating herself?" he asked admiringly. "Did she and your dad build that car together?"

Johnny said they had and then laughed. "As for what else she does. Q breaks shit. And she is the best at it."

Quaking Aspen and I turned with our arms around each other and faced the group. DeeDee snapped a photo that we would later look at and remark that we resembled giants, just as our fathers had in a photo of them at the same age.

Diane grabbed ahold of her husband's arm. She looked like she was seeing something exciting and new, and at the same time very familiar. "They remind me of Peter, John, and Vivi, Hiro."

Dad stared at us in awe, and with a tone of foreboding in his voice, remarked matter-of-factly that the world had better buckle up. "I seriously feel sorry for anyone who gets in the way of those two."

"It's going to be epic!" shouted Johnny. Q's big brother reached his strong arms around us both and squeezed. "Let's go eat, ladies. Phalaen here needs to feed, like you do, Queen Q," he said admiringly. "It must be those brains of yours."

Q and I both looked at him like we thought he was annoying. He loved it. I decided to ignore him.

"I cannot believe you're here! And that I am. You are not going to believe the time I've had the last few days!" I gushed.

"There is plenty of time for all that, Scary Ari," Johnny said without a hint of teasing in his voice. Why was he calling me that? Dad laughed and said he hadn't heard that in over a decade. Why were men so obtuse?

"Whatever," I said with a flip of my hair. "There is something I have to show you, Q. I found it on the Panacea forum a couple days ago."

"Oooh, sounds exciting. Let me get my bag." Q grabbed her backpack—the essential carryall for all geeks, and we headed for the backyard and the meat fest.

Diane, DeeDee, and the Doc assumed command of the food, while Q began to unpack her tool bag. It was like watching Mary Poppins extract items that one would never expect a person to carry around, including a soldering iron and a tin can.

"Bring me your laptop, sweetie," said Q. "I need to do a little doctoring on it before we go on any expeditions." The tin can reminded me of how we used to talk to one another. She must have read my thoughts because she looked up when I handed her my computer, nodded toward the can and said, "Still using it for secure communication," and laughed.

"Would you mind if I had a look?" Sato asked. Q told him to have a seat and then set each of the items in front of him. She took his right hand and set it on the roll of Duct tape and told him the items were in order left-to-right.

She then asked if any of us had cell phones on us. Dad did. She took the battery out and handed it back to him, holding her finger to her lips.

As Sato picked up each piece, he felt and inspected it just long enough to ascertain what it was. When he got to the tin can, his face lit up and he said, "Progresso!" which got a huge grin out of Q.

Everyone sat in silence as Q went to work with surgery precision. First she covered the web camera with a piece of black electrical tape, replacing my neon sticker.

She then removed the battery and depressed the power button for a few seconds.

Dad started to question what she was doing, but Sato reached over and touched his arm. He seemed to know what was happening by the sounds he heard, even though a seeing person would say there weren't any. He was pretty savvy for someone with dementia.

She slid on an antistatic wrist strap that had a power cord dangling from it and opened the back of my laptop using a jeweler's screwdriver. She undid several screws before popping the back loose and removing the hard drive.

Using her soldering iron, she then removed the mic, the infrared receiver, and the built-in Wi-Fi.

"What's this? An ice-cream scoop?" I asked sarcastically.

"I am not a gas station. This is a sophisticated laboratory," Q responded with a Russian accent.

We both laughed until we snorted. Johnny just shook his head. He had got stuck watching *Armageddon* three times after betting us that we could not stay awake all night so he caught our little exchange.

Plugging in the power cord, Q then looked up at Dad and gave him a wink. His jaw dropped. He was an engineer and he could see that all she had to do was yank away and the power would be lost due to the lack of battery. Unlike a fixed-wing with a deadstick, this machine had a single point of failure.

She booted up the now operational laptop with Tails Linux off of a USB drive that dangled from a chain tucked inside her Princess Leia T-shirt. She was about to introduce Dad to Tor.

Sato called out to Diane to bring his camera tripod. Q smiled handing him the can. I had never used a cantenna before but had read about it. She was going to utilize the neighbor's Wi-Fi. Sato was awarded the privilege of deciding which one. He seemed thrilled to be included and stood to set up the cantenna.

Utilizing a travel router that she connected via an Ethernet cord, Q was able to access a VPN. Now a local ISP would not be able to see that someone was using Tor, nor what sites she visited. I had not been as careful. Not even close.

I had known that Gizmo was the one who would be able to help me. And I was sure I needed Q. That they could be one in the same person was beyond comprehension.

The end of the table was filled with serving bowls of buttered corn cobs, glistening ribs and steaming chili and my tummy began to rumble while my mouth watered. I caught Johnny gazing at me. We both laughed at my insatiable appetite.

Q and I traded places and I quickly logged in to Panacea and found the post. I paused and sat back, letting everyone gather around me. Diane was the first to say something. "I know those lyrics! It's from *Alice in Wonderland*. And is that a joker?"

"It is," I answered, pulling out two sets of dual headphone mics and splitter from my backpack. I offered Sato a pair of earbuds. Q did the same, sharing hers with Johnny.

"The avatar caught my attention too, Diane," I said. "I had only seen it once before on a post that was dated the same day Mom died."

I looked around and could see that everyone but Q and Johnny were looking at the screen. They were looking at each other. Q told me to go on.

I clicked on the song lyrics, which we quickly agreed were best sung by Gene Wilder, and the screen turned to snow. Before anyone could react, Sato transformed into a commanding drill sergeant and said, "Shh!"

We all froze. He had shocked me into stillness. Only seconds before, he had seemed like just a sweet, old man, happy to have a pot to stir for family and friends.

And then he began to hum. He could hear music through the snow. Diane joined in, her eyes closed, and her hands clasped as if in prayer.

Q, Johnny, and I looked at each other. Analog was old. So were these people. For a moment, I thought they might start babbling in single syllables.

Then Johnny started to laugh. Or cry. It was hard to tell. "Phalaen!" he said. "This is it! This is the song I heard you singing to Q." Q started to hum along.

And then it clicked. Lewis Carrol had written his songs as parodies of the poems children were taught to memorize. *The Lobster Quadrille* also known as "The Mock Turtle's Song," rhymes and mimics the flow and tune of the poem *The Spider and the Fly* by Mary Howitt.

I started to type the words as I recited them aloud, "'Will you walk into my parlor?' said the spider to the fly; 'Tis the prettiest little parlor that you ever did spy, And I have many pretty things to show you when you are there.'" The snow disappeared and on the screen appeared a photo of my bedroom door.

"Oh my God!" My dad's voice sounded anguished.

240

"Uncle John, it's okay. It's just a keyfile. People who are tech-savvy use them instead of passwords." Q said. She was doing her best to calm him, but it was obvious that she too was bothered.

"Q, that is Phalaen's bedroom door. How could someone get a photo of her bedroom door? That is inside our home!" His face was red with rage.

Johnny had been kneeling at my side and he immediately jumped up, placing an arm upon my shoulder. "Is that true, Phalaen? Is that an exact picture? Are you certain?"

My heart raced. "I can't breathe," I said. "Please. Can you all just give me a second?" I put my head in my hands. I could hear someone whimpering. I felt someone's forehead press against mine and knew it was Q's. And then I realized the animal sounds were coming from me.

"Ssshhh," said Q. "It's okay. Just breathe." I am not sure how long we were like that because she just kept counting to three over and over and over again. "Inhale one, two, three. Exhale one, two, three. Inhale one, two, three. Exhale one, two, three."

She backed away when the whimpering ceased and my breathing calmed. DeeDee put a plate of food in my hands and told me to eat, assuring me I would feel better.

The hottest part of the day had passed, but it was still very warm and the sun shone on the yard, making everything look lit up from within. It gave me a feeling of warmth, even though I was still shivering. Everyone ate without talking.

"Wait!" I finally said, startling everyone from their thoughts. "That is not a picture of my bedroom door. At least not as it has been since I was thirteen years old."

Dad put his plate down, wiped his mouth with his napkin, which he then abruptly discarded on the table, before coming around to look at the screen. He said, "You're right. It's missing your sign."

"What sign?" asked Sato.

"It was a sign I made when I declared my bedroom a boundary for independence, demanding privacy. It was silly really, because I had as much privacy in my home as I wanted," I told them, as if they needed an explanation.

"What did it say?" Johnny asked.

Dad chuckled, "It is still there, and it says 'Welcome Fly, I'm Spider'."

"Phalaen, there is a good chance that you will only get one crack at this. So trust yourself. You've made it this far," Sato said.

I typed in the letters, making sure the words appeared exactly as they did on my sign and hit Enter.

The door opened. On the other side of it was a photograph of Mom sitting in a field with a very old-looking Baby Harry lying beside her. She held a copy of *The Denver Post* dated August 21 of the current year, just two days prior.

"Dad. That's Mom." I said and looked at Q in shock. "The picture was taken two days ago. How can this be?"

I felt more than saw my dad as he fell to his knees. The screams that came from him made no sound. DeeDee lunged for him and cradled his head against her chest as he sobbed.

242

Q spoke up in a still, quiet voice. "Forty-two," she said. "The answer to life is forty-two."

I swallowed hard and held back the convulsions that were threatening to choke me. I said, "What are you talking about?"

"Aunt V took me to see *The Hitchhiker's Guide to the Galaxy* when it was in the theatre. I remember she joked that she knew everything, and her proof was that she was forty-two."

I took off my bandana and wiped my eyes. "I don't get what you are saying, Q. What does that have to do with the photo?"

"It's the date," said Johnny. "8 + 21 + 13 = 42."

"That must be a coincidence," Aunt DeeDee said.

"Not with Vivi," remarked Diane, suddenly very serious.

"She and Jacob died on 11/20/11. Also 42," Q said. "Aunt V is alive." She turned to Johnny, and her face contorted as tears squeezed out from her eyes. "Johnny, do you think that it is possible?"

Johnny grabbed his sister and held her, as the two of them dared to allow themselves a glimmer of hope that their bother might also be alive. Poor Q had been sent away for daring to question the death of her brother and my mother. I had suffered loss. So had she; she had suffered punishment as well.

For the first time since we had arrived and Doc had said hello to Diane, he spoke up again. "We don't know. Photos can be doctored." Funny choice of words coming from him.

"That thing you said Mom and Jacob were working on, Johnny. Is there some way we can find out

243

who they were working with? Maybe that person knows what has happened to them," I pleaded to him hoping.

We were all sitting around the table now. Dad had moved up onto a chair, his body slumped and weary. He looked drained of life. DeeDee sat next to him, holding his hand. Always the healer, I had watched her hold my mom the same way.

The images that had been flashing through my mind like the slides from a View Master started to reveal a story. "You said that *Panacea* was the name of my mother's first sculpture." I said to Diane, more as an accusation than a question.

She nodded slowly, looking very concerned.

I looked at Sato. He sat without expression. He did not have the look of someone hiding his emotions. He looked lost. Like he had been left behind and abandoned and didn't know why. Similar to how Dad had looked after searching Mom's attic room. And then I knew.

"It was you, wasn't it, Sato? You were the third person?" His face turned toward mine and then his head dropped in shame.

Johnny and Q pulled away from each other. "No! Don't say anything, Hiro. You must never say it! It's called 'plausible deniability'," Q warned.

We all sat in the stillness of awe, knowing that some things cannot be unspoken. We seemed to know we were not ready to hear what we could not have previously imagined.

Johnny got up and walked behind Q. He bent down and kissed her head, then removed something from her hair. He handed it to me and said, "This is what you are looking for."

244

"It was my last Christmas gift from Aunt V. The stone is tremolite and is said to open us up to love and compassion," Q said.

"It's lovely Q," I said as I placed it along with the drawing on the table. I removed the pendant from under my T-shirt then slid the hairpin needle into the groove just as Rose had told me. They fit together perfectly.

"That," I said pointing to the drawing, "is Mom's twenty-first sculpture, Dad. She finished the series."

Turning to Johnny, I said, "I think we know what is in the box."

Sato began to cry. I went to him as a mother would a child, and using my bandana, I bent down to wipe away his tears. How could I be mad at him?

How could I be mad at her? I had gotten everything I wished for. I had even discovered what it was that would cause my mother to leave her family. She, together with Jacob and Sato, had changed the world, even if the world didn't know it yet.

We sat there, quietly trying to absorb the reality of what had just been revealed. The moment was too awesome for revelry. Time passed. The earth moved. We remained still.

"Hey, PAL, what is that on your arm?" Dad asked, breaking the stillness. As usual, his awkward timing made me laugh.

"It took you long enough, Dad." I lifted up my arm and showed everyone the tattoo that Mom had gotten me a year and a half before. "It is the ace of spades. It is the symbol of power. Mom got it for me for my seventeenth birthday," I told them, proud that I'd kept it secret for this long. I loved it that the secret was uncovered at the same time that Mom's was.

Q said, "I knew when I saw the avatar that it had to be Aunt V's doing somehow. You see, Phalaen, she got me one too." She lifted up her arm to reveal a queen of hearts. "Compassion," she said, eyes shining with her unspent tears.

"She, Jacob and I went together the last time she visited, just before the accident. She got Jacob the king of hearts. I didn't know what it stood for at the time," she said forlornly. "She got one too. It was of a Joker, exactly like the avatar."

Diane started laughing. "Blackjack!" she exclaimed, then stood up and began to twirl. She outstretched her arms and looked up toward the shining ball in the sky. We all watched, moved to see her joy, like that of a mother who had found her daughter. Nothing could steal the beauty of the moment. Or so we thought.

A cell phone sounded with the woman's voice saying curtly, "At the tone, the time will be" and then repeated herself without actually telling the time. It was coming from Q's bag.

Johnny said, "It's P-time," which Dad and I both knew meant that it was Patrick calling. Never late. Never early.

Q answered the phone. I could tell it was bad news when I noticed the look on Q's face. She pressed the speaker button and I recognized the sound immediately. So did my dad.

"What is that?" DeeDee asked.

"It's the sound you hear when Ms. Pac-Man is being chased and about to be eaten by the monsters," Johnny said, as he placed his large, calloused hand upon my shoulder.

I swallowed hard.

246

"What does it mean," DeeDee persisted.

Q turned to me, looking so very sad and said, "It means that Phalaen isn't safe. The ghosts are coming for her."

Epilogue

A sigh of blissful content escaped her lips as Diane gazed in awe at the view below her. Hiro felt her excitement and clasped her hand tightly. "Tell me, darling, what do you see?" he asked.

"It's magical, Hiro. There is an iridescent veil cascading down the side of the mountain, puddling on the desert floor into giant pools of Caribbean blue water surrounded by an oasis of lush green, bursting with fertility."

"God knew what He was doing when He brought us together. I see better through the lens by which you view the world than I ever did before." She kissed him on the lips and nuzzled her head into his neck.

Despite the gravity of their mission, Milan and Deedee felt the couple's joy and exchanged smiles. In the two years they'd been visiting Karim and Karl's compound, they'd never grown immune to the visual impact of the impressive wall of solar panels, nor the gift of abundance they created.

Deedee turned to look at Diane as she spoke into her headset. "Wait until you see what they are powering," she said, with youthful glee.

If the circumstances had not been so dire, the trip would have been a fun, sunset excursion with old friends. They had been a witness to each other's most intimate joys and pains decades ago. Like soldiers who had survived a war, their traumas and victories had bonded them. But it was Vivienne's secrets that had delivered them to this moment. Because her secrets had become theirs also.

Discussion Questions

1. The theme of people not being who they seem is found throughout the story.
    a. Is that a subjective or objective evaluation?
    b. As children, we perceive reality from the POV that we are the center of it. As we mature into adulthood, there is a natural evolution of thought that enables us to be empathetic to the experiences of others, including our parents. What can parents do to enable that transition to be less painful or is pain essential to the process?

2. Were Vivienne and John wrong to withhold information from Phalaen about their lives? Were they wrong to withhold information, and even lie, about Vivienne's skillset, particularly as it pertained to Phalaen? What are the nuances of lies of omission to preserve the sanctity of one's privacy versus to mislead another?

3. The Vietnam War played a pivotal role in many of the characters' lives.
    a. What is the significance of the tattoo on Phalaen's forearm?
    b. How can social media be used in PSYOP strategies by warring factions?

4. Delores, Deedee and Panacea are all names attributed to one person. How do their meanings

relate to the evolution of Vivienne's transformation?

5. Who is the voice on the other end of Richard's cell call on the train?

6. Why are Phalaen and Panacea a threat and to whom? How is creating and operating a website a crime? Should newspapers be held legally responsible for all transactions that occur via the Want Ads? Should the postal service be held liable for all products transported? Should a homeowner/landlord be subject to prosecution for any crimes committed at their home by their tenants?

7. What does the binary code on the cover translate to and what is the philosophical implication?